THE RED DANCER

Richard Skinner was born in 1965, and is a graduate of the UEA Creative Writing course. He lives in Camberwell, London and has written book reviews for the *Guardian* and the *Financial Times*. *The Red Dancer* is his first novel.

RICHARD SKINNER

The Red Dancer

First published in 2001
by Faber and Faber Limited
3 Queen Square London WC1N 3AU
This paperback edition first published in 2002

Typeset by Faber and Faber Ltd
Printed in England by Mackays of Chatham, plc

A CIP record for this book
is available from the British Library

ISBN 0-571-20934-3

2 4 6 8 10 9 7 5 3 1

Those who know the enemy as well as they know themselves will never suffer defeat.
Sun Tzu, *The Art of War*

We must not touch our idols; the gilt sticks to our fingers.
Gustave Flaubert, *Madame Bovary*

The story of a shattered life can only be told in bits and pieces.
Rainer Maria Rilke

Prologue

I am absolutely Oriental.

I was born in the south of India on the coast of Malabar, in the holy city of Jaffnapatam, the child of a family within the sacred caste of Brahma. By reason of his piety and pureness of heart my father was called Assirvadam, which means 'The Blessing of God'. My mother was a glorious bayadère in the temple of Kanda Swany. She died when she was fourteen, on the day I was born. The priests of the temple, having cremated my mother, adopted me under the baptismal name of Mata Hari, which means 'Eye of the Dawn'.

From the time when I took my first uncertain steps I was shut up in the great subterranean hall of the pagoda of Siva, where I was to be trained to follow in my mother's footsteps through the holy rites of the dance. Of these early years my mind retains only vague recollections of a monotonous existence in which, during the long morning hours, I was taught to imitate automatically the movements of the bayadères, and in the afternoons was allowed to walk in the gardens while weaving garlands of jasmine for decorating the altars.

When I reached the threshold of womanhood, my foster mother saw in me a predestined soul and resolved to dedicate me to Siva and to reveal to me the mystery of love and faith on the night of Sakty-pudja, in the following spring. It was on the purple granite altar of the Kanda Swany that, at the age of thirteen, I was initiated. Naked, I danced before the rajahs on the banks of the sacred Ganges . . .

PART I

Portrait of Margaretha as a young girl

1
Amsterdam, 1895–96

> Captain in the East Indies army, currently on leave, seeks to return to the East Indies as a married man. He's seeking a cultured young lady of pleasing appearance and gentle character. Please reply to Post Box 206, Amsterdam.
>
> *Het Nieuws van den Dag*, 1895

It was my idea to place the personal ad in *Het Nieuws van den Dag*. I thought it would be amusing to see how a womaniser like MacLeod would respond. The idea came to me while I was at Sergeant Stam's stag party at the Café Americain in February 1895. At the end of the evening, Stam was so drunk he could hardly stand up. He put his arm around my neck and told me that the only man in the East Indies who had had more women than him was MacLeod. When they were garrisoned at Padang together, Stam said, MacLeod had slept with more than fifty women. And then in Banhermassin, the figure was rumoured to be even higher. 'Damn good man,' Stam said before falling over.

At the time, MacLeod and I were captains in the Dutch army. We were both on extended leave in Amsterdam after long periods of service in the East Indies. I met him one night at the Café Americain and liked him immediately. He struck me as the kind of man who enjoyed the company of other men. He was witty and very generous – always buying drinks for everyone and proposing toasts. The other officers teased him about his reputation with women, but he derived great pleasure from it and was proud that he was still a bachelor. I'd heard other stories about him, though, uglier stories, and one or two officers warned me of his notorious temper.

Two days after Stam's stag party, I placed the ad in the personal section using MacLeod's post box number. Then I waited. MacLeod received the first reply three days later and brought it with him that night to the Café Americain. He was very amused. He waved the letter in the air and asked who had played the joke on him. I owned up straight away. He clapped me on the back and said he hadn't laughed as much in months.

I had forgotten all about it until one cold night in March, when I received a request from MacLeod to meet him at his sister Louise's house, where he was staying on leave. I walked to the house on Leidschekade, which was just around the corner from the Café Americain. MacLeod showed me into the living room and offered me a schnapps. He sat me down and indicated some letters and photographs on the table. It took me a few moments to realise that they were replies to the ad. He explained that he had received fifteen letters in all. At first, he said, he had treated them as part of the joke, but gradually began reading them in earnest. The letters had made him think about himself in an unfamiliar way. He was thirty-nine and a confirmed bachelor. Would he ever marry? Would he ever have children?

He had spent the past few weeks sorting through the letters and had chosen one in particular that stirred him the most. It was from a Margaretha Geertruida Zelle, who lived in The Hague. She was very pretty, he said, and showed me the photograph she had sent. He was right – her face was quite round and her eyes were shaped like almonds. Her dark hair was pleasantly pinned up, using a comb and a ribbon. She was as dark and beautiful as a gypsy. MacLeod said that, in his experience, dark-haired women were always more passionate than blondes or brunettes. He told me that he was thinking of writing back to arrange a meeting with her. What did I think? I wasn't sure if this was all an elaborate hoax. I looked for a hint of a smile, or a glint in the eye, but he seemed quite sincere. I said that if he thought it was a good idea, then he should go ahead with it. He nodded and clapped his hands. 'Excellent!' he said.

I spent the next five days in Flanders, visiting my brother, who had married a dull Flemish woman and settled in Gent. My brother's apparent happiness and MacLeod's change of heart weighed on my mind while I walked around the flat countryside. Would *I* ever marry? What did I want for myself? When I returned to Amsterdam, I bumped into MacLeod at the Americain, and he told me that he was meeting the girl the following morning at the Rijksmuseum. I laughed, because I knew he had no patience with the Arts, but MacLeod looked concerned. Was it the wrong kind of place? he asked. I assured him it was perfect for such a meeting. As I walked home that night, I still wasn't sure if it was all a prank to get even with me. I decided that I would see for myself whether his assignation was real.

The next morning, I went into a coffee shop opposite the museum and took a table by the window. I read the paper and watched for MacLeod, who was due to meet the girl at midday. He arrived a little early and stood by the entrance, looking up and down the street. Years of army life had taught him, like me, the value of punctuality. I suppose I was a little surprised to see him there. Just after the clock above the Town Hall struck midday, a woman turned the corner and crossed the street. I recognised her from the photograph. She was wearing a cream muslin dress and a broad hat with ostrich plumes. As she approached, her legs pushed out the skirts of her dress and something stirred in me. MacLeod offered her his arm and led her up the stairs to the entrance of the tall, red-brick building. As they walked through the main archway, I realised that I was a little jealous.

I went to the Americain earlier than usual that evening in the hope of seeing MacLeod. I'd had three whiskies before he came in, looking very pleased with himself. He ordered a cognac and knocked it back in one. Well? I said. He put the glass down and announced that he knew he would marry the girl. I stood dumbfounded. He said two things had convinced him of the fact: the first was the glances of appreciation she had received as they wandered through the museum. The second was that she had admired a particular painting, by Rembrandt, of a naked woman stepping from a bath. She had told him she liked the feeling of being naked. 'She's a woman after my own heart, Verster,' he said. Six days later they were formally engaged.

In April, the girl moved into the house on Leidschekade and they arranged to have a small celebration there. On that evening, MacLeod introduced her as Margaretha, but he called her Gerda when they spoke together. Her black hair was done up in a chignon. She was wearing an ivory-white merino dress that showed off her cleavage. She was very charming. When I asked who else would be coming, MacLeod laughed and said it would just be the three of us. He and Gerda had agreed that they wanted only me there because I had brought them together in the first place. As if reading my mind, MacLeod told me not to worry – Gerda had found the joke as funny as he had. I smiled and shrugged and raised my glass to them. What else could I do?

The next time I saw her was at the Café Americain, when MacLeod introduced her to all the commissioned officers in the bar and ordered schnapps with beer chasers for everyone. Although she was the only woman in the place, she talked easily with the other officers, all of whom cast glances at MacLeod. He leant over to me and asked me how old I thought she was. I said twenty-three or four. He shook his head. Eighteen, he said. I looked again: she was young enough to be his daughter, but she would never have passed for such. He asked if I remembered the night of the party. I nodded. He said he had plucked her cherry that night. He laughed and said she had been afraid, but he loved plucking cherries so much that he wouldn't take no for an answer. He had been in such a rush that he'd ripped off her petticoat.

Their wedding was in August. Margaretha wore a pearl-grey dress and veil. The ceremony at the Consulate was brief and attended only by close family members. When the marriage was first announced, Margaretha's father, Adam Zelle, had refused to give his blessing. MacLeod had told me he thought the old man just couldn't stand the idea of another man taking her away. Eventually, the old man had relented and attended the ceremony. The reception that followed was at the Café Americain. When everyone had sat down, it was noticed that Adam Zelle wasn't present. No one knew where he had got to. MacLeod later told me that he had paid the driver of Zelle's carriage to take him to a completely different restaurant.

When he returned from Wiesbaden, where they had spent their honeymoon, MacLeod seemed disconcerted. He explained that the spa town had been full of young German officers, to whom he often saw Gerda talking. When he was passing by on his own, they made loud remarks about what they would like to do with Gerda. He'd had to step up to one of them and remind him that Gerda was his wife. Also, the trip had been costly. Gerda had ordered several new dresses and the spa town was expensive. The whole episode seemed to worry him. He asked me if he could borrow some money. 'Just to tide me over,' he said. He seemed relieved when I agreed. He then asked me if I would look in on Gerda the next evening since he had an appointment with a young lady and would be late home.

I did what he asked and spent the following evening listening to Margaretha playing the piano badly. Louise seemed gloomy and the low-ceilinged room was stifling. As soon as Margaretha had finished, Louise left the room. Margaretha sat beside me and asked me about the East Indies. I told her about the heat, about the rain that usually fell every afternoon and the monsoon that came every September. She said the town she had grown up in had been too small for her and that she was sure life in such a faraway place would be exciting. I chose not to tell her of the constriction and boredom of colonial life. Instead, I watched her young face and, for the first time, was afraid of what would happen to her.

Five months after the wedding, she gave birth to a baby boy. MacLeod was at the Café Americain playing cards at the time. When he received the news, MacLeod ordered a schnapps for everyone and, when they had been served, he stood up and announced that his son would be called Norman after his great-uncle, a retired general.

In the spring of 1896, Queen Regent Emma held a royal garden party, to which nearly every commissioned officer was invited, as well as politicians, businessmen and celebrities. I drifted uncomfortably among the marquees and covered tables set out on the lawns, looking for a familiar face. It was with some relief that I saw MacLeod arriving with Margaretha just as luncheon was announced. She was wearing a lemon-yellow gown with a string of pearls. MacLeod presented her to the Queen Regent's young daughter, Queen Wilhelmina, who smiled and said, 'How charming.' Margaretha curtsied. MacLeod and I spent the afternoon at the bar, where MacLeod drank and I tried to slow him down. He was angry at her extravagance. Her new dress had cost forty guilders, an amount he simply couldn't afford on his captain's pay. He muttered something about bills. I looked across the garden and saw Margaretha dancing with a naval captain. Several men gathered round, waiting for the next dance.

MacLeod's leave in Amsterdam had been extended, firstly because of his wedding and then because of the baby. But soon after the royal garden party, MacLeod finally got his new posting – to Toempoeng, in Java. As was usual with a new posting, MacLeod also received his promotion, in his case to major. I hadn't seen much of him at the Americain and the word was that he was seeing a great deal of his mistress. I was with a friend at the Pink Flamingo Casino one night when I saw MacLeod arrive with Margaretha. I said hello to them, but MacLeod seemed keener to play roulette than talk. He only used one-guilder chips and put one chip on each colour as his bet. While I stood with my friend, I watched MacLeod, who was in turn watching Margaretha. She was mingling at the baccarat table. She was wearing an olive-green dimity dress that hugged her body and trailed down to the ground. A businessman was watching her. A few moments later, the businessman approached her and they began talking. She was standing close to him, looking up into his eyes. He gestured to the door; then they drifted past the velvet curtains and up some stairs. At this point, MacLeod cashed in his chips and left without saying good-night.

Early in the summer, I received my new posting. I was to be garrisoned at Magelang, a small town high up in the mountains of central Java. It would be a dull few years. Like MacLeod, I also received my promotion to major but, unlike MacLeod, I was to be posted immediately as I had no wife or family. I packed up what few possessions I owned and gave notice on my rented room. My passage was booked for mid-June. I went to the Americain several times, but MacLeod was never there and no one knew where he was. I called by the house in Leidschekade twice, but no one was home. The third time I went there, Louise answered the door and told me that her brother was hardly ever at home these days and that Margaretha spent all her time at social events. She said 'social events' as though it was a disease. I asked her to pass on my good wishes to them both and my hope that we would see each other again. But the world was too big and I never did, although I often thought of Margaretha.

2
Dutch East Indies, 1897–99

A photograph taken on 1 May 1897 on board the SS Prinses Amalia, *bound for the Dutch East Indies, shows a group of eighteen people gathered together – six men, eight women and four children.*

In the foreground are two girls sitting on the wooden deck. They are both wearing long checked dresses and one has a bonnet set back on her head. Behind them sit five women. To the right sit three in long black dresses, with black frills and tight chokers. One face is slightly blurred.

On the extreme left sits a young woman in a voluminous black skirt and white jacket with large, uneven lapels. Her hands are crossed on her lap and she is looking directly into the camera. This is Gerda. She is twenty years old. To the right of her stands a young boy with fluffy blond hair, carrying a large sabre on a leather sash. This is Norman; he is one and a half.

Standing just behind him is a short man, dressed completely in black, with a black bowler hat. He is not looking at the camera, but upwards and to his left. The lenses of his spectacles reflect the blankness of the sky.

Behind Gerda stands a soldier, wearing a kepi. The two rows of buttons running down his jacket are connected by chenille. The soldier is Major Rudolph MacLeod. He is forty-one.

All the men have moustaches. No one is smiling. The day is overcast.

By the time I received my new posting in Toempoeng, my marriage to Gerda was foundering. What had started as a response to my deepest insecurities as a bachelor had developed into a mismatched coupling. The one saving grace in all of this was my son, Norman. I loved him above anything, above my own life even. As soon as he was born, Gerda handed him over to the wet nurse. She showed him no love, and I strove to show him all the love I could in order that he might have enough. I do believe he was happy. I remember how, every morning on the boat to Java, I took him out on deck and we would practise marches and salutes together.

As a family, we spent the first year in Toempoeng – a small, dirty village as dull as rain. The garrison amounted to no more than twenty men. There was nothing to do there and no one to meet. The only person we saw was Van Rheede, who owned a coffee plantation in the hills. He doubled as the government comptroller for the region, a job which involved making sure that there was not too much corruption among the local Javanese council. We clung to Van Rheede for fear that we would go mad with boredom.

I think it was boredom, and alcohol, that drove me to Gerda after a particularly raucous night at his house. As soon as we got home, I told her to strip. She was surprised, because we hardly slept together any more, but I think she was secretly glad. She took off her dress and unbuttoned her petticoat. I looked at her body, which I had once so coveted. She pulled her hair loose and got into the bed without a word. I quickly disrobed and climbed on top of her. I spread her legs and pinned her down. For a moment we were together again, and the moment must have had some truth to it because out of it came Jeanne Louise, my beloved daughter. She was named after my sister, but we quickly took to calling her Non, a shortened version of *nonah,* the local word for 'girl'.

When old Major Bervoets retired as garrison commander in Medan, Sumatra, I received my promotion and was ordered to replace him. I breathed a huge sigh of relief that I would be put to some use after all. I immediately rode my horse over to Van Rheede's and asked him to take in Gerda and the two children while I travelled over there to secure accommodation. We Dutch took care of our own and I knew he would agree without hesitation. I packed a small case and spent three days sailing from Surabaya across the Java Sea and up the Strait of Malacca to Tanjungbalai. From there, I took a cart to Medan. As luck would have it, Bervoets was returning to Holland and giving up his villa, but not for a month at least. I wrote to Gerda that I would stay on for that month, adjusting myself to the new job and arranging for new furniture. The army refused to give financial assistance, which meant I had to auction off everything each time I moved house. It was a severe drain on my finances.

Fortunately, my promotion brought with it a modest increase in pay, which I desperately needed. I had left Amsterdam with many debts – my meagre captain's pay simply did not cover the kind of lifestyle I had enjoyed. I learnt to avoid those I owed money to – Captains Ter Stegge, Verster and Kraaykamp. Then there had been the wedding reception and the honeymoon in Wiesbaden. To make matters worse, Gerda had bought new dresses, hats, shoes and parasols for the trip, all of which were on credit. But my biggest expense of all in Amsterdam was my mistress, Johanna, whom I was seeing long before I met Gerda. When I realised the mistake I'd made in marrying Gerda, I found solace in Johanna. She made me feel appreciated every time I saw her, which was often. She cried when I told her I was leaving for Java, but her tears soon dried up when I gave her my parting gift of a diamond ring.

Medan was a small city, consisting of multi-storey buildings and excellent roads, all designed by the Dutch but built by the Sumatrans. Electric lighting had been installed five years previously. Several shops, or *tokos*, sold goods from Holland. It was paradise compared to Toempoeng. I wrote to Gerda, explaining all this, and asked after the children. I was anxious about them being alone with her. In one of her letters, she sent a picture of her with Norman and Non. She mentioned that a naval lieutenant had taken the photograph. Gerda vexed me with her flirtations, but I tried, for the children's sake, to make the best of it.

Eventually, old Bervoets left the villa and I prepared to move in. I sent word to Gerda to make the sea journey and began the laborious task of arranging the sale of what little we had in Toempoeng and moving the new furniture I had bought. Mertens, the garrison doctor, lived nearby. I had befriended him since arriving in Medan and he helped me move. Mertens had himself just arrived in Medan when Krakatoa exploded in 1883. He said it was the worst sound he had ever heard, but the sunsets for months afterwards had been a very striking purple-red. The villa overlooked the city, perched on the slopes of our very own collapsed volcano, which eventually peaked 100 kilometres to the south. Steps had been cut into the hillside and irrigated to grow rice. The clouds were always low and the atmosphere somewhat oppressive. To the north lay the Strait of Malacca, which you could only see on a clear day. I employed a maid, who came up from Medan every morning and left every evening. She collected water, cooked the rice and cleaned the house. I made sure the villa was stocked up with brandy.

On the night Gerda was due to arrive, I put the wicker chair on the verandah, lit the lamp and settled down with a newspaper. I had no idea exactly when she would arrive. She had sent a telegram, but failed to mention a time. This was typical of her, but I had grown accustomed to her bad organisation and even worse timekeeping. It was nearly ten o'clock when I heard a cart approach and saw Gerda's white dress through the gloom. I took Non from Gerda's arms and looked into the small bundle. Non was fast asleep. I stood under the lamp and saw that she was very pale. I brought Norman into the light and saw that he, too, looked unwell. When I asked Gerda about this, she said it was nothing, only that food had been a little scarce in Toempoeng. My hackles rose and I shouted that she was the wife of a major in the Dutch army and that she could have all the food she bloody well asked for! She said that I hadn't sent her enough money, to which I countered that all she had to do was ask!

I told the porter to unload the cart and left her to bring in the last of her infernal hatboxes herself.

My anger with her lasted for the next few days. I left instructions with the maid to give both Norman and Non extra food and busied myself at the garrison. There was a suspected outbreak of rabies in Medan – two dogs had been seen running wild in the streets, twitching and foaming at the mouth. I ordered a complete round-up of every dog in the city. Bill posters were put up in the city centre as well as in the outer slums, ordering every citizen who owned a dog to clamp its mouth and turn it over to the garrison. By the fourth day of the round-up, we had several hundred dogs. The compound was full of them. I arranged for two squads of soldiers to shoot them and burn the carcasses. At the same time, I arranged for another four squads to search the slums for any dogs that were being hidden by the natives. After two days, we had a further 141 dogs. One of the platoon sergeants brought a native soldier to me, saying that he had attempted to hide his father's dog. When I questioned him, the soldier claimed there was nothing wrong with it, but I was taking no chances. I docked him two months' pay and assigned him latrine duty for a week. I ignored his obvious resentment and dismissed him. Orders were orders and the natives had to understand that. In all, 739 dogs were caught and killed.

A few weeks later, I informed Gerda that we would host a drinks party to celebrate my promotion. It was a tradition that I didn't particularly relish, but one that I was obliged to observe. On the day of the party, I left the garrison at four o'clock and took a rickshaw up to the villa. When I arrived, Gerda seemed upset. She told me that she had dislodged an enormous scorpion after moving one of the potted palms on the verandah. It was pale yellow, almost white, and had its pincers raised. The maid had had to come and sweep it off the verandah. She had heard it fall into the foliage. She shivered when she told me. I shrugged and told her that was why it was important to move the flowerpots each morning.

I undressed and doused myself with cold water in the bathroom, then put on my dress uniform. My nerves were jangled, so I had a large brandy to take off the edge. Non was given her milk and put in her cot. Norman was fed his rice and vegetables by the maid and put to bed. At six-thirty, I looked in on them: they were both asleep. Gerda changed into a rust-coloured sarong and bright blue *kabaja*. I asked how much they'd cost. She said next to nothing, which I didn't believe. By seven, the first guests started to arrive. As I had instructed, the maid stood by the door holding a tray of glasses filled with sherry. Gerda was next to me as I welcomed people one by one. Most of the guests were junior officers from the garrison. I had noticed many of the sly glances they gave Gerda on our Saturday nights at the club, but although I had come to find my wife deeply unattractive, I was going to make damn sure no one else laid a finger on her.

One of the guests was a major newly transferred from a garrison further along the coast of Sumatra. He knew no one and, for half an hour, tried to impress me with his knowledge of Indonesian geography. I took long draughts from my brandy and noticed that Gerda was deep in conversation with a young naval lieutenant. I had no idea who he was or what he was doing in Medan, but I began to wonder if he was the naval lieutenant Gerda had mentioned in her letter. When Mertens arrived with his wife, I made my excuses and slipped away. I fetched some sherry for them. We talked about the lack of drugs to combat the latest outbreak of cholera. Bored by our conversation, Mertens' wife broke off and mingled. I asked Mertens if he knew who the naval lieutenant was, but he didn't.

By nine-thirty I was half-cut and the guests were thinning out. The naval lieutenant was leaving too. He smiled at Gerda and kissed her hand before he left. My teeth were clenched in fury at his impertinence. The maid was gathering up the last of the glasses. I told her to check on the children and walked over to Gerda. She said what a pleasant evening it had been and I told her to go to hell. She looked at me and I waited for her to say something so that I could get angry. I picked up a bottle from the dining table and poured myself another brandy. She was just about to say something when the maid rushed back into the room. She said that Norman was ill.

I ran into his bedroom and what I saw mortified me. He lay panting and contorted, clutching his stomach. The sheets were twisted into a knot at the foot of the bed. There was vomit on the sheets and floor. I told the maid to fetch the doctor, then knelt down beside the bed. The boy's teeth were chattering and his eyes were closed. I quickly got a blanket from the chest of drawers and laid it over him. Mertens came in. He laid the back of his hand on the boy's forehead and told the maid to get some water and towels. His wife was sent to fetch his bag.

As Mertens felt for a pulse, Norman vomited again. A white sludge dribbled from his mouth. I laid another blanket over him, even though he was hot and sweating, and asked Mertens what we should do. Mertens clutched the boy's wrist and stared at his pocket watch. I turned and saw Gerda and the few remaining guests at the bedroom door. I shouted at them all to get out. Gerda ushered the guests away. I could hear them whispering in the living room; then everything was quiet. The maid came back with a bowl of water and towels. Mertens put his watch away and said that his pulse was very weak. I shouted at him to find out what the matter was, but he told me to keep quiet. He passed his hand over Norman's swollen stomach and the boy cried out. He asked if there was any kaolin and morphine solution in the house. I ran to the kitchen to get it. I had to steady myself against the wall for a moment before going through the cupboards until I found the solution. Mertens pulled out the cork stopper and carefully opened Norman's mouth. He poured some of the white liquid down his throat, but he vomited it into a puddle on the sheets. I groaned when I saw blood in the bile.

It was an age before Mertens' wife returned with his bag. He took out a thermometer, shook it and placed it under Norman's arm. The poor boy opened his eyes and looked into the middle distance. They were large and round and bloodshot. I told him that everything was going to be all right, but he didn't respond. Then his eyes closed again and he lay still. I thought he seemed better, but Mertens frowned. He said that it was some kind of poisoning, that it was serious. He put a stethoscope to his ears and spent a long time listening to the boy's heart. I sat on the bed and took Norman's hand. It was ice-cold. His mouth hung open and his breathing was shallow. I looked at his golden hair, all matted and wet. Mertens was still checking the heartbeat when he suddenly cursed under his breath. He put his ear to the boy's heart. I held my breath. Mertens listened for a few more moments, and then said, 'I'm afraid he's gone.'

The next morning, I woke on the sofa, still in my dress uniform. My head was on fire. I sat up and smoothed down my hair. Strong bands of sunlight slid through the wooden slats on the windows, making me blink. The air in the room was hot and stale. Events of the previous night slowly came back to me. I remembered drinking brandy, while Mertens tried to console me, then the doctor leaving very late with his wife. I remembered lashing out at Gerda when she tried to comfort me. I remembered the heaviness of my breathing when I was finally alone.

I stood up and staggered to the back of the villa. In the bedroom, Gerda was still asleep. I walked to the side of the bed, where she lay curled up. Her long hair was uncoiled on the pillow. I grabbed it and pulled her out of bed. She fell on to the floor, screaming. As I dragged her out of the bedroom, I felt clumps of hair come away. She tried to cling on to the furniture and begged me to stop, but I shouted that she was a vain hag and continued pulling her along the floor. I dragged her into the living room. All she wanted to do was fuck my officers. Worst of all, she was responsible for Norman's death, and I was going to punish her for that. I let her go. She held her head and sobbed. I kicked her as hard as I could in the stomach.

I was given compassionate leave by General Biesz. With the help of the garrison pastor, I made arrangements for the funeral. I consented to a burial in the army cemetery and, after Mertens had completed the post-mortem, I put my son into the ground. He was buried with full military honours. At the service, the garrison brass band played the 'Monte Carlo March', a song that Norman and I used to march to on board the ship from Holland. I broke down; I could not help myself.

During my leave, I hardly said a word to Gerda. I slept on the sofa and spent time either in the mess halls, where I took my meals, or walking in the city. Every face I saw was Norman's. In the markets, on street corners or in bars, I heard the boy calling out. Sometimes I thought I could see him, just disappearing round a corner, or through a doorway. Such a sweet boy. I wrote to Louise, informing her of Norman's death. I wrote that his loss had cracked something inside me. I received a reply from her post-haste, in which she said I should never have married Gerda.

I was at the mess one day, drinking in the late afternoon, when Mertens sat down beside me. He had been looking for me all day, he said. I offered him a brandy, but he declined. He told me he had some news about Norman's post-mortem. The results had been negative for poisoning, but he had since discovered that Norman had been poisoned after all. He went on to say that my maid, who had contracted cholera and was being cared for in the hospital, had died the previous night. Before she died, though, she had confessed to poisoning Norman. I stared at Mertens. Words failed me. I searched my mind for a reason. Mertens said it was because of that soldier I had disciplined about the dog. The soldier had been her betrothed. She had poisoned Norman's rice the night of the reception because of the punishment I had administered.

In a matter of days, I received orders from General Biesz to transfer immediately to the Willem I military establishment at Bejoe-Biroe in Java. The general said the situation was 'too delicate' for me to stay. I cleared out my desk and gathered up the papers I needed to take with me. I said a brief farewell to my secretary and to the colleagues who were still at work this late in the afternoon. They said nothing, except goodbye. I was sure the rumours had already started. I crossed the compound, a dried mud clearing, faced on all four sides by arches. I realised that my new posting was in fact a demotion and that I would never see this compound again. I couldn't stomach the humiliation. Biesz had never liked me and now he was siding with the natives. I felt a pain behind my eyes and across my chest. I flagged down a rickshaw on the road outside the compound. As the porter ran through the streets of Medan, I felt like hitting somebody.

When I arrived at the villa, I paid the porter ten cents and walked on to the verandah. I went inside and looked for Gerda to tell her to start packing – we were to leave at the weekend. I went into the kitchen, then the bedroom, where I saw Gerda in bed with a man. I saw a uniform lying on a chair. The man looked at me, swore under his breath and got out of bed. He quickly put on his uniform. Only when he was dressed did I recognise him as the young naval lieutenant at the reception. The man stood, waiting for some kind of reprisal. I told him to get out. He left quickly and quietly.

Gerda was sitting up in bed, clutching the sheets to her breasts. I studied her. I asked where Non was and she said that the wet nurse had taken her for a walk. I took a step forward and saw her shrink away from me. I told her I wanted a divorce. She looked at me strangely, clearly not expecting that. I slapped her full across the face. She let out a cry and fell to one side. I did nothing more. I realised I was too tired. I told her again that I wanted a divorce, that I wanted it so much I would even let her divorce me. She said no. When I asked why not, she said that she wasn't going to let me rob her of her rights to a pension. I felt like spitting in her face and promised to myself that I would rob her of everything else.

3
Gamelan

In 1580, Sir Francis Drake landed in Java while circumnavigating the globe in his ship the Golden Hind. *During his stay, he visited a royal court and was invited to hear a performance of the court's 'gamelan'. In his ship's log, he described it as 'country-musick, which though it were of a very strange kind, yet the sound was pleasant and delightfull'. He was almost certainly the first European to hear a gamelan performance.*

A gamelan is described by those who play it as a single large instrument, but it is in fact an ensemble of tuned percussion instruments, consisting mainly of gongs (a Javanese word), metallophones and drums. The wooden frames of the instruments are sometimes embellished with carvings of serpents or dragons and are usually painted in the royal colours of red and gold. Gongs and drums are common throughout South-east Asia, but the gamelan tradition is unique to the islands of Java, Bali and Lombok in Indonesia.

The first gamelans were made at the behest of Java's ancestral sultans and housed in their courts. They were made of bronze, but more recent gamelans are made of brass or iron, especially those found in the poorer Javanese villages. The oldest known gamelan is the Gamelan Selonding, whose bronze bars were cast more than 2,000 years ago.

The origins of the gamelan are uncertain, as there are no written records, but from reliefs found on temple walls and ancient bronze drums, it has now been established that the use of the instrument was heavily determined by cultural influences from China and, most importantly, India. Hinduism arrived in Java from India in the first century AD. Buddhism arrived later, and the two religions dominated until the fifteenth century, when Islam spread through the islands.

The last of the great Javan Hindu kingdoms, Majapahit, was conquered by Islamic invaders around 1500. The largest and loudest of Java's court gamelans, the Gamelan Sekaten, was created at that time at the command of Java's first Muslim prince. He built two huge gamelans and ordered that they be played continuously for a week at a newly built mosque to mark the birth of Mohammed. It was hoped that the largely Hindu population would be drawn to the new Islamic faith. Today, about ninety per cent of Java's population is Muslim, but the gamelan tradition still displays its Hindu-Buddhist roots.

A complete gamelan is actually two sets of instruments, each in a different scale: one is called *laras slendro* and has five notes; the other is called *laras pelog* and has seven notes. The two sets are laid out at right angles to each other.

Each instrument within a gamelan has a clear role to play, which is reflected in the way a gamelan is laid out. A central melody is played on metallophones in the middle of the gamelan and is then elaborated on by instruments at the front. Finally, the various gongs at the back are used as 'punctuation', marking off small sections within the larger melody.

The metallophones in the middle are of two types: the *saron*, which have no resonators and are struck with hard hammers, and the *gendèr*, which do have resonators and are played with soft hammers. These instruments play the 'spine' of the melody, called the *balungan*.

At the front are the small kettle gongs (*bonangs*) and some *gendèr*, as well as various string or wind instruments, including fiddles (*rebab*), bamboo flutes (*suling*) and zithers (*siter*). These all have a wider range than the *balungan* instruments and are said to play the hidden melody 'sung by the musicians in their hearts'.

Each of the gongs at the back has an onomatopoeic name: *kenong*, *ketuk* or *kempul*. The largest gong, called the *gong ageng*, is the most important instrument because it is believed to house the soul or spirit of the gamelan and no piece of music can begin or end until it is struck.

A gamelan can be played by up to forty people at any one time, but there is no conductor. The whole is co-ordinated by a drummer who sits in the middle of the gamelan, playing a range of double-headed drums. There is no musical notation and no improvisation – each piece of music has to be committed to memory.

Each player in the gamelan learns how to play every instrument, starting with the simpler instruments at the back and working their way forwards. There are no soloists but, during very lengthy performances, the players sometimes change places or are substituted altogether. No two gamelans are alike and, in time, Javanese musicians are able to tell the gamelans apart according to their tones.

On hearing a gamelan performance for the first time, the Spanish writer Miguel Covarrubias described the music as 'an Oriental ultra-modern Bach fugue, an astounding combination of bells, machinery and thunder'.

4

Bejoe-Biroe, Java, Dutch East Indies, 1900–01

Neither for the one, nor for the other did I have any specific feeling of friendship, nor enmity. During the year and a half I used to know the MacLeod family, the conduct of Mrs MacLeod, notwithstanding the many rude insults she had to endure in public from her husband, was perfectly correct. I have often wondered whether Margaretha Zelle might not have grown into a good wife and mother, if her husband had been a more equable and sensible man. Her marriage to the uneven-tempered and excitable MacLeod was doomed to failure.

Dr Roelfsema, in a letter to the Editor,
Algemeen Handelsblad, 1920

One morning, after she and MacLeod had been in Bejoe-Biroe for several months, Gerda felt groggy and couldn't wake up. She had a stomach-ache and slept through till mid-morning, when the maid brought her some tea. Then she fell asleep again. When the maid looked in on her in the afternoon, she was still unconscious and had developed a fever. Concerned, the maid hurried to the small barracks nearby where MacLeod worked. He told her to fetch Dr Roelfsema and carried on with his duties.

Roelfsema examined Gerda for ten minutes, after which he told the maid to leave the bungalow immediately. He picked Non up, closed the door after him, walked to the barracks and handed Non to MacLeod. He told him that his wife had typhoid fever and that no one except himself or MacLeod was to enter the house until he said so. MacLeod sighed and nodded.

Gerda stayed in bed, slipping in and out of sleep. She developed spots on her arms and abdomen. The fever became worse. She could only hold down black tea or thin soup and her body weight decreased drastically. The doctor prescribed a course of aspirin and looked in on her twice a day. He had no other medication to give her, he explained – there was little else he could do.

After nearly three weeks the fever broke, but Gerda was still too weak to get up. The maid returned to help care for her. One night, Gerda woke, sensing someone in the room. She saw the maid placing hot tea by her bed. Because it was still dark outside, she was confused.

'What time is it?' she said.

The maid opened the wooden shutters and pointed outside.

'*Mata hari,*' she said.

Gerda sat up and looked out. She could see the first washes of light in the east. Dawn, she thought. The maid smiled and left. Gerda sat still, waiting for her head to clear, then drank some tea. There were large black leaves and cloves in the hot water. It smelled like jasmine.

For the first time since she had been taken ill, she felt like walking. She got up and put on her white silk peignoir. Her waist seemed so thin. Her cheeks were gaunt, but she felt better, cleaner somehow. In the living room, MacLeod was lying on the sofa with a tartan blanket covering him. She crept past and went outside. The grass was wet. She walked away from the bungalow, under the brightening sky and into the banyan trees. Her legs felt weak and unused.

The jungle was difficult to walk through: aerial roots sprouted from the trees above and sank down into the soil. Lianas and vines connected each tree to every other. She heard dripping all around her. The jungle seemed alive. The foliage quivered as water dripped from above and unseen birds uttered strange clicks and squawks. The tops of the chaotic trees were as high as a cathedral roof. She stepped carefully through the undergrowth, feeling a little dizzy but calm. Insects stopped buzzing when she approached them. She thought she could hear music, soft music, coming through the trees from somewhere in front of her.

After she had crept through the jungle for some time, the trees thinned out and she could see huts in front of her. The sun had risen now and the music was louder. She stepped out into a clearing, where there was a kampong made up of about fifteen wood-and-leaf huts. As she approached the source of the music, she could make out ten or more men sitting on the hard ground, each in front of a different instrument, which he struck with hammers. She stood a little way off and watched them.

Some of the instruments looked like rows of kettledrums topped with large balls. Others were like xylophones. She saw two gongs behind one of the men. The wooden casings for the instruments were all painted in the same red and gold. The men, dressed in simple, ragged clothes, didn't talk or look at each other, but just kept their eyes on the keys and struck softly. Gerda was captivated by the sound, so slow and soothing. There was a fire burning nearby; the smoke rose directly upwards from it, drifting through the canopy of huge leaves and vines. She could smell patchouli oil.

Then she noticed two young girls as they came out from behind one of the huts. Their pepper-red silk sarongs were trimmed with gold and trailed on the ground. They were very slim. Both wore metal headpieces and small-link chains and wider bracelets around their ankles, wrists, upper arms and necks. Their eyebrows were thick and black, their lips and long nails painted scarlet. They began dancing to the music, their bodies stiff, but their arms moving fluently, wrists turning in the air, hands fanning in and out. They turned their heads from side to side, smiling all the time. Then they bowed deeply to each other, turned around and repeated their movements. Gerda couldn't take her eyes off them.

*

When she found herself back at the bungalow, Gerda was unaware of how she had arrived there. She stepped into the living room to see MacLeod sitting with Non, feeding her. He looked ridiculous in his uniform with a child on his lap. She steeled herself.

'Where have you been? Non needed feeding,' he said.

'What time is it?'

'It's gone noon. Where have you been?'

She ignored him. 'I have to go away, somewhere warmer. I need to recuperate.'

'If you are well enough to gallivant about in the early morning, you're well enough to start feeding Non again. A bottle of milk costs thirty cents and she needs five bottles a day. I can't afford to buy any more!' he said.

'You seem to be managing very well,' she said, walking into the bedroom.

MacLeod eventually agreed to Gerda's wish that she have time to convalesce and sent her to a coffee plantation near Ulingie, owned by a friend of his. Secretly, he was quite pleased she had gone. While she was away, MacLeod spent time in the mess hall with his fellow officers. They stayed up drinking and playing cards until the mess hall closed at one o'clock, at which time they would go into one of the nearby kampongs to visit a brothel.

On one such night, MacLeod paid extra to be rough and chose the youngest girl he could see. In the squalid room, he tied her arms behind her back with one of his army belts and stuffed a handkerchief in her mouth. He barely noticed the child in the crib behind the door.

In the following weeks, MacLeod tired of the prostitutes and began eyeing the Javanese wives of Dutch officers. After discreet enquiries, MacLeod soon discovered that many of the Javanese wives or mistresses were willing to sleep with other officers for money.

MacLeod gave the maid enough money to feed Non and

slept with as many of these Javanese women as his major's pay could afford. He rarely enjoyed it. He found he could drain some of his anger by blindfolding the women, or hitting them across the face just before he came.

A year after arriving in Bejoe-Biroe, MacLeod was told by the barracks CO that his promotion to lieutenant colonel had been turned down by General Biesz. That night, he woke still drunk at three in the morning to find a young Javanese woman lying unconscious next to him. When he turned her over, he saw blood dripping from her nose and mouth. Then he realised his right hand was hurting. He quickly dressed, flung two dollars on the bed and left the building quietly.

He lay low at the bungalow for the next few evenings. He did his sums and worked out that, at forty-four years old, he had been an active soldier for twenty-eight years, which meant he was entitled to a full pension of 2,800 guilders a year – enough to live on, but only in a place where the cost of living was cheaper. This would necessitate another move. He enquired among his fellow officers and was told that he could rent a villa in Sindanglaja, further into the jungle.

All in all, he thought, it was a good decision. Bejoe-Biroe was not the paradise that Medan was, even though the locals called it the City of Light. There was nothing to look at except mountains. He detested the constant chirring of crickets, the invasions of flying ants and termites by day, and the nightly plagues of moths and mosquitoes. The nights were terribly quiet and dark, except at the crossroads, which were lit by dim lanterns. Without his almanac, he had no sense of what day of the week it was, or what date. Yes, he was looking forward to Sindanglaja where, he had been told, the climate was much healthier.

When Gerda returned from the coffee plantation fully recovered, she invited Dr Roelfsema to dinner, to thank him. Gerda wore one of her many brightly coloured sarongs. She adored their exotic colours and had taken to wearing them all the time now. MacLeod changed into his dark-blue dress uniform, which Gerda noticed was beginning to look a little worn.

At the dinner table, Gerda served the doctor some wine while MacLeod drank brandy. They ate *roti* and sweet potatoes. MacLeod complained about the food. They had a fruit salad dessert and coffee. Roelfsema listened as Gerda told him about Ulingie, where it was drier. Interrupting her, MacLeod mentioned Kitchener's victory at Omdurman.

'If we're not careful in the south, he'll take over the whole of Africa,' he said.

'Have you been back to Europe recently, Dr Roelfsema?' Gerda asked.

'Indeed I have. I went to visit my brother in Paris only six months ago.'

'Paris! How wonderful. What's it like there?'

'You've never been?'

'No,' Gerda said; 'I'd love to very much.'

'Well you should. The cafés there are quite the most beautiful I've ever seen. And the dancehalls are spectacular as well.'

'I hope to go there one day,' Gerda said.

There was a lull in the conversation. Roelfsema said it was getting late and that he ought to drop in on a nearby patient. Gerda noticed it was still early. He rose and thanked them for the meal. MacLeod said nothing. Gerda gave Roelfsema his jacket and said goodnight as he left. MacLeod opened a new bottle of brandy and sat on the sofa with a glassful. He unbuttoned his tunic. Gerda wanted nothing more to do with him and retired.

In bed, she tried to picture the dancehalls and cafés of Paris. She imagined they would be large ornate buildings, with luxurious interiors. Everyone in them would be well-dressed – the men in black and white, the women in bright, rich colours. She wondered if she would ever meet that kind of people. She stretched and turned over.

She was woken by the sound of breaking glass. Her bedside clock said it was past two. She lay still, holding her breath to listen. MacLeod was moving around the front rooms, opening and closing drawers. There was a moment of silence, then a crash as something fell to the floor. She heard him mutter. She got up.

In the dining room, MacLeod was standing in front of the dresser with the bottle of brandy in his hand. He was looking for something. The bottle was half-empty and there was a drawer lying on the floor, its cutlery spilled out.

'What are you doing?' she asked.

MacLeod looked around. He staggered a little. 'Oh, it's only you,' he said.

'What are you looking for?'

'A glass. The other one broke,' he said.

'That was the last one. You've broken all the others.'

MacLeod crouched down to hunt through the cupboards. 'No it wasn't; there's another one somewhere.'

Gerda sighed and sat down at the dinner table. 'No there isn't,' she said.

MacLeod stood up abruptly, knocking over a chair. 'If you want to go to Paris that much, why don't you just go and leave me alone!'

Gerda froze. He swayed on his feet and glared at her. She was afraid to say anything. He moved towards the bureau and opened a drawer. He seemed to find what he was looking for and studied it for a moment with his back to her. When he turned around, she saw that he had a revolver in his hand. He glared at her again. The gun was shaking slightly in his hand. MacLeod walked round the table and stopped at Gerda's side. He pointed the revolver at her. Gerda's heart turned to stone. He touched the end of the barrel against her temple and pressed so hard that her head was forced down on to her shoulder. He leant over and whispered into her ear:

'If only I could get rid of you, you harridan.'

She couldn't speak for fear. The muzzle was cold and hard against her skin. It felt terrible.

MacLeod chuckled and walked back to the bureau. He dropped the revolver in the drawer and slammed the drawer shut.

'I'm going out to find a glass,' he said as he staggered out of the door. He moved away into the night.

Gerda took several breaths. She was shaking and a cold sweat broke out all over her body. She put her hands on the table and looked up. Her gaze fixed on the dresser, with three or four patterned plates leaning upright on its shelves. Behind them was a mirror. She caught sight of herself, and was surprised at how drawn and aged her reflection appeared, as though the woman looking back had knowledge she couldn't afford to keep.

5

Amsterdam, 1902

MacLeod was upstairs in the house in Van Breestraat, folding a few shirts, underpants and trousers, which he put into neat piles on the bed. The ceiling was low and he had to stoop. He then cleared out the drawers of his shaving gear, belts, studs and cuff-links. He collected his high boots and dinner shoes from the cupboard and packed everything into a large carpetbag. Packing had always cleared his mind; it gave him patience and purpose.

When he had finished, he checked Gerda wasn't in the hallway or on the stairs and then went to fetch Non. She was fast asleep in her cot. He gathered her up in his arms and made sure she was wrapped up well. She briefly opened her eyes while he did this, but went back to sleep immediately. He walked down the narrow staircase and placed his bag just inside the reception room, where Gerda couldn't see it. When he opened the door to the kitchen, Gerda was preparing some fish and vegetables for herself. MacLeod had eaten some olives and canapés at the Café Americain.

MacLeod produced an envelope from inside his jacket. 'I'm going out to post a letter.'

Gerda placed a saucepan on the stove and ignored him.

'I thought I might take Non out into the night air, it may do her cold some good,' he said.

Without looking up, Gerda nodded.

'Right,' he said and closed the door. After waiting for a few moments, he said a low farewell, but heard nothing other than the scrape of a chair. He opened the front door and felt the wind whip across his face. It was very dark, but he could make out light on the wet cobbles. He picked up his bag, closed the door softly behind him and, still clutching his daughter, ran to catch the train for Arnhem.

In *Het Nieuws van den Dag* the next day, there was an announcement in which MacLeod absolved himself of any further responsibility for his estranged wife's debts or liabilities. The announcement went on to warn all dressmakers, milliners, cordwainers and haberdashers in Amsterdam not to supply his wife with any kind of goods, since he would no longer settle any of her bills.

6

Paris, 1903

A little after two o'clock in the afternoon, a train pulled into Gare de l'Est and shunted to a standstill. Gerda collected her Gladstone bag and stepped down on to the platform. As she walked through the crowds, steam drifted up into the joists of the iron-and-glass roof. It was cold.

She left via the main entrance and walked down rue du Faubourg Saint-Martin. The long, tree-lined boulevard was busy with pedestrians. In gaps between the buildings and on large areas of wall space were huge coloured posters. She stopped to look at one advertising the 'FOLIES BERGÈRE' and admired the scarlet and salmon-pink dresses the dancers wore on the poster.

Night was beginning to fall. A man was selling newspapers beside an arched entrance. His front teeth were missing. People placed a few coins into his palm and raced off with their papers. Another man with a face as round as a plate stood behind a counter selling oysters, crabs and lobsters. The ice sparkled and melted under three bright lamps. Gerda felt the warmth of the lamps and the coolness of the ice as she passed by.

Two women walked towards her, wearing cream crêpe de Chine dresses and grey astrakhan fur coats. The grey and cream together were exquisite, Gerda thought. Their hats were covered with tangles of white net, their shiny leather shoes were high-heeled and protected by cream duck covers. Gerda looked down in disgust at her own plain merino dress.

When she reached the end of rue du Faubourg Saint-Martin, she checked her map. She felt small and uncertain in such a large city. All the street signs were white with blue writing and soon she found boulevard Saint-Denis. The street lamps, dotted at regular intervals down the wide boulevard, were being lit. Men with ladders worked in pairs, one climbing up to light the lamps, the other holding the ladder steady.

She turned into rue du Faubourg Montmartre and stood under a street light to read a piece of paper she took out of her bag. A friend in Amsterdam had told her about a good, cheap restaurant on this street called Chartier. She checked the numbers of the buildings for number 7. She passed a busy café and a small *couturière* before seeing the restaurant. The revolving doorway was set back from the street.

Inside, each of the dozens of tables was occupied and she had to share a table with a short stocky man, more interested in his food than in her. His napkin was tucked into his collar. The high ceiling was yellow with nicotine stains. White glass lamps dropped down from the ceiling in clusters. Huge brown-framed mirrors covered most of the walls. She ordered the prix fixe of *saucisson sec et beurre* followed by *rôti de veau, courgettes à la niçoises* from the paper menu. When the food arrived, she ate quickly – she hadn't had a hot meal since leaving Amsterdam the day before. She paid and left the restaurant and continued along rue du Faubourg Montmartre which, according to her map, would lead her to Pigalle.

After MacLeod's disappearance, she had waited two days before she realised he wasn't planning on returning. She went to the local courts and asked for a legal separation. The decision, granted three days later by the Amsterdam tribunal, was entirely in her favour: Gerda was to keep Non and MacLeod was to pay her 100 guilders a month in alimony. But when the first payment was due, MacLeod claimed to have no money. She appealed to him in a private letter, but he made it clear that he would not pay her another penny. What could she do? She could take him to court over the matter, but in the meantime she had no means of living. She had no choice but to leave the child in his care while she found work, at least until she could afford a court case. But what kind of work could she get? 'Go to Pigalle,' a friend had suggested to her; 'something will come along.'

Pigalle was busy. Motor cars and commercial vehicles, their sides emblazoned with liveries, crossed the large square and disappeared down side streets. Trolley cars rattled past and a taxi sounded its horn. The pavements were crowded with people, all walking in different directions. Gerda could see dozens of bright windows and illuminated signs for *cabarets dansants*, bars, cafés and restaurants. They remained etched on her eyelids long after she closed her eyes. Many women stood on their own or in pairs in doorways and on street corners. She stopped and watched them. Men in frock coats and top hats strolled by, eyeing them furtively before passing on.

Gerda was tired after her journey. She had enough money for a few nights at a cheap hotel. From a dark street behind her, she could hear music. She looked down and saw the outline of a man in a doorway turning the handle of a barrel organ. She listened to the refrain, then recognised a tune she'd heard in Amsterdam: 'Les Fraises et les Framboises'. Amsterdam was already beginning to seem like a world away.

From out of the darkness, a short man came up to her and spoke to her in French. From his intonation, she understood that he'd asked her a question and was waiting for an answer. She looked at him. The man became impatient and rubbed his fingers together in front of her face. When she shook her head, he shouted and pushed past her.

Further down the street, Gerda saw a plaque advertising a hotel called the Régence and decided to try it. She passed by a bar. It was small, with sawdust scattered on the tiled floor. A trio of men stood in one corner playing a violin, accordion and drums. Most of the people inside stood at the zinc counter, drinking beer from wineglasses. A few others were sitting at wooden tables and were served by a waiter carrying three plates of *bifteck* along his left arm.

The lower window panes of the hotel were dirty and broken, but she was too tired to try anywhere else. The entrance smelled of absinthe and perfume. Behind a worn wooden desk, a fat lady in a silk dressing gown was reading a book. She had the last of a croissant in her hand, which she dunked into a glass of wine and ate.

'Do you have any rooms?' Gerda said.

Still reading her book, the lady reached over her shoulder and took one of several keys off its nail.

'*C'est pour un moment?*' she asked.

'No, for the night.'

The lady looked at her, then behind her. 'But you're alone!' she said.

'Yes, I'm alone. I've just arrived in Paris.'

The lady looked at her again and then chuckled. She put her book down and came out from behind the desk. Her dressing gown rustled as she led Gerda up the stairs, stopping at the mezzanine to show her the toilet. The corridor was dimly lit and the carpet made up of yellow and brown whorls. The lady breathed heavily as she walked, explaining that she was the *patronne*. She opened a door and peered inside. Over her shoulder, Gerda saw some stockings and shoes on the floor. Among the messed-up bedclothes, someone lay sleeping.

'Marie?' the *patronne* said.

A woman raised her head. She had long dark hair.

'*Oh! Excusez-moi,*' the *patronne* shrugged and closed the door. She opened the door to the next room and looked in. Satisfied that this room was empty, she motioned to Gerda. The room contained an enormous bed, a clothes-hanger by the door and a Japanese screen that hid a washbasin. A single bulb dangled from the ceiling. Gerda asked how much.

'*Deux francs la nuit.*'

Gerda looked around the room again. There were no curtains. Her heart sank a little, but it was cheap. She promised herself that she would only stay a few nights.

'*D'accord,*' she said.

The *patronne* glanced at her. 'Are you sure, *ma petite*?'

Gerda nodded.

The *patronne* sighed. 'This room has no key but you can bolt it from inside. I'll be downstairs if you want me.' She left, shaking her head.

Gerda bolted the door and opened her bag. She put her clock on the bedside table. She tried the basin: the water was ice-cold. She hung her few clothes on the hanger and looked out of the window. The organ-grinder was still there, playing the same song. It was dark. She lay on the bed and listened to him, wondering when she would be in Amsterdam again.

When she awoke, it was still dark outside. Her clock said it was just before midnight. She got up and looked out of the window. This time the street was full of people. A sign opposite her flashed 'LE PARADIS' and she saw two flower sellers standing underneath. A man shouted and then ran past. She heard a woman's laughter in the hotel corridor and someone tried her door; a man's low voice and the clinking of glasses. She stood still until the voices departed.

Gerda tried the basin again: the water was piping hot now. She washed, undressed and got into bed. She turned out the light and lay still. The bed was comfortable. In the room next to hers, a man and a woman began arguing. They talked too fast for her to understand, but she knew it was over money. Gerda sank deeper into the bed, expecting the man to hit the woman at any moment. It was quiet for a while, then a door banged.

Gerda was very tired, but she couldn't sleep. All night, doors were opened and slammed shut, people came and went. A bell rang. By early morning, the organ-grinder had left, but a woman repeatedly sang 'Mon Paris' by herself for more than an hour. At one point, there was a huge dispute between several women outside the front of the hotel. Gerda heard police whistles. The hotel and street became quiet only when dawn broke. Exhausted, Gerda fell asleep.

*

It was light when she woke again. Her clock said it was after two. She got up and washed. When she had put on her only clean clothes, she tied her hair into a neat chignon and went downstairs. Today she would look for work. The *patronne* was still at her desk, reading the same book and dressed in the same silk gown. Gerda wondered if she had moved at all.

Two young women were standing in front of the desk, as if waiting for something. One was dressed in a tight, shiny skirt. The other had long blonde hair which was very flat and very straight. So unlike the fashion, Gerda thought. She recognised the perfume from the night before.

'*Bonjour, chérie,*' the blonde woman said.

'*Bonjour,*' Gerda replied.

'Are you the one who stayed here the whole night?'

'Yes.'

'Where in heaven's name have you sprung from?' she said.

'Amsterdam,' Gerda said.

'What for?'

'I've come to look for work.'

The blonde woman looked slowly down the length of Gerda's body, taking in the cheap black flannelette skirt and duck jacket. She frowned.

'How long have you been in Paris?'

'I arrived yesterday.'

'And what kind of work are you looking for?'

'I don't know,' Gerda said.

'How old are you?'

'Twenty-seven.'

The blonde looked at Gerda's face. 'You poor love. You don't know what you're doing, do you?'

Gerda felt butterflies in her stomach. 'I'll find something.'

The blonde continued regarding her, so that Gerda began to blush. The blonde seemed to decide something. 'Listen,' she said, 'can you sit still for hours on end?'

'Yes, I think so.'

'Good. I have a friend; he lives over on avenue de Clichy. He's a painter, but he earns his money by doing posters and portraits. He might be able to use a face like yours.'

Gerda smiled.

'He works early in the mornings. We'll go and have a word with him, shall we?'

'Thank you,' Gerda said. 'What's your name?'

'Alice. What's yours?'

'Margaretha, but people call me Gerda.'

The tram signal sounded as it crossed place Pigalle. Alice pointed out the Moulin Rouge, which she had visited quite often. 'You wouldn't believe what goes on in there – it's a madhouse,' she said.

At place de Clichy, they got off and walked together up avenue de Clichy. They passed a cemetery. Gerda shivered in the cold. The city was shrouded in fog. The men and women walking on pavements looked thin and unearthly. Above them, fixed to the side of a building, a poster loomed in the mist. It was advertising the Palais de Glace on the Champs-Élysées. A woman with a figure like an hourglass glided on knife-thin skates.

Alice told her that her painter friend was quite famous in certain circles as a colourist. She emphasised the word 'colourist'. He had once told her that Apollinaire admired his landscapes, but Alice didn't know who Apollinaire was. 'Do you?' she asked. Gerda shook her head.

They stopped at a huge apartment building. Alice pressed a button and, after a few minutes, the door flew open. Gerda saw a tanned man with dark shiny hair and stubble. He was wearing a white vest underneath his black jacket. He smiled and threw his arms up when he saw Alice.

'Oh, *ma petite,*' he said and kissed Alice on either cheek. '*Ça va?*'

'Octave, this is Gerda, from Amsterdam. Gerda, this is Octave Guillomet.'

'Hello,' Gerda said.

Guillomet studied her face for a moment, then waved his arms. 'Come on, it's too cold to stand here all day. Come inside.'

He led the way upstairs, to a large room on the second floor. Huge windows at either end let in acres of light. There were paintings stacked against the wall, two easels with half-finished paintings on them. Brushes and blue and green paints lay scattered on the worktops.

'As you can see, I'm very busy, but please, sit down.' Guillomet pointed Gerda to a chair. 'What can I do for you?'

'She came to Paris looking for work,' Alice said.

Guillomet nodded. 'I see. What kind of work?'

Gerda felt his gaze on her. This man was waiting for an answer, but Gerda didn't want to appear uncertain. She could tell him the truth, or she could earn his sympathy with a lie.

'I don't know. Anything. My husband, a colonel, died in the Indies and left me with two children to look after,' she said.

Guillomet tutted and shook his head. 'Listen,' he said, 'I paint posters for theatrical productions – *Messalina, Carmen,* that type of thing. Are you interested in doing some modelling for me?'

'Yes, very much,' Gerda smiled.

'Good.' He looked at Gerda's face. 'Sit up straight for a moment.' He studied her posture, stroking his chin and nodding slowly. 'Fine, now take off your clothes, please.'

'What?' Gerda said. 'I thought you meant my head and shoulders!'

'Agh.' Guillomet threw his hands up in impatience. 'I don't need models for that and anyway, the pay is terrible. I would rather not do it either, you know? I would rather do my landscapes all day, but there is no money in that. I can see you have a good figure, but I need to see you naked. If you're not interested, then please, I'm very busy.'

Gerda looked at Alice. 'It's all right, Gerda,' she said.

Gerda stood up. Both Alice and Guillomet watched her impassively, as though they were waiting for a bus. She began unlacing her boots. The concrete floor was cold through her stockings. She unbuttoned her jacket and laid it on the chair, then removed her chemise. Underneath was a bodice, so old and worn that Gerda was ashamed. They waited without speaking. Gerda unfastened her skirt, underskirt and petticoat. She laid them on the chair, unrolled her stockings and finally removed her knickers.

When she was naked, she stood with her arms by her sides. Goosepimples formed on her skin in the cold studio. Guillomet's eyes lingered over her body.

'Yes, you have a good figure, except for your breasts – they're too flabby and pendulous. I can use you, but only in costume.'

Gerda's cheeks burned. She felt like a cow at market.

Guillomet looked at her, waiting for an answer. 'Well?' he said.

Gerda looked at him. How else would she earn money for her food and lodging as easily as this? When she realised that she had no other real choice, her gaze became cool and uninvolved. 'Yes, for the sake of the children,' she said.

'Good,' he said; 'you can get dressed now.'

7
Les Affiches

In 1798, Aloys Senefelder invented a process by which many prints could be obtained from a single design drawn on a stone surface. A back-to-front outline was drawn in black and the areas to be printed filled in with inks. The remaining areas were made ink-repellent. He called his process 'lithography' and, during the 1850s, it was used to create a new form of advertising: the large, illustrated colour poster.

The first posters were rather crude – printed in one or two colours on tinted paper. Gradually, though, the process became more sophisticated so that, by 1890, successive stones of the primary colours (red, yellow and blue) were used, followed by a fourth stone of transparent tints, made up from the complementary colours (green, violet and orange), which gave the poster a more complex colour make-up. The theory of complementary colours had recently been devised and popularised by the Impressionists and Pointillists.

Illustrated posters had their heyday at the turn of the century, when the streets of Paris were littered with them, advertising all manner of things: operas and *opéras bouffes*, ballets, the Folies Bergère and Moulin Rouge, skating rinks and the Cirque d'Hiver, pantomimes, masked balls, touring troupes and minstrel shows, the Jardin de Paris and the Musée Grévin, department stores such as the Grand Bon Marché and Halle aux Chapeaux, bookshops, magazines and periodicals, newspapers and the serialised novels of Hugo and Zola, chicory, jam, Spanish chocolate, Indian syrup, Dubonnet's quinquina and Pernod's absinthe, pastilles, glycerine toothpaste, Sarah Bernhardt's *poudre de riz* (rice powder), Roger & Gallet soaps, perfumes, hair restorer, matches and Saxoléine lamp oil.

The mass production and wide circulation of these posters was a huge industry and many artists were courted by lithographic publishing houses for commissions. But although the quality of posters became ever better, it was still poor compared to the colour reproduction of painting. Renoir, Cézanne and Sisley were all approached by the publisher Vollard to draw coloured lithographs, but they refused, agreeing only to do the 'black stones' and leaving the colour to be added by the printer.

Toulouse-Lautrec, however, was an exception. The misshapen painter trawled the Montmartre underworld of bars and brothels for subjects, and his posters are among the most evocative of the era. The influence of Japanese prints – with their strong lines and solid forms – was very evident in his lithographs. He is now as famous for them as for his paintings. Indeed, his Moulin Rouge posters are arguably more recognisable than any of his paintings.

There was one man, however, who lifted colour lithography to something more than mere advertising: Jules Chéret. In his life, he is known to have completed more than 880 posters, but probably did many more. Born in Paris in 1836, Chéret left school at thirteen to become a lithographer's apprentice, during which time he lettered brochures, flyers and funeral announcements. He carried on his studies in London, where he designed book covers for the Cramer publishing house and floral designs for the Rimmel perfumery on Wigmore Street.

After travelling through Sicily, Malta and Tunisia, he returned to Paris and set up his own lithography studio with presses brought from London. He produced the first lithograph from his new studio in 1866, for an 'enchantment' in five acts called *La Biche au bois*. It was an enormous commercial success and from then on, Chéret earned his living by designing posters.

Chéret worked in a large room, stretched over a large stone, leaning on his left arm and drawing with his right hand. He would look at his own image in a cheval glass when checking for a movement or expression, and had to look constantly in another mirror to see the reversed illustration properly. His main references were Velázquez, Donatello, the Rubens paintings in the Louvre, which he visited every Sunday, and the Turner paintings he saw at the V & A Museum while he was in London.

Chéret's output was formidable and no other artist came anywhere near the number of posters he produced. He entered a golden era in the 1890s, during which his posters were so common that they became synonymous with *la belle époque*. The laughing women he drew were called 'Chérettes'. A song was even recorded about the singer's yearning for a poster girl, described as *'la fleur du paradis, danseuse de Chéret'*. It was a huge hit.

Monet, Degas and Seurat were all open in their admiration of his work. A petition to have Chéret decorated was signed by Rodin and Massenet and, in 1890, he was made a Chevalier of the Légion d'honneur. In 1900, his eyesight began to fail and he was forced to stop his lithographs and work in much larger forms. He produced murals for the Préfecture in Nice, designed the curtains for the Musée Grévin and tapestries for Maurice Fenaille's villa in Neuilly. In 1925, his eyesight failed him completely and he retired to Nice. He died there in 1932, aged ninety-six.

Throughout his career, Chéret also produced many drawings, pastels and oil paintings. In 1933, an exhaustive exhibition of this work was held at the Salon d'Automne in Paris. Many were astonished by his ability as a fine artist.

8

Paris, 1904

Georges du Parcq was hot and agitated after climbing the hundreds of steps up to the Sacré Cœur, despite the chill in the morning air. Standing at the top of the steps, he straightened his jacket and overcoat. The streets were empty. Further up rue Lapin, a gendarme was standing outside a doorway. It was Jacques. Du Parcq got out his notebook and pencil and walked towards him. When Jacques saw him approaching, he raised his palm.

'No one inside yet, Georges. How do you people get here so quickly?'

'That's our job, Jacques; what's going on?'

'A shooting. A man's dead and the woman's inside. The usual.'

'Who's in charge?'

'Lieutenant Boileau.'

'How long before I can eyeball?'

'You'll just have to wait like the others. When they get here.'

Du Parcq sighed and looked around for a café. There was one just opening further up the street. He looked at his pocket watch: twenty-five to seven. He looked up; the bruised clouds barely cleared the highest point of the Sacré Cœur.

'A lovely morning, Jacques.'

'No it's not,' the gendarme said; 'it's a shitty morning, Georges.'

'Tut-tut. You should be more optimistic. I'll be back.'

Georges du Parcq had been on *Le Monde* for three years, covering petty crimes and misdemeanours. He hated it – long hours spent all over the city gathering information on crimes that only merited a few lines and sometimes didn't make the paper at all.

He should have been promoted to court cases months ago, but Gabert had been promoted instead. Now Gabert spent every day in the press gallery of the Justice Courts, taking long lunches and finishing early. What did he know? He hadn't grafted on the provincial papers like du Parcq had – ten years in Nice and two years on *Le Soir* in Arcueil before joining *Le Monde*. He was tired of covering insignificant cases like this.

After drinking two *express* and smoking two cigarillos, du Parcq left the café and ambled back to the crime scene. Jacques was still there, more watchful this time as he kept an eye on the six or seven reporters who had arrived. All were younger than du Parcq and wore better suits. They chatted to each other while they waited.

Lieutenant Boileau came out of the apartment building and issued a statement. A woman had shot her lover and was being detained for questioning. Someone asked if there was another woman involved. Boileau said, 'No comment.' Someone else asked if the woman would be charged. 'Probably,' Boileau said and pushed past them. Du Parcq made his notes and lit another cigarillo. The other reporters drifted away to file their copy and make the lunchtime edition, but du Parcq stood quietly by, leaning against a wall and waiting.

The crime scene doctor arrived and went into the building. Fifteen minutes later, the doctor left, which meant that the shooting was probably an open-and-shut case. When he saw that Boileau was less busy, du Parcq approached him with one or two more questions but, as usual, received no replies he could use. Boileau was such a stickler. Du Parcq hung around and caught two of Boileau's officers as they left the building. He asked them both if there was another woman involved. The first said he didn't know, but the second said, 'Of course; why else would a woman shoot her lover?'

'Do you know anything about her? Good looking?'

'By all accounts.' The officer winked and walked away.

Du Parcq wrote notes for the basic outline of his story and was about to leave for the office when someone touched his arm. Standing by him was a woman with black hair and huge almond-shaped eyes.

'Monsieur, are you from the newspapers?' she said.

'Yes, what can I do for you, madame?'

'It's about Suzette. We're friends.'

'Suzette? You mean the woman who shot her man?'

The woman nodded.

'What's her last name?'

'Harrault. What's going to happen to her?'

Du Parcq took a note of the name. 'They'll take her away and charge her. Why?'

'Because I'm afraid it's partly my fault.'

Du Parcq looked up. Her face was calm. 'Oh really,' he said, 'and why is that?'

'Pierre and I made love once.'

Du Parcq took in her sea-blue mousseline dress and black bonnet. 'What's your name?' he asked.

'Gerda,' she said.

'Can I buy you a coffee, Gerda?'

'Yes, certainly you can, monsieur.'

'Good, follow me.' Du Parcq checked to make sure no one was watching before he took her arm and led her to the café up the street.

When they were sitting down with a coffee each in front of them, du Parcq asked Gerda for a full account of the affair. Much to his delight, she was more than happy to comply.

She had met them both in a local bar one night, not long after Gerda had arrived in Paris a year ago. The bars in Montmartre are always friendly and the three of them had soon got talking. Suzette was petite and shy. She had said very little, but when she did say something, it was always very intimate. Gerda had liked her from the beginning and sensed they could become good friends. But most of the time Suzette was overshadowed by Pierre, who was a huge man with a deep voice.

They lived near Gerda's lodgings and she began to see them regularly. They were always together, though not out of choice, but because Pierre seemed afraid to let Suzette out of his sight. Gerda had thought it was strange because Suzette didn't strike her as the unfaithful type. But, she said, she understood that people could sometimes be nervous of that when there was perhaps no need to be. Du Parcq nodded. She had soon realised how belligerent and sarcastic Pierre was. He used to insult Suzette, but as far as Gerda knew, he had never hit her. It was a subtle battle, Gerda said, designed to undermine what little confidence Suzette had.

Then Gerda had begun noticing the compliments that Pierre threw her way when Suzette's head was turned or when she had gone to the ladies' room. At first, she hadn't said anything, out of respect for Suzette, but Gerda had arrived in Paris without knowing anyone and was lonely. She had next to no money and couldn't afford to leave Montmartre, so she was glad to meet these two people and, slowly, came to appreciate the attention Pierre paid her. He must have sensed this because, one night in a bar, he had put his hand on her knee and said he wanted to sleep with her. She had found Pierre attractive to look at, but she liked Suzette; so she took his hand off her knee and asked him to buy her a glass of white wine.

During all of this, she had been modelling for Guillomet, the famous artist, but the pay was terrible. She was trying to secure work as an Oriental dancer in the *cabarets dansants*, but no one was interested in Oriental dancing – they wanted acrobats, slapstick artistes or singers. She could see no way out of her predicament and there was no one to help her. One night, she was in her rooms worrying about how she would pay the next month's rent when Pierre had called on her. He had gently stroked her hair as she told him her worries and she sought comfort in his kind words. They had made love. She had felt bad about it as soon as it was over and made Pierre promise not to tell Suzette. That had been two days ago and she must have found out, for now poor Suzette was in jail.

When Gerda had finished, he knew he had the story. In return, he told Gerda about a friend of his who might be able to help her secure work as a dancer. His friend, he explained, owned a museum devoted to the study of the Orient and its antiquities. He wrote down the address and telephone number for the offices of *Le Monde* and told her she should ring him in a fortnight, by which time he would have spoken to his friend. Gerda took the piece of paper and thanked him. What a charming smile, du Parcq thought. He could understand very well what had attracted Pierre. He paid for the coffees and said goodbye to Gerda.

At his office, he spent his lunch hour writing up the story. He kept very close to Gerda's version of events and painted Suzette as a victim with no escape from a cruel three-way affair. It made page two of the Late Evening Special.

When the case came to trial two weeks later, the Counsel for the Prosecution portrayed Suzette Harrault as a calculating murderer who'd shot a man down in cold blood. The Counsel for the Defence presented the same scenario as du Parcq's story: that Suzette Harrault was the victim of a brutal sadist, hellbent on making her life a misery. The *avocat* cited Gerda's testimony in du Parcq's story as supporting evidence. The Presiding Magistrate declared that, after hearing both Counsels, he'd decided to treat the shooting as a *crime passionnel*. 'And therefore,' he said, 'Suzette Harrault is acquitted.'

Du Parcq spent that evening in the bar across from the offices of *Le Monde* and glowed with pleasure at the compliments his colleagues paid him. Later, when he was a little drunk, he told them about the mysterious woman called Gerda. 'Without her testimony,' he said, 'that girl would never have got off.'

9

Paris, 1905

I am Émile Guimet, the founder of the Musée Guimet in Paris, where Lady MacLeod gave her first performance as Mata Hari. My friend Georges du Parcq introduced me to the delights of Mata Hari's wonderful and exotic stage performances. He telephoned me at my museum one day in January and told me of a woman he had met while filing a story, a woman who wanted to be an Oriental dancer. I thought it a marvellous idea. The Orient, for so long a distant and unknown part of the world for most French citizens, was slowly becoming more familiar. Only five years before, a whole Javanese village had been reconstructed on the Champ de Mars during the Exposition Universelle. Debussy was composing music inspired by the pagodas of the East and Gauguin had lived among the peace-loving natives of Tahiti in order to revitalise his wasting senses.

It was to the Perroquet Bleu in rue Chaptal, just off place Pigalle, that Georges took me on the night of 4 February 1905. It was hardly the most auspicious venue for a professional début. It was a tall, thin building in a narrow street where *filles de joie* accosted passers-by and sly men tried to sell cheap stockings. The street was so dark that, for a moment, we couldn't find the right place. There were no illuminated signs and no doorman to show the way, just a black door on which we had to bang in order to be admitted. A scantily dressed woman pushed open the door and motioned us inside. She pointed the way forward down a rickety staircase. The fact that there was no entrance fee didn't augur well, but Georges slipped her a franc piece in any case. As we descended, I told Georges of my discomfort in such unsavoury surroundings, but he pacified me, saying, 'Patience, Émile. Patience.'

Georges had been to see her in two or three *cabarets dansants* in Pigalle and Montmartre, where she had performed free of charge during the entr'acte. On the telephone, Georges attempted to describe the voluptuous movements of her dances, but admitted he was unable to. Instead, he was telling all his friends and colleagues to go and see her. In recognition of his help, she had given Georges a silver statuette of the Hindu god Siva, which, she told him, was from Java. He put it on his mantelpiece, where it has remained, smiling benignly over the whole of his small apartment. This is what finally swayed me. When he showed it to me, I was piqued at the thought that she knew of Siva and became interested to see her interpretation of the great Eastern religions.

We found a table near the back of the dark room. There were wooden shafts and beams throughout, supporting a warped roof. In front of us were ten or so round wooden tables, like ours, and in front of those was the small dais, barely a metre away, and edged with red curtains. The stuccoed walls were cream-coloured and smeared, the roof yellow with pipe smoke. The place was nearly full and lively with the expectant shouts of men waiting for the night's entertainment. A woman with a tray ran up and down the back stairs, ferrying drinks to the tables and tucking the tips she received into her dress front. Most of the men were drinking bocks – beer in wine glasses – and absinthe. Georges ordered a cognac. I ordered my usual sloe gin with seltzer water. When the waitress left, I noticed a man on his own in one corner. He had a pad on his knee and was drawing the interior scenes.

A compère then appeared on stage and announced the attractions. The first act was a troupe of three Arabian dancers, who wore fake rubies in their navels and cavorted around the stage as though they were members of a seraglio, aiming to please their sultan. It was a grotesque and inane display, but the audience was very taken with it. Some raised their glasses and whistled; others threw centimes on to the stage, which one of the troupe made sure to collect before disappearing into the wings. The second act was a juggler, whose performance involved the use of skittles, knives and flaming torches. As you can imagine, the audience was not overly enthusiastic. The third act, 'Leo and His Infernal Violin', was even worse and doesn't merit a mention at all. I drank my sloe gin and wished I had never come.

The compère appeared again and announced a set of acrobats.

'But first,' he said, 'please welcome a sensational new dancer from the Orient – Lady MacLeod!' The audience cheered in anticipation and Georges sat upright in his chair to get a better view. When she came on to the stage, with her eyes cast down and only the merest hint of a smile on her lips, the audience settled down and everyone was agog. She was dressed in a brassière, trimmed with gold, and a short gold sarong, over which fell a transparent veil. Her black hair hung loosely, held in place by a plain hairband. She wore wooden clogs, which were similar to ones worn by geishas in northern Japan, but which must have come from her native Holland. Her attire was simple, drab even, but it belied the hypnotism and guile of the performance to follow.

She stood looking out towards a spot somewhere above and behind the audience. Her face was as still as a winter pond, as though she had done this a thousand times before. Some music started up off-stage – wailing, dervish-like music – and she began a series of slow turns and twirls, always extending her arms upwards or outwards and always holding her head steady. Several times, she remained crouching on the floor with her back to us and, on the last such crouch, she cast aside her veil and swirled round to reveal that she was naked except for her brassière. The crowd of men rose to their feet, clapping and whistling in appreciation and then, suddenly, she disappeared from the stage.

My first reaction was of immense excitement and invigoration. My sixty-nine years seemed to melt away at such an extraordinary sight. Here was a woman who had interpreted most perfectly the slow seductive dances of the *bayadères*. I had never seen it done so well before – indeed, I had never seen it done *at all* before. The whole of Paris was ignorant of such dancing and, if nurtured and directed, I realised at once that she had the potential to carve a lucrative niche for herself in the world of performance.

We sat talking our way through the acrobats and a dismal *chanteuse*. Or rather, I talked and Georges listened. I told him of the plans and projects that I had already envisaged off the top of my head. I imagined her dancing to audiences of thousands across Europe's major cities. I was so immersed in my thoughts that I did not notice Lady MacLeod suddenly materialising at our table. She was dressed in the plainest of clothes. We stood up and Georges introduced us. Her dark eyes looked at me. What a sweet smile she had! One could sense the naïveté in her manner, but also the splendour of her presence. She sat down with us and, when asked, ordered a glass of *vin blanc*. I felt compelled to tell her immediately what I thought. I told her that she had a great future, that she was perfect. I'm afraid I rambled on somewhat about the collection of Oriental jewellery and costume that I have in my museum and how I could imagine her dressed in those fine robes and shiny stones. She smiled and listened patiently.

Eventually, I asked how much she was to be paid for her performance that night. She didn't hesitate when the question came. 'Twenty francs,' she said. I told her I could secure her 1,000 gold francs a night. Well, it was a joy to see the expression on her face! She brought her hand up to her open mouth in astonishment. I told her about a room in my museum that would be an ideal backdrop for her performance. I mentioned several people I knew who would be very interested to see her. She readily agreed and I promised to make the necessary arrangements as soon as possible. I began to enquire as to her background, in preparation for any advance publicity, and she proceeded to tell me about the places she had been in the Dutch East Indies. She made great mention of the music and dance of the natives and told me how inspired she was by their art. Oh, how lucky she was to have been to Java, a place I have often travelled to in spirit but never in person. Then I remembered my sole concern: that she must have a more exotic sobriquet. I asked if she knew any Eastern or Oriental expressions for, alas, I have no knowledge of any foreign languages. She admitted that she knew nothing except one or two things in Malay. I told her it didn't matter if her stage name was Malay, Siamese or Mandarin, it just had to be foreign and exotic-sounding. She struggled to recall as much as possible and, after a kind of verbal tit-for-tat, we came up with an expression she had learnt while she was ill with typhoid in the Indies: 'Mata Hari', which means 'Eye of the Morning', or 'Dawn'. I thought it perfect and, much to my delight, she agreed.

My museum is on avenue d'Iéna, opposite the Tokyo Palace. I opened it in 1884, a year after the Orient Express began its regular service to Constantinople. The whole venture was made possible by the legacy my father left me when he died. My father was a successful financier, trading in cheap cotton imports from Indo-Chine, but he was also an amateur collector of Oriental trinkets and knick-knacks. He used to keep them in a cabinet of curiosities. As a child, I would sort through them, turning them over in my hands and imagining the far-off lands they had come from. I particularly remember a piece of Chinese jade and a Khmer figurine. When my father retired, he settled in Arcueil, a Parisian suburb. I used to visit him there on Sundays. We would have luncheon in his new 'conservatory' and then walk in the nearby park. He became more absorbed in his collection and made many new acquisitions. He showed them to me, telling me of their origins and meanings, and explained to me his baffling system of taxonomy. His collection was quite well known locally – so much so that, one morning, he woke to find the whole collection stolen. The police mounted an investigation and the local paper reported the crime. It was Georges who wrote the story. That was how he and I met. Georges interviewed my father and helped the police as much as he could, but they never recovered any of the collection. My father was never quite the same after that. I continued to visit him and encouraged him to start afresh, but he was clearly depressed over the whole experience. Less than a year after the burglary, he died.

His death seemed so senseless and sad. At that time, I had a job as an industrialist, but was bored. I longed to travel. I spent months in a dilemma, going back and forth from my work in Paris to my father's house, before making the decision to leave my job. From then on, I vowed to follow in my father's footsteps and devote my life to the collection of all things Oriental. I wanted to keep alive the spirit of knowledge he had engendered in me. I sold my father's house and began planning trips to the Orient. The first of these was to Hokkaido, the northernmost island of Japan, where I learnt the basic techniques of ikebana – flower arrangement – and brought back the first Japanese woodcuts to be exhibited in Europe. I planned and completed two further trips, during which I acquired many kimonos, *sumi-e* paintings and three complete *cha-no-yu* tea sets. Gradually I accumulated hundreds of Oriental art objects, including some Tibetan tankas, Nepalese inlaid silverwork, some early Amaravati carvings and a fine gilded figure of a dancing Dakini. I was finally able to house these artefacts in my present museum when an old trading warehouse closed down. After several years of pouring my father's money into the museum to keep it open, it is now running profitably and I have more than 1,000 visitors per annum.

In 1903, one of these visitors was Giacomo Puccini, whose latest opera, *Madam Butterfly*, was preparing for its world première. He travelled from his home in Monte Carlo to the museum in order to seek my advice on the authenticity of the costumes and stage designs. He had several drawings with him and we sat in my office, drinking sweet leaf tea and discussing the finer points of kimonos and geisha hair design. I pointed out that one of the drawings depicted a hair design called *monoware*, which has a strong sexual reference in its resemblance to a split peach. Puccini paled somewhat and left our meeting more thoughtful than when he had arrived. I was very honoured to receive an invitation from him to attend the première at La Scala in Milan and made the journey wondering what effect our conversation had had. As I sat in the magnificent red and gold auditorium watching the performance, I quickly realised he had decided to omit any hint of *monoware*. When I returned to Paris, I wrote to him thanking him for the invitation and said I hoped he hadn't been offended by our meeting. I was somewhat relieved to receive a reply from him saying that, on the contrary, he had found our discussion extremely stimulating. My only other contact with him was in 1906, when Mata Hari was at the height of her success. She had been booked by Monsieur Antoine, the Director of the Opéra in Monte Carlo, for a performance of Massenet's *Le Roi de Lahore*. Thinking he might be interested in its Oriental setting, I wrote to Puccini inviting him to the opening night. Much to my delight, he accepted and I later found out he was so impressed that he sent her some flowers with his felicitations, describing her as a *charmante artiste*.

Before this, however, Mata Hari had performed under her new name for the first time on 13 March, five weeks after that fateful evening at the Perroquet Bleu. As a venue, I chose the museum's rotunda on the second floor, which houses the library. My assistants and I transformed the airy cylindrical space into an Indian temple. The eight columns holding up the balcony were garlanded with flowers, and sheets of gauze were hung from them to provide a backdrop. The museum's centrepiece, a one-metre-high bronze statue of Siva Nataraja, originating from southern India and dating from the eleventh century, was wheeled into the library and dozens of candles placed about it. The candlelight was reflected in the sapanwood wainscotting, steeping the whole library in a lustre of red.

I compiled the small guest list with care. In the end, I sent out invitations to twenty-five people, including the actress Cécile Sorel, the theatrical agent Maître Clunet, the Japanese and German ambassadors, Madame Kiréevsky, who was organising a benefit for the Russian Ambulancemen, and the journalist Édouard Lepage. On the evening in question, my assistants showed the guests to their seats and served them Turkish pastilles and sherbets made from mangoes and pomegranates while they waited. I selected Mata Hari's costume from the museum's collection of clothing and jewellery – a white cotton brassière covered with jewel-studded breastplates, bracelets for her wrists and upper arms and an Indian diadem that curved backwards over her hair, which was knotted *à l'espagnole*. From the back of her brassière to the wrist bands, a sarong was attached so that it flowed over her hips when her arms were wrapped around her and opened into a fan when her arms were outstretched. The rest of her was bare. She looked exquisite.

When she was ready and the hired orchestra of Javanese gongs and drums were in position just off-stage, I introduced her to the illustrious audience by talking a little bit about the *bayadères* and religious dances of India. When I had finished, the electric lighting was turned off. Standing behind my guests, I watched her emerge from behind a column and take her place by the candlelit Siva. The orchestra began its soporific and sombre rhythms. As Mata Hari outstretched her arms and stood on tiptoe to begin her dance, I was reminded of Botticelli's Venus. The same pose, the same proportions. I made a mental note that Mata Hari must have her portrait painted presently, and I knew several good but poor artists who would be more than happy to capture her on canvas. Yes, I thought, her beautiful image must be immortalised for ever.

> Suddenly Mata Hari appears, The Eye of the Day, the Glorious Sun, the sacred Bayadère whom only the priests and the gods can claim to have seen in the nude. She is tall and slim and supple like the unrolled serpent which is hypnotised by the snake charmer's flute. Her flexible body at times becomes one with the undulating flames, to stiffen suddenly in the middle of her contortions, like the flaming blade of a kris.
>
> Then, with a brutal gesture, Mata Hari rips off her jewels, tears her veils. She throws away the ornaments that cover her breasts. And, naked, her body seems to lengthen way up into the shadows! Her outstretched arms lift her on to the very tip of her toes; she staggers, beats the empty air with her shattered arms, whips the imperturbable night with her long heavy hair . . . and falls to the ground.
>
> Édouard Lepage, 14 March 1905

10

La Presse

I have heard vague rumours about a woman from the Far East, who has come to Europe laden with perfume and jewels, to introduce some of the richness of the Oriental colour and life into the satiated society of European cities. There are supposed to be scenes of veils encircling and being discarded, giving a suggestion of naughtiness that such a display should take place in a private drawing room.

The King, 1905

Lady MacLeod, that is to say Mata Hari, the Indian dancer, voluptuous and tragic, dances naked in the latest salons. She wears the costume of the bayadère, as much simplified as possible, and, towards the end, she simplifies it even a little more.

La Vie Parisienne, 1905

I know nothing of the East, but was thrilled with the beauty of her body. She interprets the admirable poesy of the Malayan race. I predict a great future for her.

Camille de Sainte-Croix, Revue Théâtrale, 1905

The little breasts only were covered with chiselled brass cupules, held in place with thin chains. Glittering bracelets, encrusted with precious stones, were on her wrists, arms and ankles. The rest of her was bare, fastidiously bare, from the nails of her fingers to her toes. Dominated by the ornamental bust, the plastic and firm stomach showed a sexless suppleness in symmetric curves which from the armpits under the raised arms, traced themselves to the haunches. The raised legs were ideal, like two fine columns of a pagoda. The kneecaps, amber-coloured, seemed plated with gold leaf that had rosy reflections. I can never forget her dancing. With serpentine movements, Mata Hari turned smiling the while towards the sleeping god (a standard prop in the *mise en scène*), and prostrated herself three times. Then turning again slowly, she took from her left wrist in the same rhythmic fashion, the large metal bracelet she wore. We could see then in place of this copper bangle, a thin natural bracelet, tattooed in blue on the pale gold skin, which represented a snake swallowing its tail.

Louis Damur, 1905

Seeing Mata Hari so feline, extremely feminine, majestically tragic, the thousand curves and movements of her body trembling in a thousand rhythms, one finds oneself far from the conventional *entrechats* of our classical dancers. Mata Hari dances like David before the Holy of Holies, like Salambo before Tanit, like Salome before Herod!

Gaulois, 17 March 1905

Mata Hari dances with veils, bejewelled brassières, and that is about all. The tall Mrs MacLeod wore the dress of the bayadère with incomparable grace. From Java, on the burning soil of which island she grew up, she brings an unbelievable suppleness and a magic charm, while she owes her powerful torso to her native Holland.

No one before her has dared to remain like this with trembling ecstasy and without any veils in front of the god – and with what beautiful gestures, both daring and chaste! She is indeed Absaras, sister of the Nymphs, the Naiads and the Walkyrie, created by Sundra for the perdition of men and sages.

Mata Hari does not only act with her feet, her arms, eyes, mouth and crimson fingernails. Mata Hari, unhampered by any clothes, plays with her whole body. And then, when the gods remain unmoved by the offer of her beauty and youth, she offers them her love, her chastity – and one by one her veils, symbols of feminine honour, fall at the feet of the god. But Siva wants even more. Devidasha gets closer to him – one more veil, a mere nothing – and erect in her proud and victorious nudity, she offers the god the passion which burns in her.

And, sitting around her, the Nautsches excited her further in uttering terrible 'stâ-stâ-stâ' sounds and finally the priestess, gasping for breath, sinks down at the feet of the god – where her dancing girls cover her with a golden sheet. Then Mata Hari, without any feeling of shame got up gracefully, pulled the holy veil around her, and, kindly thanking both Siva and the Parisians, walked off amid thunderous bravos!

Afterwards, Mata Hari, now dressed in an elegant evening gown, joined the public and, playing with a Javanese *wajong* puppet which she held in her hands, told us gaily the story of the prehistoric drama of Adjurnah.

La Presse, 18 March 1905

The door opened. A dark figure glided in, her arms folded upon her breast beneath a mass of flowers. For a few seconds she stood motionless, her eyes fixed upon the statue of Siva at the end of the room. Her olive skin blended with the curious jewels in their dead gold setting. A casque of worked gold upon her dark hair, she was enshrouded in various veils of delicate hues, symbolising chastity, beauty, youth, love, voluptuousness and passion.

The next dance was equally impressive. She stands before us a graceful young girl, a *slendang* – the veil worn by Javanese maidens – around her waist. In her hand she held a passion flower, and she dances to it with all the gladness of her sunny nature. But the flower was enchanted, and under its charm she loses command of herself and slowly unwinds the *slendang*. As the veil drops to the ground, consciousness returns. She is ashamed and covers her face with her hands.

Nothing inanimate will render the emotion conveyed by the performer, nor the colour and harmony of the Eastern figure. It was a tropical plant in all its freshness, transplanted to a Northern soil. The Parisians who witnessed the performance were struck with the unconscious art of the dancer, and with the intelligence and refinement she displayed. Miss Duncan is Vestal, but Lady MacLeod is Venus.

Frances Keyzer, *Daily Mail*, 1905

Miss Isadora Duncan reincarnated Greece. With the music of Beethoven, Schumann, Gluck and Mozart she restored the pagan dance movements. All Paris salons wanted to have Miss Duncan. Then, like everything on earth, she disappeared. She, her mother and her long-haired brother who accompanied her on the violin, went to conquer Berlin.

This season we have Mata Hari. She is Indian, with an English mother and a Dutch father, all of which is a little complicated. Yet she is Indian. Miss Duncan apparently danced with only her feet and arms showing, while Mata Hari is entirely naked, with only some jewels and a piece of cloth around her hips and legs. She is charming – a rather big mouth, and a pair of breasts which make many a spectator, too heavily provided for comfort, sigh with envy.

La Vie Parisienne, April 1905

At the salon of Emma Calvé, the dances of Mata Hari are not of a moving or impressive interest or perfection. However, although Mata Hari dances in the nude, do not believe that her dancing is indecent or that the sight of the beautiful Indian woman might provoke inappropriate thoughts – even though she danced naked from head to foot, with big eyes, and with a smiling mouth that is set into her face like a cut in the flesh of a ripe apple.

Écho de Paris, 1905

I have seen her dance at Emma Calvé's. She hardly danced in the real sense at all. She arrived fairly naked at her recitals, and with graceful movements and downcast eyes shed her clothes, and would then disappear enveloped in her veils. She even appeared at a Hindu fête in a garden, bare under a great June sun, riding a big white horse, richly caparisoned with saddlery encrusted with real turquoises. Her skin amber by night, seemed mauve by daylight, but patchy from artificial dyeing. She moved her long, thin and proud body as Paris has never seen one moved before. Paris swallowed her, and raved about her chaste nudity, retelling anecdotes that Mata Hari had uttered about her hot Asiatic past. She was invited everywhere, men fought to pay her way.

Colette, *Figaro*, December 1923

PART II

11

Orient Express

> On last Friday evening at 7:30 the new quick railway service between Paris and Constantinople, via Vienna and Giurgevo, came into operation. For the present it will be a bi-weekly service both ways, leaving Paris at half-past 7 p.m. on Tuesdays and Fridays; and the train will consist of three saloon carriages, fitted with 42 beds, a refreshment saloon, and a sufficient number of luggage vans, in which the luggage will be so arranged that it can be examined in the vans by the Customs officers at the frontier stations, thus avoiding the delay and annoyance unavoidable when the luggage has to be removed from the train. There will be no change of carriages between Paris and Giurgevo, and it is expected that the entire journey between Paris and Constantinople will be completed in about 75 hours.
>
> *The Times*, October 1883

Georges Nagelmackers was a large man, close to six feet tall. His eyes were piercing. His large moustache, sideburns and massive, hoary beard were the fashion for men in the late Victorian era. Photographs show him wearing a thigh-length frock coat of brushed fustian, and a double-breasted cream waistcoat. He carried a black polished cane and wore a high, silver-grey top hat.

Born in Liège in Belgium, a city built around its iron and steel works, he trained as an engineer. In his early twenties, his profession led him to the United States, where the Americans were building the Union Pacific Railroad, the world's first transcontinental railway. While Nagelmackers was there, he witnessed the completion of the final section through the Rockies between Omaha and Sacramento, thus linking the Pacific with the Atlantic.

Nagelmackers was greatly impressed by the efficiency of the rapidly expanding American railroad system. In particular, he admired the new sleeping cars used on long-distance trains, which were designed by George Pullman. The tables between the seats used by day in these cars were designed to be removed and the seats pulled towards each other, so that a kind of bed was formed. Curtains could be drawn along rods that ran along either side of the central aisle, making the whole carriage into a dormitory. By comparison, the European trains of the 1870s were like cattle trucks and Nagelmackers resolved to use Pullman's example to create a brand new form of luxury travel.

On 4 October 1883, thirteen years after Nagelmackers' trip to the United States, the newly christened Orient Express stood at Gare de l'Est, ready to begin its inaugural run. Nagelmackers had had posters advertising the new service displayed in London, Paris, Brussels and Vienna. In Constantinople, Nagelmackers had every poster emblazoned with the letters 'O–E', painted in the colours of the Ottoman Empire, thus engendering the idea that the new train linked Moslem Turkey and Christian Europe.

Gilt-edged invitation cards had been sent to the First Secretary of the Embassy in Paris for the Ottoman Empire, Belgium's Minister of Public Works, the General Manager of the Belgian State Railways and the Chief Controller of the French Minister of Finance to attend the departure of the train. The first passengers would be a group of forty international diplomats, publicists and pressmen.

There were five coaches in total, each resting on two assemblies of four wheels placed at either end of the coach. These assemblies, called 'bogies', were a recent invention of Nagelmackers'. The four wheels of each bogie were arranged to cushion bumps and provide a much smoother ride. He boasted that passengers would now be able to shave safely at eighty kilometres per hour.

The rear coach was the *fourgon*, or baggage-wagon, which also carried provisions and other necessary stores. Next to the *fourgon* was the *wagon-salon-restaurant* car, half as long again as any other coach in the world, with crystal-clear windows that stretched along almost the entire length of the carriage. Each window had its own spring-loaded pull-down blind as well as a set of pleated damask curtains.

The whole of the interior of the dining-parlour-car was panelled in oak and maple. The edges of the panelling, doors and door arches were decorated with scrolls and curlicues. In each corner was a swag of gilded flowers, set against geometric designs carved into the wood. Net racks, for hats and small items of luggage, ran the length of the coach and were supported by ironwork brackets. All doorknobs, window-catches and handles were made of brass.

At one end was a small parlour for women. Adjacent to this was a 'snug' – a smoking room with easy chairs for gentlemen. This snug could, if necessary, be cleared and fitted with tables and chairs to accommodate an extra number of dining passengers.

The dining room proper had tables for four running along the whole of one side of the carriage and smaller tables, set for two, along the other. Each was spread with a white cloth and the napkins were folded into shapes of birds and butterflies. On every table were two cut-glass decanters filled with burgundy wine and a vase of fresh, brightly coloured flowers.

The silver cutlery and crystal wine glasses on each table reflected the bright light given off by gas-lamps fixed to the sides of the carriage. Each of these lamps, made by Pintsch, had eight gas-jets, which were fed by cylinders hanging beneath the coach, between the bogies. These lamps had been designed to imitate the crystal-and-gilt chandeliers of the Paris salons.

All chairs were free-moving and upholstered in dark,

embossed leather, with brass studs the size of doubloons running along the edges of the mahogany frames. These chairs stood on wall-to-wall carpeting, which was dark red.

Next came the two sleeping cars. These were both as long as the dining car and contained two-berth, three-berth and one or two four-berth compartments. The lower berths were fixed and doubled as sofas during the day. The upper berths were lowered at night, using a hinge system that Nagelmackers had designed. The underside of the upper berths were panelled in oak so that, when fixed to the wall, they matched the rest of the oak interior. Each compartment window had heavy damask curtains, which matched those in the dining car.

A dark leather armchair was placed by each window, with just enough space to allow for the swing of the wardrobe doors, on the inside of which were mounted full-length mirrors. Above each berth, another Pintsch gas-lamp and a small counter-top were placed within easy reach. A glass and water jug rested on the counter-top.

Separating the sleeping cars from the engine was another *fourgon*, in which the mail was carried. Nagelmackers had secured the monopoly on mail-carrying over the distance from Paris to Constantinople and the fees his company received from the participating governments were a sizeable offset to the overall running costs.

The locomotive itself was the latest design, called an 'EST 2-4-0'. Above the actual furnace was a brass steam-dome and a tall stove-pipe chimney, which was flared to allow steam to escape easily and so avoid super-heating in the pipes. Along its sides ran the control-rods, levers and linkage. Below these were the exterior cylinders and brass-rimmed wheel-splashers. The cab had a roof, but it was too small to afford any real protection. The driver and fireman could only keep warm if they stood close up against the firebox.

On the outside of each of the five coaches, painted along the top, was the name of Nagelmackers' dream: *Compagnie Internationale des Wagons-Lits et des Grands Express Européens.*

12

Vienna, 1906

The Orient Express left Gare de l'Est promptly at 7:30 p.m. on a cold Tuesday evening in December. The whistle blew and echoed around the station where Mata Hari had arrived from Amsterdam three years previously. She sat in her compartment, facing the window, and looked out as the spectators on the platform slid past. All wore long, dark overcoats. Some had brought their children to watch the departure. Two or three people waved sadly as the train pulled out of the station, then the platform ran out and all she could see were the street lights shining along the diverging tracks and dark walls looming.

Out of a small wooden box she took a gilt clock and placed it next to her bed. She put her lavender packet, soap, *masque de boue*, powder puff and rouge stick next to it. Under her bed, she placed her Chubb safe-box and jewellery case. She sorted through her trunks, hanging dresses in the wardrobe and her dressing gown on a hook behind the door. On the bed, she laid out three dresses to choose from for her evening in the dining car.

Just before nine o'clock, she entered the dining car wearing a sateen dress the colour of magnolias, and a matching hat and boa. A waiter showed her to a table. As she followed him, Mata Hari scanned the dining car: nearly all men, sombrely dressed and deep in discussion. Only two women. She hoped she wasn't going to have a dull evening. The waiter pointed to a seat at a table where two men were already eating. They put down their knives and forks and stood up. The man next to her was small, but stocky. The other was much taller and more handsome. As she took off her hat, they both nodded to her and smiled.

'*Enchanté,*' the taller one said.

'Good evening,' she smiled back. 'May I sit here?'

'Of course. Allow me to introduce myself,' he said. 'Oleg Jankovsky. And this is my friend Pierre Nozière.' He pointed.

'I'm Mata Hari,' she said and sat down.

As he sat down, Nozière looked surprised. 'The dancer?'

'Yes, that's right.'

'Very honoured to meet you, madame.'

'Thank you.' She settled in her seat and smoothed down the front of her dress.

'Are you travelling for a performance by any chance?' Nozière continued.

'Yes, to Vienna. I have engagements at the Secession Art Hall and the Apollo Theatre.'

'Oh,' Nozière said.

'If there's anything I can do to make your passage as agreeable as possible, please don't hesitate to ask,' said Jankovsky.

'You're very kind.' The train swayed slightly, making the glasses on their table clink together.

'Wine?' Jankovsky held up the bottle of red.

'No, thank you,' she said. 'I hardly ever drink.'

'Because of your profession?' Jankovsky inquired.

'Yes. I have to treat my body with care.'

Jankovsky smiled. 'I'm sure you treat your body with the utmost care,' he said and filled his own glass.

The lights in the dining car suddenly dimmed, hiding the faint smile on her face. White shirt fronts and the gold finishings in the carriage stood out in the gloom before the lights flicked back on. The waiter appeared. She looked briefly at the menu.

'The lamb is very good,' Nozière said.

She followed his advice and ordered the lamb. The waiter nodded and left. 'Are you gentlemen travelling on business?' she asked.

Jankovsky spoke first. 'I'm an industrialist. My firm has an office in Stuttgart, where I have some business. And Pierre here is taking a holiday in Buda-Pest.'

Nozière smiled. 'I've never been,' he said.

'I hear it is like Paris, but without the trees,' she said.

'I was telling Pierre that the Gellert Hotel spas are excellent. They keep one bath at thirty-four degrees and another at thirty degrees. You alternate between the two, then every once in a while, you plunge into the *bain froid*.'

'That sounds wonderful,' she said.

Jankovsky was looking at her. 'It's very invigorating.' He picked up his glass and drank the wine in one gulp.

After the main course, the train slowed down. The other diners parted the curtains at their table to look out. Nozière did so as well and announced that the train was pulling into the little station of Epernay. The train came to a stop with a hiss at the bright platform. The three of them saw a *conducteur* overseeing the loading of mailbags into a coach further up the train. He hurried the men up; then they heard the closing of doors. After a few minutes, the train crawled out of the station and into the night once again. A waiter appeared and left with their empty plates. The train picked up speed.

'Before you arrived, Oleg and I were talking about the Dreyfus affair,' Nozière said, taking a sip.

'Dreyfus?' she asked.

'Alfred Dreyfus.'

She looked blankly at him.

'Oh, perhaps because you are from the East, you do not know who Alfred Dreyfus is?'

'No, monsieur, I do not.'

Nozière looked at Jankovsky. 'Well,' Nozière said, 'he was an artillery officer in the French army. A Jew. He was found guilty of passing on documents to the Germans and sent to Devil's Island eleven years ago. But then, a man called Picquart, who was head of counter-espionage, declared that

Dreyfus was innocent. There were all sorts of ridiculous trials organised by the army to convince the public that Dreyfus was guilty, but the public refused to believe it. Dreyfus was brought back to France seven years ago and given a new trial, but they still found him guilty. It dragged on and on, and then President Loubet finally pardoned him. It was only a few months ago that his guilty verdict was finally quashed and he was fully exonerated.'

'Why was he treated so?' she asked.

Nozière fidgeted in his seat. 'Well, because he was a Jew.'

'Pierre is a journalist with *L'Aurore*,' Jankovsky said.

'Yes, that's right. We published the famous letter by Zola.'

'Pierre is also a republican,' Jankovsky said.

'And I fear Oleg is a monarchist!' Nozière laughed too loudly.

'Was he innocent all along?' she asked.

'Oh God, yes!' Nozière said.

The waiter arrived with an assortment of cognac, cheeses and fresh fruit. The colours of the cheese and the plums complemented each other, she thought. 'And what is Dreyfus doing now?' she asked.

'He's been restored to the army, with the rank of major,' Nozière said.

Jankovsky poured some cognac for himself. 'Do you like the theatre, madame?' he asked.

'Very much,' she smiled. 'I would like to try my hand at the theatre.'

'Which actress do you most admire?' he said.

She considered his question. 'Lillie Langtry, I think.'

Both men concurred.

'I saw her once,' Jankovsky said, 'some years ago in London. The play was called *The Degenerates*. It was terrible, but she was superb. I do believe she is the most beautiful creature I have ever seen.' His eyes twinkled. 'Until tonight, that is.'

A warmth suffused her stomach. Everything became sharper and brighter for a moment.

Nozière poured some cognac into his glass. 'Do you remember when she dropped a spoonful of strawberry ice down King Edward's back? She was ostracised by society for a week. How absurd the English Royalty is!'

Jankovsky laughed and raised his glass. 'Here's to the spirit of the lady!'

'Is she still the king's mistress?' Nozière asked.

'Yes,' Mata Hari said.

Jankovsky shrugged. 'Who can blame him? If I were king, I'd do the same!'

'I think the English are lucky to have a Royal Family,' she said. 'I wish France still had a monarchy.'

'I quite agree,' Jankovsky said and produced a cigar from inside his grey jacket.

Back in her compartment, she watched the train pull out of Châlons-sur-Marne. She had left the dinner table when Jankovsky and Nozière began arguing about the French Revolution. She idled on her bed and thought about Lillie Langtry. She had seen photographs of her in society magazines, reclining on a chaise longue, dressed in red crushed velvet and diamonds, with rose petals strewn about her feet. She had never seen such a beautiful woman. She thought about King Edward. What would it be like to be the king's mistress? She often dreamed of marrying into nobility. MacLeod used to call her an upstart, which had upset her more than anything else he said. Lola Montez had King Ludwig I and Cléo de Merode had King Leopold II, so why not her?

Earlier that year, MacLeod had sent his lawyer, Mr Heijmans, to Paris to secure an agreement for a divorce. MacLeod had asked several times via his lawyer, and each time she refused. Heijmans was clever: it was several days after their first meeting that he even bothered to bring up the subject of the divorce. She had declined once again, at which point he sighed and put his briefcase on his lap. He opened it and, with reluctance, handed her a piece of paper.

It was a photograph of her naked body. She remembered it had been taken a year or so after she had arrived in Paris. She'd been paid very well for her poses – three in all. She knew such photographs exchanged hands for a great deal of money in Parisian salons.

Heijmans smiled. The picture, he explained, had been sent to her husband by a friend of his. She looked at him. He shrugged his shoulders and said that not even a liberal judge in Amsterdam would allow her to have custody of Non or remain married to MacLeod in the light of this photograph. If she agreed to a divorce without any fuss, she could have the photograph back. She realised she had little choice. A month later, Heijmans sent her the final papers.

She was still lying on her bed when there was a knock at her door. She knew very well who it would be. She looked at her clock: 11:55. She stood up and opened the door. It was Jankovsky, reeking of cigar smoke.

The train shunting into motion woke her with a start. She slipped out of the bed and peeked through the curtains. It was just daylight. Cold and grey. She saw a sign pass slowly by: MÜHLACKER. A few people stood motionless on the platform, watching the Orient Express draw out of the station.

'Where are we?'

She turned and saw Jankovsky stretch. 'Mühlacker,' she said. 'You have to go now. We'll be arriving at Stuttgart in an hour.'

'I went to Mühlacker once. It's an awful town.' He yawned.

The train clacked across points and picked up speed. She stood for a few moments by the window, looking out. She wondered what Vienna was like – if it was as cold as they said.

'Oleg, you have to go now.'

He looked at her, in her peach silk nightdress, and nodded.

When he was dressed, he took out his wallet. For a moment, she thought he was going to give her money, but he gave her a card. It had his name and address in Paris on it. He seemed about to say something, but instead he just looked directly at her for a few moments and then left. Before the door had closed, she knew she would never see him again.

Vienna was indeed very cold. A heavy snow was falling on the city as Mata Hari alighted from the train at Westbahnhof. She found a porter, who arranged her three trunks on his trolley and took her to a taxi.

Outside the station she stood with her hands in a muff, watching the large snowflakes fall through the morning air. There was no wind. Two children, in coats and gloves, were laughing and gathering the snow up into piles.

The city seemed quiet. There was little traffic and any noise was deadened by the snow. A little black taxi pulled up beside her. When the porter had unloaded her luggage, she tipped him and got in. The taxi pulled away, slipping at times along the deep ruts.

She gazed out of the window at the long lines of tall buildings. Each had a lead roof, with rounded corners, and an ornate entrance. Snow had collected on the balconies and window sills. A man walked through the snow with his head down. A lady with a small child disappeared into a doorway. Mata Hari recited the German street names, trying to familiarise herself with this strange language. The driver smiled and corrected her pronunciation.

At the Hôtel Bristol, the car pulled over. A doorman appeared from nowhere and supervised the unloading of her luggage. She paid the taxi driver, who waved as he drove away. The doorman showed her through a revolving door into a plush green foyer. When she had checked in, the receptionist confirmed her interview with the *Neue Wiener Journal* for three o'clock. She decided to rest till then.

In her room, she sat on the bed and took out Jankovsky's card from her purse. She turned it over in her hands. In bed with him the night before, his eyes had been two points of light, his teeth flashing in the darkness. She could still feel his hands on her skin. She stood up and walked over to the full-length mirror, where she took off her dress and underwear. When she was naked, she stood in front of the mirror and placed her hands on her stomach, then her breasts. A shiver passed down her spine.

A few minutes before three o'clock, Mata Hari entered the hotel bar, wearing a robe of sapphire-blue chiffon trimmed with chinchilla. Her pearl earrings bobbed as she walked and her hair shone under the clusters of bright lamps. Already seated at one of the tables was a young man in a dark suit and wire-frame glasses. He was so busy writing something that he didn't notice her approach.

'Are you from the newspaper?' she said.

He looked surprised as he got to his feet. 'Yes. Madame Mata Hari?' He held out his hand.

She nodded and shook his hand.

'Please sit down,' he said.

She sat opposite him and leaned back in the green leather armchair. A waiter in a white jacket appeared.

'Would you like some coffee? Or tea perhaps?' the journalist asked.

'I would like a mint julep with a little sugar.'

The journalist ordered another coffee and the waiter disappeared.

'First of all, I'd like to welcome you to Vienna . . .'

His French was good. 'Thank you, monsieur, you are too kind.'

'And to say that I am looking forward very much to your performance tomorrow evening at the Secession Art Hall.'

'You have a ticket?'

'Oh yes, your agent Maître Clunet was prompt in supplying me with a seat in the front row.'

'Good. Would you like another for a friend?'

'No, that won't be necessary, thank you,' he blushed.

'As you wish.'

'I hope you won't mind my taking notes?'

'Not at all.'

'Good. I'd like to begin our talk by clearing up the confusion surrounding your birthplace. Where were you actually born?'

'I was born in the Indies, and lived there till I was twelve years old. My parents were of European extraction, but my grandmother was the daughter of a Javanese prince.'

'And what about your upbringing?'

'My childhood memories are very clear. I remember my first years amidst the marvellous tropical vegetation. At the age of twelve, I went to Wiesbaden. Later, I got married. With my husband, a colonel in the Dutch colonial army, I returned to my native country, where I spent my time horseback riding, gun in hand, and risking my life. I have Hindu blood in my veins. Dancing is in my blood. Although I have become a woman, my eyes still enjoy the sights of my youth.'

'Could you tell me a little about your art?'

'My art? It is really very simple – the most natural thing in the world. Nature itself is simple; only man complicates it. One does not need things that have been complicated to the point of being ridiculous; the sacred Brahman dances are symbols, and all their gestures must correspond to thoughts. The dance is a poem, and every gesture is one of its words. I have been taught from my earliest childhood the deepest meaning of these dances, which constitute a cult, a religion. In Batavia, I often came in contact with rich princes who would invite us, my husband and myself, into their homes. These men, who are very religious, have famous dancers whom they hardly show to anyone. These dancers know the most secret Brahman dances, which are executed around the altar, and I have been able to study with them for a long time.'

'It's been claimed that no one before you has been able to give such a complete impression of sacred art.'

'In my dancing one forgets the woman in me, so that I offer everything and finally myself to the god – which is symbolised by the slow loosening of my loincloth, the last piece of clothing I have on – and stand there, albeit only for half a second, entirely naked. I have never yet evoked any feeling but an interest in the mood that is expressed by my dancing. I have travelled all over the East, but can honestly say that nowhere have I seen women dance while holding a snake or some other object. This I first saw when I came to Europe, and it struck me with dumb amazement.'

The waiter came holding a tray and served their drinks. She took a sip of her julep and set the glass down. The journalist stirred his coffee while he searched through his notes.

'Is it true that you assisted Monsieur Guimet in the preparation of his lecture which preceded your dance at his museum last year?'

'I have to confess, yes. I studied Orientalism, lived with it, thought in it and dreamt about it. I know the music of these countries, I could go through all the harp variations that accompany my dances, and I even compose. I helped him a lot.'

'Why did you go to Paris, not anywhere else?'

'I don't know. I thought all women who ran away from their husbands went to Paris.'

'I wonder what you would have done if, when you arrived in Paris, you had not succeeded?'

'I had a gun ready and my decision was taken,' she smiled. She sipped her julep. 'I have a character which is always apt to follow a sudden impulse.'

'And how did you come to arrive so suddenly in Paris?'

'I arrived only a year and a half ago from Holland, with half a franc in my pocket. I went to the Grand Hôtel. It is quite a story, oh, not a very pleasant one!'

'But very impressive. Please tell me something of it.'

'I did some modelling for a time, and rode horses in a circus. But I felt I could do better, that the glow and the arts of my holy country were deep within me. Only those born and bred there become impregnated with their religious significance, and can impart to them the solemn note to which they lay claim.' She laughed. 'Now I am in Paris and mix with a thousand people every day.'

'And what are your impressions of European society in general, and Parisian society in particular?'

'My impressions are not flattering. Having remained close to Nature for so long, which is simultaneously innocent and simple, I look upon your worldly behaviour as if it takes place on a stage where everything is false and on the surface only. Women wearing make-up and false hair, compliments that are nothing but lies, all this inspires in me an amazement that borders on hilarity. I am astonished that your women do not have the customs of my country, where women may have to suffer inferior treatment like being whipped, but where at the same time we are superior, because we can sew, make our own clothes, are good cooks, can shoot straight, can ride horseback and are capable of doing logarithms and talking philosophy.'

'I've read somewhere that four ministers of state invited you to supper, and that in the intimacy of their dining room you regaled them with your art.'

'I differ from other artists. I am at one with my public; I am on the same social level. I not only *dance* in the best Paris salons, but am received there as an equal, and I myself at times entertain my hosts.'

'I'm curious to know whether you don't look forward to a time in your life beyond dancing in public – a return to the Brahman temples maybe?'

She nodded her head. 'I fully agree. I do have such an ideal. I confess that I might say goodbye to my dancing career soon.'

'Really?'

'Yes.' She paused and looked at the journalist, who was writing quickly to keep up with her. 'A better prospect has appeared on my horizon. I have been asked for my hand in marriage by Count T–y, who is a Russian officer attached to Grand Duke Michael.'

He looked up. 'Congratulations! You must be very happy.'

'Thank you. I am.'

'Can you tell me something about your plans?'

'Plans? Well, for the moment, I have so many of them. I've had several offers from abroad, including London and St Petersburg, which pleases me enormously. I am preparing three new Brahman dances. I would like to get an apartment of my own, with my own furniture and bouquets of flowers. I adore flowers. The Eastern dances such as I have witnessed and learned in my native Java are inspired by flowers, from which they take their poetry. I would like to get away from the uninteresting atmosphere of the boarding houses I usually stay in – please don't misunderstand me, the Hôtel Bristol is wonderful – I mean the *pensions* in Paris. But above all, I want to work, to work and study.'

'What about the theatre?'

'The theatre? I do not know yet, but I have had many proposals from impresarios.'

'You've been received warmly here in Vienna. Is there anywhere else you would like to perform?'

'Do you mean in Europe?'

'Yes.'

'As I said, I may go to London and St Petersburg. I would like to go to Spain; I have an idea that the landscape there would suit me. Maybe Buda-Pest. I'd like to visit the Gellert Hotel to try their spa baths.'

'What about Berlin?'

'Berlin? I wouldn't dance in Berlin for *any* amount of money!'

'Why not?'

'My agent, Maître Clunet, has told me that they would not appreciate the nature of my performances there. No' – she shook her head – 'in Europe my affections reside in Paris.'

> I wonder if these dances, in their oriental calm, are real – whether they have anything Indian at all. But even if they do not, there is much to admire, for this body, which is formed like a work of Art, and which moves with gestures of caressing charm and yet priest-like, is highly provocative. Whether it is provocative in the artistic sense only is a matter of taste.
>
> *Die Zeit*, December 1906

> I would have to lie if I were to say that the performance is more than that of an amateur.
>
> *Wiener Deutsches Tageblatt*, December 1906

> The new Art of the Dance, which Mata Hari for the moment more feels than expresses, is still waiting for its great exponent.
>
> *Arbeiter Zeitung*, December 1906

> If she had not had the advantage of 'nude publicity', she would not have been a success.
>
> *Deutsche Zeitung*, December 1906

> Isadore Duncan is dead! Long live Mata Hari!
>
> *Neue Wiener Journal*, December 1906

13

Berlin, 1907

> Are we still living in the times of Louis XVI, who arranged a majestic and enthusiastic reception for a foreign ambassador who turned out to be none but a Marseilles shopkeeper?
>
> François de Nion, *La Prensa*

He was a short, slim man, his thinness emphasised by the way his dark-blue serge suit hung loosely from his shoulders. His face was younger than his years and she imagined it had always been that way. He had the most extraordinary eyes. They bulged slightly and were brilliant blue, drawing in everything around him. When she looked into his eyes, the rest of his face grew vague. Two taller men stood silently behind him.

'Good afternoon, madame. My name is Traugott von Jagow. I work for the city police.' His French was excellent.

'Good afternoon. My name is Mata Hari.'

'Yes, I know that, madame,' he said.

'Is this a social or professional call?'

He smiled. She made her question sound like an insult. He glanced around the dressing room. It was small and cramped, with mirrors along one wall and clothes hanging from hooks in the walls, the door and from hat-stands. Two trunks, open by her feet, were half-spilling on to the floor.

'I hope you are comfortable. Our shabby theatres are old and are hardly the most salubrious.'

'I've been in worse places than the Metropole, I can assure you,' she said.

'And the Hôtel Cumberland?'

'Perfect.'

'*Bon*.' He almost bowed. 'As to your question, it is my misfortune that my call has to be professional. I'm sure the manager of this music hall has informed you that, in Germany, we have the regrettable duty of inspecting the costumes worn by all foreign artistes, such as yourself.'

He waved his hand, as though brushing away a fly.

'Normally, I would designate this repugnant duty to one of my least senior officers, but, with so esteemed a guest in our country, I felt that nothing else would suffice except to perform this inspection personally.'

'I'm honoured that you should take the time.'

'With such a reputation, madame, it's the least I can do. I've heard of your performances at the Folies Bergère and Trocadéro in Paris. They precede you.'

'You're too kind. And what do you think you will find in my chest, Herr von Jagow?'

There was a hint of a smile on his face. 'I'm sure there are many joyous and exotic messages from the Orient in your chest, madame, and I'm sure they are all legal. May I?'

'Please.' She opened her arms.

He signalled to the two men standing behind him. They searched a trunk each, lifting the veils, sarongs, skirts and shawls and gently prodding underneath. All the while, she looked at von Jagow, who held her gaze. She couldn't tell if he was in awe of her or disgusted with her. The two men finished, saying they had found nothing. Von Jagow nodded to dismiss them.

'Everything appears to be in order, madame.'

'Good.'

'How long will you be staying in Berlin?'

'I'm not sure. I have no engagements following this as yet and I would like to explore your wonderful city, so I may stay for a few weeks. I will do as my impulse tells me.'

'Please allow me the honour of showing you the sights. My office has a motor car which we use for special guests. It is very comfortable.'

She assented with a smile.

'Excellent. Tomorrow morning perhaps?'

'Tomorrow afternoon?'

'Fine,' he said, then bowed in a quick, jerky movement. 'Goodnight, madame and good luck.' He turned and strode out of the room, shutting the door behind him.

Mata Hari took her time undressing, pausing to hang up each article of clothing while she considered how best to deal with von Jagow. She could tell by his bearing that he was an important city official and that, if there was a future for herself in Berlin, she would have to get along with him. For now, though, she decided it would be best to wait and see.

Standing naked, she sorted through her travelling baggage and found her saffron-coloured sarong. The silk was embroidered with red flowers on golden vines. She twirled this around her thighs and tied it in a loose-fitting knot which just concealed her pubis. She stood straight and then pulled the knot – the sarong fell to the ground. Satisfied, she twirled the sarong again around her body and tied it with the same knot.

From her Gladstone bag, she took out several pieces of jewellery and placed them on the dressing table. She attached bracelets, made of filigree, on each wrist, upper arm and just below each knee. She put in the earrings – yellow garnets dropped on tiny silver chains. Covering her breasts, she put on a yellow cloth bodice, cupped with seashells, and clasped its hooks behind her. She placed a choker around her neck and straightened the beads hanging on threads from the ribbon. Finally, she took a casque of worked gold out of a felt bag and placed it in her hair.

As she was finishing dressing, there was a knock at the door. One of the cabaret dancers came in holding a large bouquet of orange flowers. They glowed in the dark room like Chinese lanterns.

'These just came for you! Aren't they beautiful?' the dancer said.

Mata Hari took them. The petals had black spots and left orange dust on her fingers when she touched them. She put the bouquet down and opened a little envelope. Inside, there was a card:

> A great but diffident admirer of yours who, in order to watch you, has stayed two days longer in Berlin than he intended, ventures with great deference to ask you to accept the accompanying flowers as a sign of his admiration.
>
> Alfred Kiepert, Lieutenant in the Second Company of the Eleventh Westphalian Hussars Regiment.

'Well, who is it?' the dancer said.

'Lieutenant Kiepert. Do you know him?'

'Kiepert? Are you joking? He's only one of the richest landowners in Berlin. He has a huge estate just outside the city!'

'Really?'

'Oh, you're so lucky!' the dancer said.

> You can scarcely credit the mystic frenzy produced by her lascivious attitudes. Her nervous tremors, her violent contortions, were terribly impressive. There was in the performance something of the solemnity of an idol, something of the loathsome horror of a writhing reptile. From her great sombre eyes, half-closed in sensuous ecstasy, there gleamed an uncanny light, like phosphorescent flames. She seemed to embrace an invisible being in her long shapely arms. Her braceleted legs were glossy and well moulded, they so quivered through excessive effort that it seemed the tendons must burst through the enveloping skin. To witness the spectacle was to receive the impression that one had actually been present at the metamorphosis of a serpent taking a woman's form.
>
> An anonymous spectator, Berlin 1907

*

After the performance, Mata Hari sat on her trunk, breathing heavily and trembling slightly. It was always some minutes before she could recover from a dance. There was a knock on her door. Without waiting for a response, the door opened and the stage manager told her in his faltering French that she had a visitor. He asked if he should show the man in. Mata Hari nodded and stood up.

When the stage manager beckoned, a soldier appeared, dressed in a dark-blue jacket decorated with red epaulettes and bands of yellow chenille. His cream jodhpurs were stretched taut over his thighs and, even in the dim light, she could see his knee-high black leather boots shine. He held his hussar's cap, also banded with chenille, to his chest. She had never seen such a magnificently dressed soldier.

Sensing her appreciation, the soldier clicked his heels. 'Lieutenant Alfred Kiepert, at your service, madame.' He took her hand and clumsily kissed it.

'Thank you for the flowers, Lieutenant. How did you know that tiger lilies were my favourite?'

Kiepert looked confused for a moment. 'I didn't,' he said.

'Are you a good guesser then?'

'I must be!' he laughed awkwardly. He fiddled with his cap and took a deep breath. 'May I invite you to Adlon's for dinner?'

She saw that his hair was damp with sweat and his cheeks flushed. He couldn't have been more than twenty-one or two. But he was very rich.

'I would be delighted,' she smiled. 'Give me a few minutes to get ready.'

The restaurant was almost full. Several officers, with uniforms the same as Kiepert's, sat smoking cigars and talking. Beside each of the officers sat a woman, dressed in evening wear and listening. Clouds of smoke gathered above the tables.

The maître d' nodded briefly to Kiepert and showed them to a table for two towards the rear of the restaurant. As they followed him, several people nodded or raised their glasses. Mata Hari smiled back, without knowing who they were.

Once seated, Kiepert leaned across to her. 'Madame, your Dance of the Seven Veils tonight was an exquisite experience.'

'Thank you, Lieutenant.'

'Please call me Alfred.'

A waiter appeared from nowhere. Kiepert ordered a bottle of Vernis Mordore Dore and a caviar hors d'oeuvre.

When the champagne arrived, Kiepert insisted on opening it himself. There was a loud pop. He filled their glasses, spilling some, and toasted the Kaiser.

'And to the Crown Prince!' she said.

Kiepert laughed. 'We call him "Little Willie", you know.'

'Have you met him?'

'Of course.'

'I would love to meet him,' she smiled.

'Maybe I can arrange it for you. Let me try.'

'I'll tell you something about me that few people know.'

He leaned forward. 'Go on.'

'I'm the daughter of King Edward and a Hindu princess.'

'Really?'

'It's been necessary to be discreet, for the sake of my father, but since I found out, I've traced my family tree all the way back to Azo IV.'

'My God!' Kiepert said. His round face went red with excitement.

'Yes, it's true. Azo IV founded the House of Zelle in 1000 AD. Then, in the sixteenth century, my family split into the British Royal House of Guelph and the German Hohenzollerns. So, you see, the Crown Prince and I could be related.'

'Amazing! I'll drink to that.' He guzzled his glass of champagne and quickly poured another.

*

After dinner, they walked to one of Kiepert's apartments, on the Nacodstrasse. Inside, he was still flushed and excited. She kissed him slowly and told him to wait for a few moments, then went into his bedroom. She took off her turquoise satinette dress, her lace *cache-corset* and stockings. Hanging on a piece of string inside her dress was a small sponge. She took it off and, lying back in his big bed, inserted it into herself. She called to Kiepert. He tore his clothes off and jumped into bed. Within seconds, he was inside her. His head was buried in her neck and he was moaning on top of her. She pushed on his shoulders to slow him down – he was hurting her – but he took no notice. A few minutes later, he shuddered and slumped on her. Then he fell asleep.

Kiepert left early the following morning, but told her she could remain in the apartment as long as she wished. He had some business to attend to on his estate and would be back in a few days. She thanked him. When he had gone, she telephoned the Cumberland and arranged to have her things sent over. Then she called von Jagow, who arranged to pick her up at two o'clock.

Von Jagow arrived punctually and was waiting by a motor car when she stepped out on to the street. He announced that it was the newest hand-made Benz Motorwagen and that, like Berlin itself, it was a wonderfully modern machine. He ushered her into the rear cabin and ordered the driver to take them on a tour of the city. The driver released the handbrake and the car sped away. Von Jagow inquired after her health and told her that the morning papers had been positively ecstatic about her performance. She thanked him and looked around the cabin. The entire interior was padded in olive-green buttoned quilting. The pull-down blinds on the windows were purple. The driver in the open cabin up front was wearing a peaked cap and goggles.

As they drove down Unter den Linden, von Jagow pointed out the Brandenburg Gate. The car passed underneath the gate, then crossed the river. Barges and smaller boats steamed up and down. He showed her the Reichstag and the old university, where he had been a student. The domes and steeples were black with grime. As they rounded a corner at speed, a startled student crossing the street had to jump clear. The driver swerved, then pumped the rubber horn angrily. Mata Hari looked through the rear window and saw the student get to his feet. His books were strewn across the road.

They crossed the river again and entered a residential area made up of massive houses and apartment blocks, all partially hidden by huge trees. Von Jagow explained that they were reserved exclusively for the diplomats, civil servants and military personnel working in Berlin. She was looking at the impressive buildings when von Jagow tapped on the glass partition and the car came to a halt by the pavement.

'Let's look inside this one, shall we?' von Jagow said as he opened the door.

Mata Hari glanced out and saw a huge lime-stucco house. She counted four floors and several windows.

'What a strange colour. Won't we disturb the residents?' she asked with surprise.

'Don't worry, madame,' von Jagow smiled; 'this one is owned by the city police. Please, let me show you around.'

As she stepped out of the car, a gust of wind blew in the treetops, making the leaves rustle. She held on to her hat and looked either way down the wide street. There was no one about. The noise of the trees increased the impression she had of being away from the city centre. Von Jagow told the driver to wait, then led her to the entrance, which was covered by a portico. Taking a key from his waistcoat pocket, he unlocked the door and waved her inside.

The hallway was painted in a deep forest-green. It smelled fresh inside, as though the house was tended to regularly. Von Jagow closed the door behind him and led her through the rooms on the ground floor. There were two reception rooms, one lemon-yellow and one orange, a magnolia dining room with a table that could seat up to twelve people and a book-lined study with burgundy walls.

The kitchen was an antiseptic white. The thick wooden work surfaces had been scrubbed clean; glistening pots and pans hung from hooks on the wall. Standing isolated in the centre was the oven. The hotplates were spotless. It was more like a kitchen for a hotel than a house.

Upstairs, there was a dove-grey reception room with a fireplace large enough for two firedogs. At the other end of the room were a raised platform and a patterned screen. Padded chairs were placed along the walls. A set of doors led through to an adjoining snug, with a smaller fireplace and a card table. Further down the corridor, von Jagow showed her the first of the bedrooms. Each of the rooms, he explained, was named according to its colour and all in all the house could sleep up to thirty guests.

Presently, they came back down the stairs to the hallway. Mata Hari was amazed. She had never before been inside such a luxurious house.

'Why are you showing me all this?'

His blue eyes twinkled. 'Do you like it?' he asked.

'Yes, very much.'

'Would you like to live here when you are in Berlin?'

She didn't know where this was leading.

'Don't worry, madame, it's an honest question,' he said.

'I would love to stay here, yes.'

'Then you can.' He snapped his fingers. 'Just like that.'

'Why me?'

'Because you are a famous artiste, and because you could be very helpful to me. You have many imitators now, but I want the real thing.' He opened his arms and indicated the high-ceilinged hallway. 'All this can be yours, in return for a small favour.'

'Favour?'

'Yes, a favour. Several favours, actually.'

'What do you mean?'

'All I ask is that you make yourself at home here and, from time to time, entertain some people.'

'Soldiers?'

Von Jagow chose his words carefully. 'Yes, soldiers. But other people also.'

'Such as?'

'Oh, diplomats, couriers, that kind of thing. People who have certain "information" I need.'

Mata Hari considered his proposition. She looked at him and he returned her gaze, without flinching.

'I could show you great wealth and comfort, if you were willing,' he said.

She remembered how poor she had been when she had first arrived in Paris. She remembered Guillomet, the painter, who had said he could only use her with her clothes on; Alice, who was probably still staying at the Régence Hôtel. She remembered the lawyer, Heijmans, and the naked photograph of herself that had left her so powerless. She thought of MacLeod and his accusation that she was an upstart; his cruel temper. And then she thought of Non, whom he had stolen from her, and wondered what she looked like now.

'I'll do it.'

'*Bon,*' he smiled, 'you've made a wise decision, madame. Let me take you to Adlon's to celebrate. We'll have fresh trout and the most delicious white wine you have ever tasted.'

Late the next morning, Kiepert telephoned to say he had returned to Berlin and would see her in an hour. She replaced the heavy receiver and slid out of bed.

Kiepert's bathroom was panelled in mahogany. There was an ottoman against one wall and a wicker chair in the other corner with a bidet next to it. Built at one end of the deep, long bath was a mahogany cabin. When she turned on the taps inside, the water came out of a nozzle above her, so that she could stand while she washed herself. Kiepert had called it a *douche*. She had never used one before and spent a long time soaping every inch of her body. When she had dried herself, she put on a transparent white negligée trimmed with marabou feathers and scented her hair with rose pomade. She puffed up the pillows and lay in bed, waiting for Kiepert's return.

When he arrived, he came straight into the bedroom. He was carrying a briefcase and his expression was crestfallen.

She sat up. 'What's the matter, Alfred?' she asked.

'Things are difficult,' he said.

'What do you mean?'

'Things are difficult because you are French and I am German.'

'But I don't understand. I don't mind that you are German.'

'That's not it.'

'What then? Please, Alfred, tell me.' She sensed that he was trying to be determined about something.

'My family have insisted that I should break with you.'

'Why?'

'If I don't, they will disinherit me.'

'What?'

'Please try to understand.' He put the briefcase on a table and opened it. 'Perhaps this will show you the degree of my regret.'

She frowned at him. 'What is this, Alfred? I thought I pleased you.'

'You did, but I can't see you any more.'

She looked at the briefcase. There were neat piles of banknotes inside.

'There's 300,000 marks. Take it, please,' he said.

14
The Green House, 1908

> Two and a half years ago I made my first appearance at a private performance at the Musée Guimet. Ever since that memorable date ladies, styling themselves 'Eastern Dancers', have sprung out of the ground and honour me with their imitations. I would feel highly flattered with this mark of attention, if these ladies' performances were accurate from a scientific and aesthetic point of view. But they are not.
>
> Mata Hari, *The Era*, 1908

Viktor Sokolov knew his journey from St Petersburg had been announced to Russian agents based in Berlin. His imminent arrival would have been telegraphed by his superiors in St Petersburg. The Russian military kept an office in Berlin, and it was the office's job to protect emissaries such as himself, whether they were in transit or staying for a period of time. The German authorities knew of this office – it was an open secret in the city – but as long as peace prevailed, they raised little protest.

When his train had pulled into Friedrichstrassebahnhof, Viktor carried his small suitcase and his diplomatic pouch outside, where he queued for a taxi. He told the driver to take him to the Russian Embassy. He had an appointment with the Consul, with whom he had been instructed to leave his diplomatic pouch. The Mont Blanc fountain pen he had been given, however, was to be kept with him at all costs. Viktor checked the inside pocket of his jacket: the pen was safe. He sat back and realised how tired he was. His journey had taken two days. He'd had nothing to do except look at the snow melting in the flat, bleak landscape.

At the Embassy, he was met by an assistant to the Consul and shown to the Consul's office on the first floor. The Consul was a rotund man, with greased hair and round spectacles. He smiled and said, 'Welcome back to Berlin, Viktor.' They embraced. The Consul then opened a safe behind a picture hanging on the wall, and deposited Viktor's diplomatic pouch inside.

They sat and talked about St Petersburg. The Consul asked how life was in the city, Viktor answered that everything was fine. The Consul said he missed St Petersburg, but was enjoying life in Berlin. He said it was very civilised. One could buy so many fine things here. He showed Viktor his new 'wristwatch', made by Cartier, a Frenchman. It was the latest fashion. Viktor admired it. The Consul asked Viktor how long he would be staying, Viktor replied that he didn't know. The Consul nodded sagely and told him that a room had been booked for him at the Adlon Hôtel.

Viktor's superiors in St Petersburg had told him that there was a leak somewhere within this Embassy. Information from files deposited in the Consul's safe was known to have been passed on to German agents. Viktor was certain that the documents in the diplomatic pouch contained nothing important. The pen he was carrying, on the other hand, was something entirely different. But he still wasn't sure if his superiors thought the Embassy's staff, or the various couriers passing through Berlin, were to blame. During his two days on the train, Viktor realised that his journey had been set up to ascertain this. Either way, he was under suspicion as much as the Embassy staff. Viktor had been told not to divulge too much to the Consul about his instructions and he had no intention of disobeying. He thanked the Consul and asked if a taxi could be ordered.

As he was checking in at the Adlon Hôtel, Viktor was greeted by two German officers he'd met on a previous visit to Berlin. He was struck by the coincidence. He shook their hands and accepted an invitation to join them for a drink in the lounge bar. To refuse would have been inappropriate, and therefore suspicious. There were several German military men in the bar, as well as a few Frenchmen. They were all drinking vermouth. Someone asked him what he was doing in Berlin and he answered as vaguely as he could. One of the officers ordered a pepper vodka for Viktor.

There followed a discussion about entertainment for the coming evening. Someone suggested a cabaret at the Metropole, another a casino. They asked Viktor, a visitor to the city, for his preference and Viktor sensed that they were eager to impress him. Meanwhile, a German captain informed everyone that he had just spoken to Mata Hari on the telephone and she had agreed to make up the party. Everyone seemed to settle for that as a solution; more vodka and vermouth were ordered.

Viktor had heard of the woman. The headlines from German newspapers were telegraphed every day to St Petersburg. He knew that she was Indian, that she was a celebrated dancer and that she was very beautiful, but little else. He was curious to meet her.

They carried on drinking and talking for another hour, at which point Mata Hari arrived. She was dressed from head to foot in white lace, with a fox-fur wrap around her shoulders. The animated conversation amongst the group of officers died down while she was introduced to those she didn't know, including Viktor. She had very dark hair that was braided and clipped back into extravagant curls. She smiled at him. Her large oval eyes were olive-dark and regarded him lazily as she returned Viktor's greeting. He felt his neck tingle. Despite himself, Viktor was indeed impressed.

She turned to the group. 'Gentlemen,' she said, 'may I suggest that we adjourn to my rooms where we can all continue our revelries. I promise I can furnish you all with an evening's entertainment better than any cabaret in the city. And, what's more, I guarantee the freedom afforded by the privacy of my rooms . . .'

There was a low murmur of assent among the men – they needed no further persuasion. On his way out, Viktor arranged for his suitcase to be taken to Mata Hari's rooms.

He travelled to her apartment in a motor car with his two officer friends. They drove out of the city, to an area he didn't know. He was told it was the Wilhelmstrasse district. The long, tree-lined roads were quiet and impressive. Huge villas and mansions were set back in calming foliage. Their destination was a lovely large house, with a curious green exterior. As Viktor walked to the front door, he noticed that every window was lit. Once inside, Mata Hari gathered her guests in the hallway and announced that a late buffet would be served shortly in the first-floor reception room, which allowed her guests time to settle in their rooms.

Viktor was shown up the central stairs. A valet led the way, carrying Viktor's suitcase, which had arrived a few moments after Viktor. The place was enormous: two corridors led off each landing and, looking down them, Viktor could see several doorways. His room on the fourth floor was very fine, small but tastefully lit and painted cherry-red.

The valet placed Viktor's case on the bed and produced a form from inside his waistcoat. He explained that Viktor should check the contents of the case and sign the baggage receipt to verify that nothing was missing. It was a requirement for all foreign diplomats staying as guests, he said. Viktor nodded and opened his suitcase. Searching through it, he could find nothing amiss. The valet smiled and handed Viktor the receipt, which Viktor signed with the Mont Blanc pen. The valet asked for the pen to sign it himself. Viktor hesitated. He would draw too much attention if he refused, so he offered the pen up without fuss. The valet turned and leant on the dressing table while he added his signature, then handed the pen back. He thanked Viktor and left. Viktor checked the pen, looking at the brown marbling and unscrewing the barrel to find the piece of paper inside. Satisfied it was the same one, he put it back in his jacket pocket and decided to freshen up before heading downstairs.

When Viktor entered the first-floor reception room, the buffet was already under way. The room was very warm. Some of the guests were standing in pairs around the fireplace, others were seated in groups of armchairs, talking and eating. A waitress stood behind a long table, which displayed an array of cold meats and salads. Viktor chose some pork and bread sauce and found his German acquaintances.

A minute later, he saw Mata Hari come into the room and he watched as she mingled with her guests. She had changed her clothes. She was now wearing a coral-pink silk dress and a magenta shawl. Her bare arms were pale and slender and her open neck was flushed with the heat. Her hair was pinned up into a conch and her diamond earrings glittered in the firelight. Viktor couldn't take his eyes off her. She spoke to each of her guests for a moment, before moving on.

When she approached Viktor, he nodded to her and said how beautiful she looked. She smiled and thanked him. She told him that the evening's entertainment was about to start and that he should find himself a seat. Viktor nodded. Her eyes lingered on him before moving on to inform the others.

The party arranged the chairs into rows and sat down. A large screen was stretched across one end of the reception room, behind which Viktor could hear people getting ready. The waitress came round with a tray of small glasses filled with schnapps. Smiling, she offered one to Viktor, who took it. The drink smelled of peaches. It reminded him of his father's *dacha*, with its peach trees in summer. One of his German friends sitting next to him knocked the schnapps back in one. Viktor sipped his, the alcohol burning his tongue and warming his stomach.

When everyone was settled in their seats, the electric lighting was hastily dimmed, then switched off altogether. Voices died down. Clusters of candles on either side of the screen were the only illumination. Two women folded the screen up to reveal four or five women in costume, standing still on a small stage. Nearby sat two East Indian men with instruments: one was a kind of upright guitar; the other was a set of small timpani. Viktor saw Mata Hari, standing to one side of the stage, give the musicians a nod.

The music began. It was unlike anything Viktor had heard before: slow and sedative. The women started dancing. Their languorous movements were hypnotic to watch. In the half-light, Viktor slowly realised that the women were wearing nothing under their costumes. The tightly-fitting bodices were thin and gauzy. He could see their full breasts and dark nipples, and their black pubic hair. Viktor found himself shocked, but aroused. Nothing like this could ever happen in St Petersburg. He drank his peach schnapps and strained to get a better view.

The next morning, Viktor woke to see his room wildly disordered. His clothes were strewn over the floor, a chair was overturned and the bedclothes were horribly dishevelled. He had a splitting headache. He thought back over the night before. All he could remember was dinner and the cabaret afterwards – the half-dressed women appearing from behind a silk screen. He tried to concentrate, pinching his nose and rubbing his temples, but could recall nothing after that.

Suddenly, he remembered the fountain pen and felt a surge of panic. He looked around the room and saw his jacket on the floor by the dressing table. He jumped out of bed and went through the pockets: the pen was still there. Thank God. He slumped to the floor and sighed heavily. He looked down at himself, naked in a wrecked room. What did he think he was doing? It was time to leave. He quickly dressed and threw things into his suitcase. On his way out, he saw none of the guests or the staff. The place appeared to be empty.

Within two hours, Viktor was sitting on a train bound for Brussels. Two things struck him. Firstly, he was shocked at how long he had slept. When he had left the apartment in Wilhelmstrasse, it was past 4:00 p.m. Even the worst hang-overs had never kept him asleep that long and his headache felt as if it was the consequence of more than just alcohol.

Secondly, he realised that his room had been ransacked, but made to look like the results of an eventful night. He had somehow managed to extricate himself from a potentially disastrous situation. Anything could have happened after he lost consciousness, but the pen was safe. That was the most important thing. Viktor realised he had been very lucky. All the same, he wished he could recall what had happened after the cabaret.

His train would arrive in Brussels the following morning at 7:30 a.m. Once there, he promised himself he would find a quiet hotel room and lie low for a few days. He would see no one. Then, he would board another train, this time for Paris, which was his ultimate destination. His instructions were to travel leisurely to Paris, via Berlin and Brussels, and to spend some days in each city in order to attract as little attention to his movements as possible. This was exactly what he intended to do. His head still throbbed. He settled down in his seat and slept.

In Brussels, Viktor found a small hotel just off La Grand' Place. For two days, he tried to enjoy his walks around the city, but was prevented from doing so by the thought of how close he'd come to real danger. He didn't dare think about what would have happened if he'd lost possession of the pen.

On his last evening in Brussels, he went to the Théâtre de la Monnaie to see a revue. His French was excellent, but not good enough to understand some of the jokes and double entendres. He left the theatre with the rest of the audience, which gradually thinned out, so that he found himself walking alone back to his hotel through the narrow, half-lit streets. He was booked on the morning train to Paris and was going over the journey in his mind when someone tapped him on the shoulder. Viktor turned around and saw a man standing with his hands in the pockets of his overcoat. It took Viktor a few moments to realise it was the valet from the house in Berlin.

'Good evening, monsieur,' the valet said.

Viktor stared at him.

'I have something of yours,' the valet continued. He held up a brown Mont Blanc fountain pen. Viktor looked at it. He reached inside his jacket and pulled out exactly the same pen. He tried to say something, but the words wouldn't come.

'Trust me, the pen I have is yours. If you unscrew the barrel, you'll find the draft of the treaty intact.' He handed the pen to Viktor.

Viktor took it, unscrewed the barrel and pulled out a piece of rice paper. He carefully unfolded it. Sure enough, it was the treaty. The valet took the false pen from Viktor and put it in his pocket. 'Now we each have what belongs to us,' he said.

'Who do you work for? The Germans?'

'They think so, but in fact I'm a free agent. The details of the treaty will now go to the highest bidder.'

Viktor broke out in a cold sweat. He closed his eyes. He was trying to comprehend what all this meant, but was failing to do so.

'By the way,' the valet said, 'if you are in Berlin again, try to avoid the house in Wilhelmstrasse. Have you never heard of it before?'

Viktor shook his head slowly.

'It's called the "Green House". Have you heard of a man called Steiber?'

Viktor shook has head again. He was way out of his depth.

'Well, it was his legacy to the German police. It's constructed entirely of secret panels, revolving mirrors and tapped telephones. It hasn't been used much since Bismarck, but the German police seem to have rediscovered it. They must think there's going to be a war.'

The valet waited until this had sunk in, then said, 'Goodnight, monsieur,' and walked quickly away.

Viktor watched him disappear round a corner. He looked at the piece of rice paper in his hands. It had tiny inscriptions on it. He pictured the other pen in the valet's overcoat. This is the end, he thought, and shivered.

15
Juju

juju n. **1** an object superstitiously revered by certain West African peoples and used as a charm or fetish. **2** the power associated with a juju. [C19: prob.< Hausa djudju evil spirit, fetish]

In West Africa, every tribe strives to make its art unique, since it embodies that tribe's values and beliefs and creates its self-identity. Despite this striving for differentiation, however, all tribes do in fact produce some similar forms of art. Scarification, body-painting and ceremonial dancing, for example, are common throughout the tribes from Sierra Leone, Ghana and Togo and round the Gulf of Guinea to the Democratic Republic of Congo. But the art form most common to all these tribes is sculpture.

African sculptures have been made from almost anything – stone, metal, ivory, pottery, terracotta, raffia and mud – but they are usually made from wood and turned into masks, small figures or tools. The masks, often half-human, half-animal, are used in tribal dances and religious ceremonies to represent ancient spirits or ancestors. Some are tied to the face with raffia head coverings; others are larger and rest on the head or shoulders. A small number have handles attached so that they can be held up to the face.

Wooden figures, too, are used for ritualistic or religious purposes. They are thought to embody spirits, or are believed to be sites of spiritual forces. They are also used for their healing powers, or as protection against evil. Among the Yoruba tribe, for instance, a wooden figure is kept until adulthood by a child who has lost his or her twin.

In May or June 1907, Picasso saw such wooden masks and figures for the first time at the ethnographic exhibition at the

Palais du Trocadéro in Paris. Although Matisse had already begun collecting African tribal art, Picasso had not, until that moment, paid any attention to it. Years later, Françoise Gilot recounted what Picasso had said about the African masks and manikins he saw that day:

> Men had made those masks and other objects for a sacred purpose, a magic purpose, as a kind of mediation between themselves and the unknown hostile forces that surround them, in order to overcome their fear by giving it a form and an image. At that moment I realised that this was what painting was all about. When I came to that realisation, I knew I had found my way.

At the time of his visit, Picasso was completing a painting that was later named *Les Demoiselles d'Avignon*. It was the first of his paintings to show the influence of African sculptures and masks on his work. The painting depicted five nudes but, after his visit to the museum, Picasso repainted the heads of two, now making their faces into angular, mask-like forms. The arms of two other nudes were now raised behind and around the head, a position that showed clear stylistic parallels with the reliquary figures of the Kota tribe.

That autumn, on 1 October, a memorial retrospective was held at the Salon d'Automne for Cézanne, who had died the year before. The exhibition contained fifty-six works, mostly oils, and included a group of unfinished canvases. Picasso almost certainly attended the exhibition, since he had taken his cue from Cézanne, learning from him the value of simple form. Picasso described Cézanne as 'my one and only master'.

Towards the end of his life, Cézanne's work displayed a great attention to geometry. In a letter to his friend Émile Bernard, Cézanne wrote that painting should 'treat nature by the cylinder, the sphere and the cone'. In his late paintings, Cézanne had attempted to synthesise surface and depth by collapsing foreground and background, while simultaneously trying to incorporate different viewpoints gathered together over a period of time. He called his process '*passage*'. He advocated an abandonment of perspective, realising that it chained the viewer to a single viewpoint, and thus disallowed any conceptual understanding of form.

In November, Guillaume Apollinaire took Georges Braque to Picasso's studio, nicknamed the 'Bateau-Lavoir', where Picasso showed him *Les Demoiselles d'Avignon*. Braque was horrified by what he saw, but he also understood what Picasso had attempted. The painting was so fractured that it had lost all internal consistency. On his return to his own studio, Braque put aside a collection of Cézannesque landscapes and started anew.

Inspired by Picasso's painting, he imagined himself moving inside a canvas, feeling the spaces within and between objects. Braque liked to call these spaces 'tactile'. He chopped up Cézanne's cylinders, spheres and cones and then superimposed, overlapped and interlocked them into two-dimensional planes. In making such radical reassemblies, Braque squeezed out any tactile space and the new image was represented without a single viewpoint.

In September 1908, Braque submitted six of these highly abstract landscapes to the Salon d'Automne. All were rejected. Sitting on the jury was Matisse, who noted that Braque was merely making 'little cubes'. Picasso, however, was impressed and quickly adopted Braque's work methods. During the winter of 1908–09, Picasso and Braque worked extremely closely, so much so that Braque later commented they were 'like roped mountaineers'. They carried on from where Cézanne had left off and assimilated the continuing influence of African sculpture into the work.

Braque had some of these new paintings exhibited. Reviewers complained that the multiplicity of detail unloaded in such a limited space crushed the viewer, making it physically impossible to grasp the whole. Picasso countered their complaints by claiming that a painting should be 'a horde of destructions'. It was after this exhibition, in 1909, that Apollinaire coined the term 'cubist' to describe Braque's paintings.

Mata Hari's portrait by Paris artist Franz-Namur, 1909

16

Paris, 1909

> She was not really pretty. Her features lacked refinement. There was something bestial about the lips, cheeks, and jaw. Her brown skin always had the appearance of having been anointed in oil or was exuding perspiration. Her bust was flat and drooping and always concealed from view. Only her eyes and arms were absolute in their beauty. Those who said she had the most beautiful arms in the world did not exaggerate. And her eyes! Eyes that were magnetic and enigmatic, ever changing, yet ever of velvety softness, commanding and pleading, melancholy and mean, those terrible eyes in whose depths so many souls were drowned, actually merited the adoration awarded them. The most striking thing about her was the astonishing fact that this spoiled darling, upon whom destiny had showered gifts, grace, talent, fame, rarely lost the expression of inmost sadness. Frequently she would recline in an armchair, dreaming of secret things for perhaps an hour. I cannot recall that I ever saw Mata Hari smile.
>
> Paul Frantz-Namur, Mata Hari's portrait painter

Picasso looked up from where he was seated to the gilded ornament in the corners of the white ceiling above him. The walls of the room were vermilion.

'This reminds me of the restaurant in the Hotel Colón in Barcelona.' He turned to his companion. 'Not bad for an embassy.'

Frantz-Namur chuckled. 'How many embassies have you been to?'

Picasso shrugged. 'None,' he said. He crossed his arms and looked again at the ceiling for some time. 'But, you see, one needn't do things in order to know about them.'

'You think not?'

Picasso thought for a moment. 'No, maybe not,' he said. Both of them laughed.

'If you had said yes, I would have called you a liar,' Frantz-Namur said.

Picasso nodded, then looked at his watch.

'It'll start soon,' Frantz-Namur said.

'I have to be somewhere by ten.'

They watched the audience trickle in through the double doors to one side of the small, raised dais. Frantz-Namur and Picasso were sitting on the end of the back row. The ten or so rows of loose chairs in front of them were slowly being filled as people took their seats. Picasso turned to Frantz-Namur.

'So you think she's bona fide?' he asked.

'Yes. You'll see.'

'How is she at posing?'

'Good. She hardly moves and she never smiles.'

Picasso nodded in agreement. 'I hate women who smile when they're sitting for me. I feel like they're mocking me.'

Frantz-Namur was tempted to ask him about that, but let it pass.

'How many portraits are you doing?' Picasso asked.

'Two. One in costume, the other a dance pose in the nude. The costumed pose is better. She's wearing an Indian diadem and a collar of emeralds and topaz – very beautiful.' Frantz-Namur leaned towards Picasso. 'The diadem I mean.'

Picasso smiled.

'She's as superstitious as a Hindu,' Frantz-Namur continued. 'Once, while she was disrobing, a jade bracelet slipped from her wrist. She turned quite pale and said, "That will bring me bad luck. You'll see. It is a presentiment of misfortune. Keep it. That horrible bracelet, I never want to see it again." She was so upset.' Frantz-Namur shook his head.

'No, I understand what she means. Certain objects do have magic, I believe that,' Picasso said.

'Well, you should meet her.'

A woman was watching them. She was wearing an indigo dress, which shone like coal.

'Have you been to see Bonnard's exhibition yet?' asked Frantz-Namur.

Picasso waved his arms in the air. 'Agh. Don't talk to me about his "work" – it's execrable.'

'You really think that? I think it's fine.'

'It's nothing but a pot-pourri of indecision. Please, let's change the subject.'

They remained silent for a few moments. Frantz-Namur looked around the room, at the smiling faces taking their seats. It wasn't really Picasso's favourite milieu, he thought. He wondered what Picasso would think of the performance. 'How's the move going?' he asked.

'Horrible. I hate the upheaval, but the new apartment faces north and overlooks the trees of avenue Frochet, which I love.'

'You're moving up in the world, Pablo.'

'Kahnweiler came yesterday and took everything I've done in the last four months. It was depressing to see everything go at once.'

'Any buyers?'

Picasso nodded. 'Vollard. He bought them all.'

'That's wonderful.'

'Perhaps.' Picasso frowned. The row in front of them was filling up. 'You know, even after all the paintings I've sold, nothing can match the day my father gave me his palette and brushes and paints and told me he would never paint again. That still is the best moment in my life.'

'That he would never paint again?'

Picasso shook his head with impatience. 'He used to let

me finish the paintings he'd started. He taught me to draw the painting first using oil, then apply colour as if it had weight. "It's about weight and texture," he said. Then one day, he looked at a painting I had done for my art teacher and gave me his palette and brushes and said he would never paint again. A beautiful gesture.'

'How old were you?'

'Thirteen.'

Frantz-Namur watched Picasso's large head, bowed heavily towards the floor. His dark hair was thick and glossy. Suddenly Picasso glanced up.

'And you, my friend?'

Frantz-Namur sighed. 'Maybe I should go back to art school. I haven't sold anything in six months.'

'Everyone tells me these portraits you're doing are good.'

Frantz-Namur shrugged. 'I don't know how much to charge her.'

'There's an old trick for that. Just don't say anything about the money at all and when she finally mentions a figure, act like you're a bit surprised and then take her next offer.'

Frantz-Namur smiled. 'Good advice,' he said.

All the seats in the salon were now taken and people began shuffling along the walls to make room for new arrivals.

'How are the floods down in Pigalle?' asked Frantz-Namur.

'Not too bad, yet. It's the embankments that are the worst, but they say the water will keep rising.'

'Guillomet told me he saw two wine barrels in the Seine which couldn't pass under the Pont Neuf.'

Picasso nodded. 'I know, I know. I've heard the lower quays by the Pont de l'Archevêché and some métro stations are flooded. They say the river is going to burst its banks if it keeps raining. If it does, the city centre will have to be evacuated.'

'Shit.'

'I should have stayed at the Bateau-Lavoir,' Picasso said.

The murmur of voices suddenly died down and, when they both looked up, they saw that a small man with a tanned face and shiny black hair had stepped on to the dais. He buttoned up his jacket and looked around the room.

'The Chilean Ambassador,' Frantz-Namur whispered.

The Ambassador raised his arms. 'Good evening, ladies and gentlemen. I scarcely need to introduce Madame Mata Hari to you – her name and her art are well known. You are all probably aware that this Indian name hides a personality of lofty birth. Born on the banks of the Ganges, she shares her time between her country and a small villa here in Paris where, though in the midst of commerce, she isolates herself in a Brahmin communion with animals and flowers.

'Four years ago, at the Musée Guimet, she showed us the "Dance of the Devadasis", a word which refers to the sacred art of expressing, by harmonious gesture, the far-off mysteries of vanished cults. It was a dancing entertainment of which the deep spiritualistic meaning could only be understood by a chosen few.

'Tonight, she is going to show us an art of the most delicate charm, and at the same time nearer to our understanding. The legend she will present is called "The Legend of the Princess and the Magic Flower". It is one of the most popular and poetic dances of India. Ladies and gentlemen, please welcome Madame Mata Hari.'

There was loud applause. People craned their necks to see the stage. The lights went down.

> Tall and slender, she carries a marvellous neck, flexible and the colour of amber, a fascinating face which is a perfect oval, and whose sibylline and tempting expression strikes all at first sight. The mouth, firmly outlined, traces a mobile line, disdainful, very alluring, under a nose, straight and fine, the nostrils of which quiver above two shadowing dimples. Her magnificent

eyes, velvety and dark, are slightly slanting and set with long curling lashes – they are enigmatic, seeming to look into the beyond. Her black hair, divided in two bands makes for her face a dark wavy frame. The effect is voluptuous, tremorous, full of unexpected seduction, possessing a magic beauty and an astonishing beauty of outline.

An anonymous spectator, Paris

When the lights came back up, members of the audience began talking to each other. Frantz-Namur noticed that people were animated. Some of the audience began leaving via the double doors. Picasso stood up and looked for a way out. He spotted a small set of French windows partly hidden behind curtains. He nudged Frantz-Namur and pointed to them. Together they moved against the flow of the crowd and slipped outside into the Embassy gardens. It was still raining. The evening was refreshingly cool; Frantz-Namur hadn't realised how warm it was in the salon.

They trod across the wet grass, not speaking. The murmuring of voices could be heard behind them. Frantz-Namur turned his jacket collar up. Picasso had his head down; he seemed not to be bothered by the rain. A perimeter wall led them to the front gates, which were wide open for the departing guests. A guard nodded to them as they walked through. The boulevard outside was shiny with water. Frantz-Namur looked at Picasso.

'Well, what did you think?'

Picasso didn't say anything immediately. Then he looked directly at Frantz-Namur. There was hostility in his black eyes.

'My dear Paul,' he said, 'I was appalled. From the first moment, it was clear to me that Mata Hari does not know how to dance. She has absolutely no *disponibilité*. She's an impostor. I hope I never see her dolorous face again.'

Frantz-Namur felt a coldness creep over him. He had no

idea what *disponibilité* meant. He didn't know what to say. It was obvious that for Picasso there was nothing more to say. They continued in the rain down the boulevard. Picasso was walking quickly, as if he were alone. Frantz-Namur realised he'd probably forgotten about her already.

17

Lörrach, Baden Württemberg, Germany, 1910

My name is Maria Ann von Heinrichsen, *née* Lesser. To the French, I was known as 'Mademoiselle Doktor'. Colonel Nicholai, the head of the German espionage service in the years leading up to the First World War, called me the 'mistress of spies' and, for once, he and I were in complete agreement. At the Academy at Lörrach in Baden Württemberg, southern Germany, I taught Mata Hari everything she knew.

I was born in Berlin, probably in 1889, though I can't be sure. My father had a terrible memory. He was an art dealer and used to spend his time travelling around Europe, negotiating the sale of his clients' pictures. He was a well-known figure at Christie's and Hôtel Drouot auction houses. He was happy and successful at his job. I never knew my mother. She left my father when I was very young and I haven't seen her since. My father became taciturn every time her name was mentioned. I don't even know if she's still alive. It doesn't matter now anyway.

At school, I didn't perform well. The only subjects I enjoyed were foreign languages. I excelled at French, English and Russian. I even learned a little Spanish, which was rare in those days. When I finished school, I used to accompany my father on trips to Paris. He planned a business trip to St Petersburg and suggested I go with him in order to perfect my Russian accent. Of course I accepted. I was seventeen at the time.

While I was there, I met a military attaché, a Prussian cavalryman, and we became lovers. My father didn't seem to mind. When the time came for us to return to Berlin, I told my father I wanted to remain in St Petersburg. I remember seeing him off at the railway station – he said he had known he wouldn't keep me for much longer. He knew how headstrong I could be. One evening at his apartment, this Prussian officer told me that the Russians had a new artillery gun and that it was his job to find out about it. He was very clever – he didn't tell me outright, but let it emerge gradually. A few weeks went by and then he introduced me one evening to a Russian officer, who paid me great compliments throughout the evening. He said he loved my Teutonic beauty – my blonde hair, red lips and fair complexion. In front of my lover, he offered to pay me a great deal of money to sleep with him. I realised by my lover's lack of protest what was expected of me. During the night I spent with him, the Russian told me about the gun, and I in turn told my lover. He was very pleased with me, and told me that Berlin would be very pleased with me as well. He suggested I return to Berlin. He told me to go to an organisation called Abteilung III. I didn't know then that this was the German Secret Service.

When I returned to Berlin, I was courted by personnel from Abteilung III. They put me up at the Adlon Hôtel and took me to Adlon's restaurant. It was there that I met Mata Hari for the first time. I was introduced to her by Traugott von Jagow, who had just secured her services. To me she seemed rather gauche, but she had promise. Soon afterwards, they sent me to Lörrach for training, with the recommendation that I be trained for intelligence work. They seemed to like me there. When I finished, I was sent to Antwerp as an intelligence agent. I had a suite of rooms, where I interviewed agents sent to me by Abteilung III and allotted missions for them to undertake, as well as undertaking many independent missions of my own.

I flourished as a spy. I loved the adventure. It furnished me with all the mental satisfaction I could have wished for, but I found I had to be extremely scrupulous. I met a great deal of resistance from certain men who could not tolerate being given instructions from a nineteen-year-old woman. I learnt to be ruthless when necessary.

On one such occasion, I enlisted as my assistant a young Belgian man who had managed an efficient system of counter-espionage among Belgian patriots. One of my most highly trusted recruits was dispatched to France on a mission that had entailed much careful preparation. He was arrested the moment he arrived in France. When I received the news, I sent for my Belgian assistant and reminded him that there were only two people in the world who could have jeopardised the mission: me and him. I told him it wasn't me. I told him that whoever had betrayed my recruit would have to suffer the consequences. By the expression on his face, I knew he wasn't sure what to expect. I drew out an automatic pistol from the drawer of my desk and shot him once through the heart.

After spending two years in Antwerp, I was recalled to Lörrach, where I met Mata Hari for the second time. I was to instruct new recruits in preparation for the war. These recruits were mainly chosen from the army and navy reservists, but not exclusively. Occasionally, the academy would receive individuals, like myself, who had been recommended by agents already working in the field. Mata Hari was recommended by von Jagow. None of the recruits had any specific qualifications. We were looking for particular kinds of men and women, rather than for particular experiences. We looked for signs of independence. We wanted people who displayed discretion, patience, resource and industry, but also people who could act quickly in moments of emergency. Most of all, they had to have no strong political affiliations or aspirations. They had to have an easy conscience. Most of the people we eventually recruited were officers – espionage was considered honourable in those days. The hall porter at the Hôtel des Indes in The Hague, for example, was the brother of Baron von Wangenheim, the Ambassador to Turkey.

There were four main areas of instruction. The first, and most important, was the methods of passing on information. Contrary to what one imagines, the main difficulty facing an agent isn't the acquisition of information, but the relaying of it. So, they were shown ways to do that and encouraged to invent their own. They were taught how to invent codes, ciphers and cryptograms. We used examples of already existing codes, such as the fruit code. One agent in England had used an ingenious code involving the sale and purchase of fish. A dreadnought was a cod with head, whereas a large cruiser was just a cod, and so on. He would then send this information using picture postcards of the naval towns in which these ships were docked. The date and time written on the postcard referred to the date and time of sighting. With just a dozen postcards, we had an accurate sense of naval ship layout.

We taught them how to use invisible inks. There was a laboratory in Antwerp that specialised in their production. The most useful type was a mixture of perchloride of iron and water, which looked like cognac. Information was written *en clair* on the lining of envelopes or under postage stamps. We taught them how to prepare their own reagents, using easily available substances such as powdered oxide of copper, alcoholised water, iodine vapour, heat, even tobacco smoke.

The other main area of training was in technical knowledge. Recruits had to be able to calculate heights, distances and angles without the use of instruments. They were taught to measure distances by accurate pacing and heights by the length of shadows in relation to the position of the sun. Using these methods, it is easy to calculate angles to a relatively accurate degree and get the dimensions of a bridge, for example. Nothing could be written down, everything had to be carried in the head.

This was the main body of their instruction. The recruits were then 'finished'. This involved learning to adopt the etiquette, mannerisms and traits of the country to which they were being sent. To illustrate this, I told them the story of how we were able to trap a very skilled Allied agent through a very small detail. This agent was travelling as a fully accredited representative of an established Berlin commercial house. While having lunch one day in Munich, he said 'Thank you' each time the waitress served him a course of his meal. The waitress grew suspicious, because German salesmen tend not to be so courteous to waitresses. She reported her suspicions to the police who, in turn, informed us. We immediately arrested him, much to the embarrassment of the Deuxième Bureau.

Finally, the academy gave them a run-through of basic acting techniques. We found this to be invaluable. The authenticity of their performance depended entirely on how far they were willing to enter into the role. The deeper they entered into it, the less likely they were to be exposed. The French have a word for this willingness, they call it *disponibilité*. I taught my recruits never to think of themselves, never, as anything other than what they appeared to be. Spying is the highest form of acting. This was the last thing they learnt. They were then ready to be sent out.

We knew where each agent was to be sent even before they arrived at Lörrach. It was most important that the agent already knew someone in that country, and that they were sent there via a place that would attract the least attention. Agents going to England, for example, were sent via Holland, Spain, Scandinavia or America. Once they arrived, they began their work procedure. Their instructions were to act independently, and not under any circumstances with other agents or friends in the locality. They were told to frequent workplaces – factories, railways, and other places like bars and cafés – where they would come into contact with officials, military personnel or even soldiers. Above all, they had to travel as much as possible and enlist the unconscious help of everyone they met. We never saw them again. From

the moment they were sent abroad, no agent was ever known, even to the highest officials, by name, only by a codename.

Mata Hari's codename was H21. She was instructed by me, so the letter 'H' referred to my surname, and she was my twenty-first woman recruit to graduate from the academy. Mata Hari was a perfect student in every way, except for the fact that she was a *parvenue* – it was her only weakness. She talked a lot about the British Royal Family and we were aware that, in the past, she had pretended to be related to Edward VII. When she was at the academy, she heard of his death and became positively hysterical. We knew the social connections she boasted of were nonsense and we had to stop this, so we did. We informed her that she would fail at Lörrach if she persisted. If recruits failed during training, they were sent to either Königsberg or Spandau prison. She never mentioned Edward VII again.

When I had to give Mata Hari her instructions after she graduated from Lörrach, I realised she was a rather special case because she had already been in contact with many high-ranking military or public figures. I decided that she ought to resume her career as a vaudevillian so that she could be sent to various cities and continue being a courtesan for these men. We arranged many performances for her – Madrid, Milan, Monte Carlo – but mainly Paris, as that was where she was best known. Her situation was ideal. The preeminence of these men made it very difficult for the Allies to prove any allegations of Mata Hari's espionage activities.

On the last of their eight days at the academy, I gave a speech to the graduating recruits, including Mata Hari. I told them that, when I had first been recruited by Abteilung III, I had had a magnificent instructor. He was a life-long student of and expert in physiognomy. He had told me that I would experience many difficulties in the profession, but that I was exactly the kind of person who would excel at it. He had taught me to be intuitive, but circumspect. He had also taught me to be a student of character – other people's as well as my own. He had said I would receive no credit if I was successful and no mercy if I failed. The ultimate accolade as a spy was not to be known. I told them that all this was potent and sophisticated to a seventeen-year-old and I never forgot his words. I urged them all to heed his words too and, with that, I said goodbye. After she left the academy, I never saw Mata Hari again.

18
Virgula Divina

Ancient Chinese manuscripts refer to army generals plunging their swords into the ground in order to find water. If they were successful, an encampment would be set up around the water source. Chinese Buddhist monks, living in the same age, used to carry tin canes with them. The canes were also driven into the ground and, if a water supply was found, the spot was used for the establishment of a new monastery. This physical link between settlement and water is also a semantic one in the Chinese language: the expression 'to plant one's tin' came to mean 'to stop'.

Europe has a similarly long tradition of water divination. Central to the foundations of Norse myth is Yggdrasil, the 'world tree' that linked together heaven, earth and hell with its roots and branches. It is an evergreen ash with three wells at its base, one of which is the source of all wisdom. Odin, the lord of all gods, was willing to lose an eye in order to obtain the powers of its waters. Subsequently, the ash has always been the preferred tree from which to cut dowsing rods in Scandinavia.

But of all the trees attributed with divining powers in Indo-European culture, none has been assigned as much as the hazel. According to Vedic lore, rods cut from hazel trees were carried by the Brahman priests of ancient India. The first European account of the use of hazel was recorded in the first century AD by Cornelius Tacitus, a Roman historian, who noted its use by Germanic tribes along the boundaries of the Roman Empire. It is a specifically European feature that twigs used for water divination had to be cut only from hazel trees that bore fruit or nuts.

Tacitus was the first known person to use the term *virgula mercurialis*, the 'wand of Mercury', for a divining rod. It wasn't until the Middle Ages that the term *virgula divina*, or 'divine wand', first appeared. In 1518, Martin Luther condemned the practice of dowsing as Black Magic and therefore the work of the Devil.

Condemnation from the church, however, didn't stop Elizabeth I from using dowsing in her pursuit of wealth and power. She elicited the help of German dowsers and sent them to the West Country, and Cornwall in particular, to assist in the location of lost tin mines. The first English term for dowsing, 'deusing', came into use during her reign. The roots of this word are unclear, but it is probably a loan word from German mining parlance, or a mining word from the old Cornish, which was related to Gaelic. In Cornish, *dewys* meant 'goddess' and *rhodl* meant 'tree branch', a combination that gives us the modern English equivalent 'dowsing rod'.

The veracity of dowsing has always been questioned by scientists. One of the most famous experiments to help solve this problem was held in Paris in 1913. Armand Viré, a biologist who specialised in the life of subterranean animals, published a book which stated: 'Anything concerning dowsing seemed to me wholly cock-eyed and unjustifiable. The art was practised mostly by simple countrymen who operated on the basis of more or less unfathomable instructions which they ill-understood or seemed unwilling to explain.'

One evening, while in his laboratory in the catacombs beneath the Jardin des Plantes, Viré was visited by a geographer named Henri Mager, whose book on dowsing Viré had read and dismissed. Mager explained that the Second Congress on Experimental Psychology being held in Paris wished to hold a dowsing test and wanted Viré to organise it. Intrigued, Viré agreed.

After some research into an appropriate site for such a test, Viré found that the quarries dug under Paris during

Roman times had been recorded on large-scale maps, which had remained unpublished. None of the dowsers could possibly know of the existence of these quarries and so Viré decided to use them for the test. He told Mager to assemble his dowsers at the Daumesnil Gate a few mornings later.

The test site was an area of lawn, just inside the gate, under which the criss-cross of quarries lay at depths of between sixteen and twenty metres. Viré instructed the three dowsers to lay stakes in the lawn where they located any voids or waterways. He watched in astonishment as they walked across the lawn in large S shapes, laying stakes exactly on the boundaries of all the quarries and connecting tunnels. One of the dowsers even found a previously undiscovered gallery.

After the experiment was over, Viré published his findings, stating: 'I admit it was not without great inner struggle that I gradually confronted the evidence which at first sorely vexed me. But the facts stared me in the face and I was forced to proclaim, *urbi et orbi*, that the dowsing ability was real and that there was just cause to take dowsers seriously . . .'

19

Zermatt, Switzerland, 1911

At 8:20 a.m. on a bright January morning, Mata Hari and her ski-instructor, Jacques, came out of the Hotel Europa, put on their boots and bindings and began trudging through the snow. Although the cafés and bars had been open since first light, the town was quiet. Most of the chalets were still closed and warm with sleep.

They said little as they walked past these buildings, separated by alleys filled with snow and silent shafts of air. He walked calmly ahead, carrying two sets of skis and poles over his shoulder. She followed behind, her breath clouding in front of her and the hem of her long brown coat picking up snow.

The chalets gradually thinned out as they walked to the gondola station high above the town. The station had just started operating for the day and was empty except for themselves and a handful of others. They stood on the loading platform, watching the gondolas drift down from the mountain and into the station. An operative opened the door of one and they climbed inside. The gondola turned round and left the station as gracefully as it had come in.

As it swung clear and started climbing gently, Mata Hari looked at the town laid out below her. It was completely covered with snow and seemed much smaller than she had imagined. She saw trails of chimney smoke. A dull river wound through the town and through other clusters of villages along the valley, crossed by stone bridges all the way. Jacques told her it was called the Vispa and was a main tributary of the Rhône river, which fed Lac Léman more than sixty kilometres away.

As they climbed more steeply, Jacques pointed out the four peaks that enclosed the valley: the Weisshorn, Dom,

Dufourspitz, which the Italians called Monte Rosa, and the distinctive peak of the Matterhorn, standing out against the blue sky as a broken triangle. Along with Chamonix-Mont-Blanc, Zermatt had the finest high-altitude skiing in the whole of the Alps, he said. The gondola continued its slow, pendulous climb above the hollowed-out blanket of white.

Since it was her first day of skiing ever, Jacques taught her how to snowplough. He skied backwards, in front of her, watching her as she slid slowly over the snow. The mountain air was still and cold, with nothing in it except birdsong and the swishing of skis. He told her she was doing well.

After a few trips down the same slope, they stopped at a mountain refuge for an early lunch. The refuge was a log hut, built against a rock face and buried under snowdrifts, so that it remained unnoticeable unless one stood directly in front of it.

Inside, they sat down at a long wooden bench and were served glühwein and stew by an old woman whom Jacques introduced as Mathilda. After serving them, Mathilda returned to her seat by the fire, over which hung a huge cauldron. They were alone inside the hut.

Jacques answered Mata Hari's questions about himself. His French mother had come to Zermatt in the summer of 1881 with her mother to 'take the air'. His Swiss-Italian father had been their mountain guide. At the end of five days of low-altitude walking, his parents had fallen in love and he had persuaded her to remain with him in Zermatt. They were married a year later and Jacques had been born in 1886.

His father belonged to the École des Guides, the famous school for guides based in Chamonix but with offices in Grindelwald, St Moritz and Nauders as well as Zermatt. When Jacques was young, it was never questioned that he would follow in his footsteps and train to become a ski-guide by winter and mountain-guide by summer. His father had taught him that to be a high-altitude climber, one had to live in a horizontal world: think only of the distance to be covered, never the height to be climbed. He had also warned him never to spend too much time in the mountains, because too much snow could cause amnesia.

One night, when Jacques was seventeen, his father had been called out on a search and rescue. Two skiers had fallen down a crevasse and, while lifting them out, his father had slipped and fallen. He was never found, but the skiers had been saved. Mata Hari said she was sorry. Jacques shrugged. Like his father, he'd come to accept the risk – it was a simple exchange. He said he believed his father lived on in him, guiding him when he was unsure of which direction to take and showing him what to do in moments of difficulty.

They left the warmth of the refuge ready to ski again. Outside, Mata Hari looked across the valley and sensed the depth and breadth of the clear blue air. It seemed like the top of the world. She tied the straps of her skis and, on his signal, followed Jacques away from the hut.

They skied slowly across the mountainside to a button lift at the apex of the next valley along. From there, they were dragged uphill to the top of a large swathe of clear piste. She stood looking down the white funnel and felt her stomach tighten, a feeling she hadn't had since her first performances at the Folies Bergère.

'It looks much steeper than it is,' Jacques said. 'I'll be behind you, don't worry. Ready?'

He smiled to her. She put her goggles on and leant forward.

'Good,' Jacques said.

The snow began to slip under her skis. She felt as if she were on a moving carpet and kept her gaze fixed on the snow in front of her. As she picked up speed, she heard the wind in her ears and her stomach rose to her chest.

'Not too fast,' Jacques shouted behind her.

The wind blew into her open mouth and her tongue went dry. Her legs rocked as she hit small rises. She was going faster than she had done before lunch. It felt good to be slightly out of control and she became aware that her whole body was tense.

'Good,' Jacques shouted.

This wasn't as hard as she thought. She smiled and relaxed her body. She looked down the slope and saw the hollow groove rising and dipping ahead of her. The trees either side whipped by. Her nose and cheeks were numb with cold. She raised her head – the sky was too blue. It seemed unreal.

Just then, she hit something and her left leg dragged. She waved her arms as she tried to bring her skis together. She leant heavily on her right leg and started to veer left. She didn't want to go that way – the piste was ahead of her. Her left leg caught the snow again and skittered. She leant even more heavily on her right leg to stop herself from falling. The snow became much rougher, splattering on to her face and goggles. I'm off piste, she thought. Some trees flew by. Somehow she managed to bring her skis together and now tried to avoid the trees. Another flew by. Then the trees disappeared and the slope got steeper. She had to stop before she picked up more speed. She saw something out of the corner of her eye. Another person. It was Jacques. Oh, thank God, she thought. He was shouting at her, but she couldn't hear anything. Her eyes locked on to the slope. Suddenly it fell away from under her skis and she was flying. She could hear nothing except the wind. The whole world had gone silent. As she somersaulted, her stomach rose out of her mouth and she thought of her son, Norman. Through her goggles, she saw whiteness and snatches of blue. Norman. Norman. She hit the ground and the breath left her body.

From the foyer of the Hotel Europa, the *Empfangsdame* stood by the window, looking out on to the street. The sky was deep violet and darkness was gathering in the village. She turned on the overhead light and returned to her seat behind the reception desk. Many of the guests had already returned from the mountains, but one or two were still to come.

She went through the orders for breakfast and checked to see if any guests were leaving in the morning. The Christmas season was nearly over and many of her rooms would remain empty until Easter. She should remember to tell Eva to give them a good clean.

Business was good and her hotel was attracting more customers each year. It had been a wise decision to invest in the hotel. The first thing her customers saw when they entered the Hotel Europa was a poster of a woman skiing downhill. She was wearing a long green dress. It said: 'LES VERTIGES DE L'ÂGE D'OR'.

When the clock struck six, the *Empfangsdame* became worried. It was dark outside now. All of her guests had returned except two: Madame Mata Hari and her instructor, Jacques. As was required by law, they had filled out the log book that morning with details of their whereabouts and when they would be returning, which was an hour ago. It wasn't good to be out on the mountain in the dark. Perhaps they had stopped at a bar for a glühwein. If they had, Jacques ought to have told her – he should know better.

At quarter to seven, she decided to alert the École des Guides. She shouted at the cook to keep an eye on reception and picked up the log book. She walked on the packed snow to the school, situated further up the street towards the gondola station. Inside, the duty guide had just started the night watch. She informed him of the lateness of their return and showed him the log book. The guide nodded and told her a search party would be sent out.

When Mata Hari opened her eyes, there was darkness all around and she thought she was dead. It was totally silent. Her face was cold. When she heard her own breathing, she realised she was still alive. Thank God. Tears welled up in her eyes and she began to sob.

'Madame?'

She stopped crying and raised her head. 'Jacques?'

'I'm over here. Are you hurt?'

Her mind travelled over her body. Legs. Arms. She thought she was all right. She put her palms on the snow and pushed herself up. Her face was still cold, her cheeks numb. She shivered. She felt dizzy and her head throbbed.

'I think I'm all right,' she said.

'I'm over here.'

His voice was ten or so metres down the slope from her. To her left and behind her, she sensed a huge and forbidding presence. She looked in that direction, but could see nothing in the darkness. Then she realised it was the mountain. She sat on the snow and slid slowly down towards him. Her boot hit something. She reached out.

'There's a ski stuck upright in the snow.'

'Grab it,' he said.

She pulled it out and carried on sliding down. The snow was cold to sit on and she realised her tears had frozen.

'You're near me now.'

His voice was close. She heard him shivering and saw his dark shape on the ground.

'Stick the ski in the snow again,' he said.

She pushed it into the snow as far as she could. It was difficult to get it in very deep.

'Give me your hand,' he said.

She reached out towards his dark form and searched for his hand. When she found it, he clasped hers tightly and then squeezed it.

'You've been unconscious for hours. Are you all right?'

'I'm cold.'

'Can you feel my leg? It hurts, but I can't do it.'

'Which one?'

'The left.'

His trousers were covered with snow. She touched his left leg at the knee and gently felt his shin. He screamed out. She leant forward and realised that his left foot was pointing the wrong way. She swallowed bile and broke out into a sweat.

'Jacques?'

He was breathing hard. '*Merde!*' he said. 'I've been shouting out but no one can hear us. We're too far up.'

'What are we going to do?'

'They'll send a party out.' His teeth were chattering.

'But how will they find us? It's so dark.'

'Listen. I need you to do what I tell you. All right?'

Whatever had risen to her mouth was gone now. She nodded.

'All right?'

'Yes,' she said.

'Get that ski and start digging a hole into the mountain side with it. We have to build a bivouac.'

'A what?'

'Never mind. Just start digging a hole big enough for us both. I'm freezing.'

When she started digging, he told her not to stop talking to him. It was important for him to stay awake, he said. He asked her questions about her life. Where was she from? Holland, she said. He told her he'd never been to Holland. What was it like? She said it was flat. When she realised they were on a mountain, she laughed a little, then stopped. She carried on digging. Her head throbbed with the effort. He asked her about her family. She told him that her father was a hat-seller, that she hadn't seen him for years. Why not? he asked. She replied that he'd published a book about her without her consent. It was a horrible book. She thought about Java, about the heat and the dense foliage, the strange bird sounds. So long ago.

'Which city have you enjoyed living in the best?' he asked.

'Paris.'

She thought about what she could be doing at that

moment in Paris. She could be having a warm bath, with perfumed water and a soft sponge. She could be eating *escargots* wrapped in *jambon*. She could be strolling in the Jardins du Luxembourg. She stopped digging and started to laugh. The digging was taking so long it was absurd. She couldn't help laughing – it felt good.

'Madame!' he shouted. 'You must keep digging!'

Finally, with a great deal of effort, she finished. He told her that she must drag him inside, no matter how much he yelled. She pushed the ski into the snow as far as she could and picked him up under his arms. The strength had left her body. She dug her heels into the snow and began pulling him, but he was too heavy.

'Again!' he shouted.

She pulled with all her strength and immediately he screamed. It was hard to ignore, but the second time she pulled him he didn't scream as much. Little by little, she managed to haul him across a metre of snow to the hole. He used his arms to drag himself in. He told her to crawl inside after him.

'Now unbutton your coat and lie on top of me,' he said.

She did so, settling on him. He was shivering worse than before. His buckle dug into her. She could feel his breath on her face. He put his arms around her, inside her coat. They remained huddled and said nothing. He groaned occasionally. She rested her head on his shoulder and began quietly to cry.

The first group of six guides was sent out at 7:20 p.m. and returned to the school at 11:15. It had been dark for six hours and in winter, as all the guides were taught, missing people had to be found before dawn to stand a more than reasonable chance of survival. But Jacques would know what to do. They all knew him well.

The search party leader, Wim, told the five new guides who had just arrived to get their skis, torches and stretchers ready. He would lead them out in fifteen minutes. Wim left the school and trotted down the street towards the town centre. He was going to try Hans Herzog, the town's dowser, but he didn't want the others to know; he would never live it down.

Wim's father had always sworn by dowsing. He used the rod to find all sorts of things, not just water. He had once found a gold pendant on the shores of Lac Léman. The museum in Basle had dated it to pre-Christian times. They had asked his father's permission to exhibit it, but he had declined and it remained on the mantelpiece right up until he died. Now Wim had it. He wore it round his neck for luck.

When Wim came to Herzog's house, he saw lights on inside. He banged on the front door. Herzog wasn't trusted by the townsfolk. He kept to himself too much for people's liking. But Herzog and Wim's father had been on many dowsing expeditions together. A short, elderly man with white hair answered the door. His expression remained the same as Wim explained what had happened. Without a word, Hans waved him inside. From a bookshelf, he took down a large-scale map of the mountain and spread it on the table. He asked Wim to show him where exactly. Wim indicated a circle on the higher slopes.

Hans opened a cupboard and took out a thin, L-shaped piece of metal, pencils and a ruler. He lit a gas-lamp and placed it on the map. Sitting down over the map, he held the piece of metal in his right hand and sat still. Wim watched the rod: it remained still. A minute passed. Hans continually changed its position very slightly when, all of a sudden, it swung of its own accord and pointed across the valley. Hans drew a line on the map in that direction and picked up the rod again. He held it still for a few minutes more and, this time, the rod aligned itself up the east slopes. He drew another line and pointed to where they crossed. He told Wim to look there.

Nearly two hours later, Wim and the other guides were fanned out, skiing by torchlight, when one of them shouted. Wim skied across the slope to where the guide was crouching and saw a bivouac. He held the flame up and saw Jacques and the woman inside. He whistled for the stretchers and then talked to them. Jacques's nose was blue, but he was smiling. The woman was weeping. It was 1:40 a.m.

20

Neuilly-sur-Seine, Paris, 1912–14

> From the first, we saw with stupefaction that Mata Hari did not know how to dance. It was all sacred nonsense. She was just a big decorative savage.
>
> Monsieur Antoine, Director of the Opéra in Monte Carlo

My name is Aurore Bessy. I'm twenty-two years old and unmarried. I was Mata Hari's maid for two years. My mother knew a dressmaker in Paris who worked for Madame Mata Hari, and whenever she came to collect the dresses, she was by all accounts very gracious. My mother heard from her friend that Mata Hari had bought a villa in Neuilly and was looking for staff, so my mother's friend suggested me to Madame. When she heard that my name was Aurore, she asked to see me. I went to the villa one bright winter morning in 1912 and we sat in the drawing room and talked. I noticed she had a portrait of herself in costume hanging on the wall. She was beautiful. After just a few minutes, she asked me if I knew what her name meant. I shook my head. She said it was Malay for 'dawn', just like my name in French, and for this reason she wanted me to accept a job with her. She said it was a good omen. I was very glad to accept her offer and moved in the following day. My mistress was kind to me from that first day and I felt very friendly towards her.

The Villa Remy, as it was called, was number 11 rue Windsor in Neuilly, a leafy suburb of Paris between the Bois de Boulogne and the Seine. The front gate of the villa, with double doors, opened on to a small courtyard. The house was built in the Normandy style. The plaster walls were criss-crossed with wooden beams that were painted black. It was made to look like an English Tudor house. The ground floor had two large rooms, both facing the garden, and a small kitchen. Upstairs had three bedrooms and two bathrooms. My room was high up in the attic, tiny but warm. There was a very big garden with huge trees and a high wall surrounding it entirely. There was a patio and benches along the wall.

At the other end of the garden were the stables where my mistress kept three Indian thoroughbreds. Her favourite was called Cacatöes. I remember because my mistress had to spell it for me. She was very proud of these horses and the interior of the stables was lined with red plush. She used to ride side-saddle in the Bois, wearing her riding jacket and either a *chapeau melon* or a top hat. She looked so grand in her get-up and her picture often appeared in society magazines. She used to go to the races as well. At Easter, she went to the Auteuil races to see the Grand Prix, and in June she went again to see the Grand Steeple Chase. She once confided in me that, before she became famous, she used to ride horses in the Cirque Molier.

My duties around the place were straightforward enough. I served my mistress's meals, did all the laundry, polished the silver and attended to her guests. There were a lot of guests. My mistress wasn't usually pernickety, not like some I had before her, but for some reason I never could fathom, she was very particular about her morning coffee. She insisted that none of the staff could have any until she'd taken hers. Every morning between nine and ten, I would make it and bring a cup to her bedroom. Her bed was in the centre on a raised platform, shrouded in mauve canopies. You had to walk up a few steps to it. When I got back down to the kitchen, I used to shout at everybody, '*Le jus est prêt!*' and we would all sit around the table and drink it.

There were four of us in all: me, the groom Eric, the cook Marthe and the gardener Hippolyte. I was the only one who had a room in the villa, the others left every evening. Eric only came indoors for meals and was always quiet when he did. He was older than the rest of us and you got the feeling that he was waiting to retire. Marthe was only thirty, but she was old before her years. She was a stickler for discipline and thought of herself as the head of the house. Hippolyte was a year younger than me and cheeky with it. The day he started working here, he came through the back door whistling. He never took Marthe seriously and always made faces behind her back. But he was a beautiful gardener and took great pride in it. He knew all the Latin names of flowers and butterflies and birds and could reel them off just like that. Though I'd never show it, I liked him a lot.

He used to walk me round the garden and show me what he'd done. He pointed out the arbutus, syringas and guelder-roses in the flowerbeds near the patio. Along the walls, he had espaliered the honeysuckle and clematis. Down by the stables was a quince tree that he pruned back in the winter. In the south corner, he showed me the rosary that he'd prepared. He pointed to the roses in turn: white, blush, white musk and damask. My mistress used to say that the only thing she loved above horses was flowers and she spent hours talking with Hippolyte in the garden, planning what to plant for the following season. My mistress had a real soft spot for him and he knew it. He used to brag about it. But the thing he loved the most wasn't a flower or tree. It was a small statue my mistress had placed in a far corner, among the rhododendrons. She told me it was a 'Siva'. It had six arms and sat cross-legged and was always smiling.

During my first summer at Neuilly, the summer of 1912, my mistress had a lot of evening recitals for her friends. She danced for them, sometimes accompanied by a single Asian man playing a strange-looking guitar, sometimes on her own. She always made sure there was a full moon rising for these recitals. I remember the actress Cécile Sorel coming once. What a shock we all got seeing her in our own garden!

Another time there was a General Méssimy come to watch. He looked very grand in his red and blue uniform. Eric, Hippolyte and I would put out chairs for the guests and then I'd hurry upstairs to help my mistress with her costume. What beautiful clothes she had. I always enjoyed helping her dress so I could feel the lovely cloth in my own hands. She wore long bejewelled robes and tulle veils that trailed down to the ground. She wore brass bands on her arms and legs, and earrings. Oh, she was a picture when she was all dressed up! Eric and Hippolyte had usually gone home by the time her guests were settled, whereupon she would introduce her Magic Flower Dance. I peeked from an upstairs room and watched her twirl and throw herself about in the air. I'd read in the papers about the meaning of such dances but I could never see it myself. But it was pleasant enough to watch.

Come the autumn my mistress received an invitation to travel to Monte Carlo to see the head of the Ballets Russes. She said she would perhaps meet Nijinsky while she was there. It should have been good news, but she was agitated because she'd already had one bad experience in Monte Carlo. The director of the opera there, Monsieur Antoine, had been staging a play that featured a ballet danced by Cleopatra in the final act. My mistress had been invited to perform it. During rehearsals, Monsieur Antoine complained about her conduct and sacked her. My mistress was outraged and sued him. It was all nonsense of course and she won her case, but she couldn't forget how she had been treated. On the morning of her departure, I helped her choose a dress to wear. Eventually, we settled on her red velvet dress. She said it made her feel like Lillie Langtry. Red was her favourite colour. She once told me how, when she was a young girl, she had worn a red dress to school, which had caused quite a scandal. I think she enjoyed it – it was in her nature to be the centre of attention. When we had finished packing her *valises*, I wished her *bonne chance* and off she went.

It was lovely and warm while my mistress was away, a real Indian summer. They said it reached 100° Fahrenheit in Paris, but it was cooler among the leaves and open spaces of Neuilly. Hippolyte and Eric did their work as usual in the garden and Marthe was less bossy than was her wont. One evening, I was locking the doors to the garden when Hippolyte suddenly appeared. It gave me quite a shock, since I thought everyone had gone. I unlocked the door and he gave me a flower. He said it was an eglantine and would spoil soon, so he thought I should have it. He was always giving me little flowers for my room. It smelled beautiful. He said he had another surprise for me. He took my hand and led me upstairs. In my room, he tied several pieces of blue ribbon to the window catch and opened the window. They fluttered in the breeze. He said we had to wait until just before the daylight faded. We lay on my bed together and he kissed my neck. He whispered flatteries in my ear and said, 'Sex without love can be an empty experience, but love without sex is a waste of time.' He loved talking in riddles. Just then, I noticed a butterfly by my window. Its wings were the palest blue and had black edges. Soon, there were six or seven butterflies, all flapping around the ribbons. He smiled and said the ribbons attracted the butterflies to mate. That night Hippolyte stayed with me. It was the sweetest night of my life.

When my mistress returned, she was in a terrible temper. The Ballets Russes had turned her down and she was infuriated because she had never been turned down in her life. I'd never seen her so angry. When a new wardrobe arrived a few days later, the delivery men had an awful bother getting it up the stairs. They complained so much that, when they put it down to rest, my mistress pushed it back down the stairs in a fit of rage. It made a terrible noise and ended up in pieces. 'Won't go? Well it will now!' she screamed and ran into her room. After the men had gone, I filled a bath with valerian and camphor and suggested my mistress should soothe herself in it. She was crying in her room, saying that her trip to Monte Carlo was a bad omen, but I managed to coax her into the bath.

My mistress was very superstitious. When things were going badly, she said her life was blighted by bad omens and ill-luck. Once, I remember, she had two new mirrors hung on the walls of her bedroom. It was two days before either of us noticed that the mirrors were facing each other. She flew into a fit, saying that it was bad luck to have mirrors facing each other and ordered me to move one of them. Another time, when I brought her morning coffee, she said she had slept very badly and was feeling irritable. She asked me with great concern if it had been a windy night. When I said that indeed it had, she immediately turned maudlin. I asked what the matter was. She told me that in China, the liver is related to anger and that the wind is said to injure the liver. After a windy night, she said she always felt irritable. Well, I didn't know what to say. Eventually, she put on her black silk peignoir and complained to me that Paris no longer loved her. I said that was nonsense, but she was still sad. She asked me if I would ever like to travel to the East and I had to admit that the idea seemed unappealing to me.

In the winter, my mistress received a letter from a man called Paul Olivier. She was excited and told me that he was a journalist for *Le Matin* who had been asked by a university in Paris to address its members on the subject of Oriental temple festivals. He had asked her if she would be kind enough to perform one of her dances at his lecture. My mistress spent a few days happily organising an orchestra to accompany her and very soon everything was ready. On a cold night in December, she kissed me on the cheek and left the villa for Paris, but she returned home much earlier than expected and went straight to her room. I knew that something was wrong. The next morning, I brought her coffee in as usual and, to my astonishment, saw that my mistress was on the floor in tears. Her mattress had been slashed open with a knife and her costumes were everywhere. When I asked what the matter was, she told me through her tears that the orchestra had failed to appear for her performance because they had received a better offer from Sarah Bernhardt's latest production. She was inconsolable and let out a string of insults against 'all her imitators'.

It was after this that my mistress began behaving more and more strangely. Monsieur Olivier came to see her to organise another lecture. As I was serving them coffee in the room facing the garden, my mistress began complaining that her husband had recently dragged her about and beaten her. She even partly disrobed to show him the bite marks and bruises. Both Monsieur Olivier and I were shocked at such behaviour, but I knew, even if he didn't, that she hadn't seen her husband in years. Lord knows where the marks came from. Monsieur Olivier made his excuses and left with a worried expression. My mistress began leaving letters lying around. There was one from a Parisian jeweller's for unpaid bills of 12,000 gold francs. I saw another to a Maître Clunet, offering to sell her villa and horses for 30,000 francs. This worried me, for I didn't know what would become of me if my mistress sold her villa. One day, she gave me a gold watch and an address in Arnhem to send it to. She said it was a present for her daughter. A week later, it came back unopened. She often disappeared without notice for two or three days and would return and carry on as if nothing had happened. Hippolyte told me that a friend of his had seen my mistress going into a building that was known to be a well-to-do brothel. I didn't believe it, but Hippolyte shrugged and said, 'Needs must when the devil drives.'

During the early months of 1914, my mistress wrote and received a lot of letters to and from Berlin. She did nothing that winter except ride occasionally and drink white wine in the evenings. The hoarfrost every morning was like icing sugar in the garden. Rain fell. The nose of the little Siva in the east corner broke off. Hippolyte was most upset. In the spring, the same officer that had attended her recitals, General Méssimy, began visiting her regularly. I heard him trying to leave the villa quietly in the early mornings. Hippolyte and I smiled to each other, as we had been doing the same thing. In July, my mistress announced she was going to Berlin to perform at the Winter Gardens. 'If Paris no longer wants me, then Berlin does,' she said. We prepared her baggage for the trip and she left the next morning, saying she would be back in two weeks.

After three weeks, she hadn't returned and there was no word from her. Eric said he was worried, but we all decided to stay put for the time being. On the day that Germany declared war on Russia, a telegram arrived from Berlin: it was my mistress asking me to bring her a basket full of costumes and jewellery, as she had secured a run of performances at the Metropole Theatre. She said she was in good health and not to worry. We were all relieved and I set about collecting her things and preparing the train ticket. I left Gare de l'Est for Metz late on the second of August and arrived at the border on the evening of the third. When my train tried to cross the border, some German soldiers stopped it and announced that, as Germany and France were now at war, no passengers would be allowed to go any further without the correct transit papers. The train reversed back along the track into Metz. I was quite frightened. I sent a telegram to my mistress's hotel and waited in Metz for two days, but I didn't get a reply from her, so I went back to the villa. I didn't know what else to do.

A week went by, then another. Marthe left, then Eric. Me and Hippolyte stayed put for another week or so, but there was still no word. Hippolyte said things would get bad now that the war had started and that we shouldn't stay any longer. He knew about these things and I trusted him. He said we should go away, so I closed up the villa and we went south to Tours, away from the Boches. With all the men gone to war, Hippolyte got a gardener's job easy enough, at a château just outside Esvres. With the few savings we had, Hippolyte told me to stay at the village hotel for a while. I spent the days walking by the river, or nosing around the markets in the village. After a couple of weeks, he spoke about me to Monsieur Rousseau, the owner. He lied to him, saying that we were married. I was lucky; Monsieur Rousseau was very kind and gave me a job as a maid.

I didn't know then that I would never see my mistress again. I would like to have, for she was good to me. Working for Monsieur Rousseau was pleasant enough, but I loved working for my mistress. I have heard a lot of people say that she was not pretty to look at. Well, that's not true. Just have a look at her portrait that hung in the drawing room of the villa and you'll see. All dressed up, she was as pretty as they come. Hippolyte used to tease me about my attachment to her. He didn't miss the villa at all – the château was more than enough to keep him occupied. The only thing he missed was that silly little statue in the garden. He had a curious liking for it, but I've never fathomed why.

21
The Black Hand

In June 1903, King Alexander and Queen Draga of Serbia were assassinated. Disgusted with the king's autocratic and corrupt rule, a group of young army officers stormed the palace and found the King and Queen hiding behind a secret panel in their bedroom. They were shot, mutilated and then thrown naked out of the palace windows. One of the coup's leaders was twenty-six-year-old Lieutenant Dragutin Dimitrijevic, also known as Apis, the Serbo-Croat word for 'bee'. While storming the palace gates, Apis received three bullets from the palace guards, which he carried for the rest of his life. In Belgrade, he was a hero and branded 'the saviour of the fatherland'.

When Bosnia-Herzegovina was annexed by the Austro-Hungarian Empire in October 1908, many of Serbia's top government officials and military personnel met to discuss the ramifications for the Serb majority living in Bosnia-Herzegovina. These meetings, which remained clandestine, gradually evolved into a society dedicated to the unification of all Serbs into one domain. The group decided it needed a leader and approached Apis, who didn't hesitate for a second. In May 1911, the ringleaders, including Apis, met to agree a constitution.

Each member was made to swear 'by the sun which is shining on me' to organise 'revolutionary activities in all territories inhabited by Serbs' and to serve the cause of Serbdom 'to the grave'. A name was chosen for this secret society: *Ujedinjenje ili Smrt,* which translates as 'Union or Death'. Funds were raised by kidnapping wealthy people and ordering them to pay a ransom, or by blackmail. Anyone who had money procured from them was given a small symbol of a black hand, which ensured against further molestation. For this reason, the society became known as 'The Black Hand'.

The group became powerful and continued to plot against the Hapsburgs. They found a perfect opportunity in the official visit to Sarajevo by the heir to the Austro-Hungarian throne, Archduke Franz Ferdinand. His visit was planned for 28 June 1914, St. Vitus's Day, the day in 1389 that the Serbs had been crushed by the Ottoman Turks during the Battle of the Field of the Blackbirds and which had led to five hundred years of Ottoman rule. It was the perfect day for a show of Serb defiance, but rather than risk being caught themselves, they decided to find others to assassinate the Archduke.

Gavrilo Princip was born in 1894, the son of a shepherd from the Grahovo Valley in Bosnia. As a boy, he was introverted, preferring to read and memorise poetry than help his father tend the flock. When he was thirteen, he made the brave decision to go to Sarajevo, where he studied at the Merchants School and became involved in the writings of anarchists and nationalists. He began participating in anti-government demonstrations. During one such student battle with the Sarajevo police, he was wounded by a sabre and expelled from school.

He drifted to Belgrade, living rough and taking part in café discussions about the prospect of imminent war. The Slavs, Bulgarians, Montenegrins and Serbs were united against the last remnants of the Ottoman Empire. In October 1912, when he was eighteen, Princip attempted to enlist in the Serbian army but was rejected because he was considered too small and weak. He took the rejection badly. In the spring of 1914, his friend, Nedeljko Cabrinovic, showed him a newspaper clipping reporting the Archduke's planned visit to Sarajevo. Princip read the article but said nothing. While sitting on a park bench later that evening, he calmly announced to his friend that he would kill the Archduke. He asked Cabrinovic if he would join him. Cabrinovic didn't hesitate and the pair shook hands.

Cabrinovic was six months younger than Princip and had a similar background. He too had become interested in nationalistic and socialist writing and had even published essays in political journals. For his part in a violent printers' strike, Cabrinovic had been arrested and jailed. The authorities had pressed him for the names of the strike leaders, but Cabrinovic had refused to co-operate. He had eventually been released but was banished from his native Sarajevo for five years.

The two young men decided that they needed a third man. They chose Trifko Grabez, another young Bosnian with a history of rebellion. The son of an Orthodox priest, Grabez was seventeen when he had struck one of his school teachers and was expelled. Like Princip and Cabrinovic, he had drifted to Belgrade, where he had performed brilliantly in his studies. When he was approached by Princip and Cabrinovic, he needed no persuasion. He was nineteen at the time.

The main problem now facing them was how to get hold of the bombs, guns and poison to carry out the assassination. Grabez was in all probability a member of the Black Hand and it was through a series of introductions and debriefings that Apis, by then a Colonel on the Serbian General Staff, was informed of the young anarchists' plan. What he may not have known is that all three were suffering from tuberculosis in varying degrees. Cabrinovic and Grabez both had weakened lungs, but Princip's case was worse: the TB was eating his bones away.

Without ever meeting the trio, Apis organised their training and, during May 1914, all three took pistol practice at a secret location just outside Belgrade. Princip was a particularly skilful marksman – he could hit his target six times out of ten at a distance of two hundred yards. At sixty yards he never missed. When they had finished their training, they were given four Belgian revolvers, six bombs, three vials of cyanide and were sent to Sarajevo.

In the early morning of 28 June, they met at a pastry shop on the corner of Apple Quay, in Sarajevo. The archduke's route had been printed in the newspapers and the three of them agreed to disperse themselves at various stages along it so that, if one failed, another would have a chance. Security was minimal and each was able to mingle freely in the crowds while choosing the best spot to lie in wait.

At a quarter past ten, the six-car royal entourage approached the Mostar Café on Apple Quay, near where Cabrinovic had positioned himself. As the procession neared, Cabrinovic asked a policeman, 'In which car is the archduke?' The policeman pointed to Franz Ferdinand, standing out clearly in his blue tunic, high collar and plumed hat. Cabrinovic thanked him and moved off. Hidden in the crowd, he took out his bomb, knocked off its detonator on a nearby lamp-post and threw it at Franz Ferdinand's head.

As he had been shown during training, Cabrinovic should have waited twelve seconds before throwing the bomb, but he didn't. The twelve-second delay saved the Archduke's life. He deflected the bomb with his elbow and it fell in the street where it exploded, wounding the passengers in the car behind and injuring several people in the crowd. Cabrinovic swallowed the cyanide he was carrying and leapt into the Miljacka river below. Unfortunately for him, the river was at low tide and the cyanide did nothing except make him very sick. Four men leapt in after him and dragged him out. One of them was so incensed that he wanted to kill Cabrinovic. The police intervened and Cabrinovic was taken away for interrogation.

After the explosion, the police attended to the injured and cleared a way for the entourage to get to the Town Hall, where there was to be a formal reception. Seeing

Cabrinovic's failure, Grabez had second thoughts and fled the scene, depositing his bomb in a nearby basement. Princip's resolve, however, was still strong. Unnoticed in the confusion, he crossed the street and waited in front of a delicatessen on the corner of Apple Quay and Franz Joseph Street.

On leaving the official reception, the entourage was due to turn right into Franz Joseph Street on its way to visit a museum. But before anything else, Franz Ferdinand insisted on visiting those wounded in the bombing, who were now in a military hospital. This meant continuing along Apple Quay. Had the Archduke's driver been told of this change of route, there might never have been another attempt on the Archduke's life. As it was, the driver turned right into Franz Joseph Street and was immediately instructed to stop and reverse.

While the driver was selecting the gear, Princip had his chance. He realised there wasn't enough time to throw a bomb. Instead, he stepped forward and drew out his revolver. He was no more than five feet away from the car. He took aim and fired two shots. The first hit the Duchess of Hohenburg in the abdomen. The second pierced the jugular vein in the Archduke's neck. Both died of their injuries within minutes. In the ensuing struggle, Princip was prevented from turning the gun on himself and was nearly strangled to death. The police used swords to dispel the mob surrounding Princip, who lay injured on the ground. Princip did, however, manage to swallow his cyanide but, like Cabrinovic's, it did nothing more than make him violently sick. Princip was eventually taken away to police headquarters.

After two days of interrogation, Cabrinovic and Princip told the police the names of all who had helped in the assassination. They mentioned nothing about Apis or the Black Hand, however. On 1 July, Grabez was arrested and a trial for all three was fixed for 12 October, to be held in Sarajevo but conducted under Austrian law. The verdict, delivered on 25 October, found all three guilty on charges of treason and murder and the judge sentenced them each to twenty years' hard labour. There was a special condition for Princip: that he was to spend one day a month and every 28 June in solitary confinement.

During the winter of 1916, both Cabrinovic and Grabez died of cold and hunger while in prison. In his prison in Bohemia, Princip was in and out of the hospital because of his TB and eventually had to have an arm amputated. He died on 28 April 1918.

Although he managed to avoid any connection with Franz Ferdinand's murder, Apis was arrested in 1916 by order of the Prince Regent, because the Regent feared that Apis was plotting to kill him. Ironically, the Regent was the son of the king Apis had placed on the throne after the assassination in 1903. At his trial in Salonika, Apis confessed to his role in the assassination of Franz Ferdinand and was sentenced to death. In June 1917, he was shot at night in front of an open grave. His last words were: 'Long live Serbia!'

22

Berlin, 1914

'Welcome back to Berlin, madame,' von Jagow said. 'The city has missed you.' He poured some wine into her glass and proposed a toast to old acquaintances. His dark-blue serge suit was the same. His tie was neatly knotted and his dark hair slicked back. Apart from the crow's-feet appearing around his blue eyes, his childlike face hadn't changed at all.

She raised her glass to him. 'Thank you,' she said and took a sip. The wine, as usual at Adlon's, was superb.

'Ah, here come the truffles.'

A waiter laid a silver tray of *truffes à la timbale* in the centre of their round table and began serving the dish.

'They are the most commendable comestible ever discovered. Nobody has the faintest idea what they are, only that they are delicious. They do something wonderful and peculiar to the body,' he said.

The waiter finished serving them and wished them a good meal. Von Jagow began eating. He sat back and kissed his fingers.

'*Parfait*,' he said and sipped his wine. 'I'm afraid food is my one and only weakness. But, much as I love truffles, I love fish even more.'

'Yes, I remember.'

Von Jagow thought for a moment, then began eating again. 'When I was a boy, in Essen, I saw a fishfall.'

'A what?'

'A fishfall. I remember my mother standing at the sink peeling potatoes one summer morning when, suddenly, there was a huge crash outside, like breaking glass. She cried out and ran to the front door. I followed her and stood with her, looking out on to the street. Blocks of ice the size of shoeboxes were falling from the sky, each one with a fish in it. Some fell and skidded, others smashed open. Up and down our street, fish lay wriggling on the cobblestones. I recognised them at once – my father used to take me fishing – they were freshwater carp. They stopped falling as quickly as they had started. We found out later that it was just in our street. Then someone started picking them up and my mother picked two or three up herself. We had them for dinner that night. You should have seen my father's face when she told him where they'd come from. He refused to believe her, so she had to get the neighbour in to tell him the whole story again.' Von Jagow laughed.

A string quartet began playing in one corner of the restaurant.

'How do you explain it?' she asked.

'No one knows,' he said. 'People say that it's a freak of nature – something to do with vacuums over lakes and seas – but no one really knows. I considered it a lucky omen.'

When they had finished their main course and were waiting for dessert, von Jagow excused himself and strode away. Mata Hari sat back in her seat and looked up at the fan above the table. It was rotating slowly, too slowly to do anything except push the hot air around the room. The blades reminded her of propellers.

She looked up at the white-clothed tables around her. Army officers and city officials murmured over their food. She was the only woman there. A man noticed her. She couldn't tell if she knew him or not. She looked away and found it difficult to breathe. It was too hot and there were so many faces, always watching her and waiting. She was tired of being looked at.

A small crowd had gathered outside at the windows, looking in at the diners. She frowned. What were they doing there? She noticed that many of the other diners were looking at the crowd and smiling. An army officer stood up and toasted them.

Von Jagow returned to their table and sat down. He poured more wine for them. She felt his eyes on her.

'Are you a little sad this evening, madame?'

'A little, perhaps.'

'I trust your performance at the Winter Gardens last night went smoothly?'

'Yes. I'm tired, that's all.'

'When do you start your performances at the Metropole?'

'On the first of September.'

Von Jagow pushed his plate away and glanced around the restaurant. The chatter had become more animated.

'I have a mind to perform less often, actually,' she said.

Von Jagow looked at her. 'Really? Why?'

'It holds no interest for me any more.'

'Nonsense,' he said. 'Mata Hari is a famous star who will remain in the public eye for ever. You just need a change. After you have completed your engagements you should return to Paris. I know how you love Paris.'

A uniformed man appeared at von Jagow's elbow and whispered something into his ear. A faint smile appeared on von Jagow's face. He dismissed the man with a nod and looked at Mata Hari. He patted his mouth with his napkin, which he then folded carefully and laid on the table.

'Madame, the War Office has just made the announcement. We will not allow France to mobilise with our enemy, Russia. As of 18:45 today, Germany is at war with France.'

An hour later, Mata Hari left the Adlon restaurant with von Jagow. Many of the diners nodded to them; some stood up and shook von Jagow's hand as they threaded their way through the tables. At the entrance to the restaurant, they waited while their coats were collected and placed around their shoulders and the doors opened for them. Outside, the heat coming off the street hit her face. They paused in front of the large crowd that had gathered and that now cheered and clapped them. The faces in the crowd looked ecstatic.

She saw hats being thrown into the air, then the crowd began to sing 'Deutschland Über Alles'. Von Jagow's official motorcar stood waiting by the kerb. She noticed that it was a newer, bigger model than the one she had been driven in seven years before. It better suited von Jagow's new position as Chief of Police. As they descended the stone steps, the crowd let them through. She sensed that the crowd wanted to touch them, but they kept a respectful distance – partly out of awe, but also fear, she guessed.

The following morning, Mata Hari woke up in a sweat, the sun burning her through a crack in the curtains. She stumbled out of her huge bed and closed them. The sheets were wet where she had been sleeping. She lay back down, attempting to recall von Jagow's every sentence and gesture over dinner, to find what possible meanings they contained; but just as she remembered them, they slipped away. All she could hear in her head were the war slogans and songs that had been yelled in the streets as she was driven to her hotel in von Jagow's car. She felt oppressed in Berlin, unable to take hold of herself. Her actions were in the hands of others.

Her carriage clock ticked incessantly. It was past eleven. She knew she would be unable to sleep any more, so she rose from the bed and went into the bathroom. She stood in front of the mirror and looked at herself. She too had wrinkles appearing around her eyes. She looked for some kind of sign in her reflection to say that today would not be as bad as she thought, but she saw none. She splashed water on her face; the coldness made her gasp. She poured more water on her shoulders and arms, and around her hot neck.

Wearing an emerald-green velvet dress, she walked down the stairs to the foyer of the Cumberland, which was busy with guests checking out. At reception, she asked if there were any messages for her. The receptionist handed her two envelopes. The first was from Aurore to say that she had been refused entry into Germany at the border. She was stranded in Metz. Mata Hari groaned. How was she supposed to prepare for the rest of her performances without the costumes and jewellery Aurore was bringing with her?

The other message was from Schulz, the Director of the Metropole. He said that the theatre was going to close until further notice because of the war. What was happening? War seemed to have descended on the city overnight. Whatever opportunities Berlin had to offer her were being taken away and she desperately needed money. Standing in the foyer clutching the two messages, she decided she must leave at once and return to Paris. She could make up for the lost income by selling her furniture at Neuilly. Yes, that was the right thing to do.

She returned to her room and opened her trunk. Her belongings were scattered around the room in anticipation of a long stay and it took some time to pack them. At reception, she ordered her trunk to be brought down and then left the hotel. A minute's walk brought her to a bank, where she had deposited her best jewellery and the 30,000 marks von Jagow had given her.

The cashier looked dismayed when she requested her belongings from her safe deposit box and asked her to wait. A few moments later, the manager appeared and ushered her into his office. He softly explained that all personal belongings of French nationals had been seized the moment Germany declared war on France.

This news threw her. 'But I'm not a French national,' she said.

'You are considered a French citizen because you have been living in France for more than ten years, madame.'

'This is ridiculous! Do you know who I am?' she shouted.

He concurred that he did.

'I had lunch with the Chief of Police yesterday and if you don't allow me to collect my belongings, I'll have you sacked!'

'Madame,' he said patiently, 'the order is by the authority of the Chief of Police.'

Her heart leapt to her throat. She pleaded with the manager, but he was adamant. He opened his arms in a gesture of helplessness.

'I'm sorry, but there's nothing I can do.'

She walked back to the Cumberland and, at reception, ordered a telephone line to the city police headquarters. The phone clicked and a man said, 'Hello.' She demanded to speak to von Jagow. The man asked who it was and, when she replied, told her to wait. When he returned, he apologised and said, under the circumstances, Herr von Jagow was very busy. She didn't know what else to say. The man said he would tell Herr von Jagow that she had called. The line went dead.

Mata Hari drifted slowly to a corner of the foyer. She couldn't think what this latest development meant. Men and women were filing past her, leaving the hotel with their cases packed. She felt one step behind events. She was stuck in Berlin, her money and jewellery confiscated, with little money on her and a heavy trunk to carry. The few costumes she had with her were in her dressing room at the Winter Gardens. 'This is a crisis,' she thought. She tried to remain calm but waves of panic swept through her and, before she knew it, her eyes were brimming with tears. Her mouth went dry. Through her tears she felt a hot resentment towards von Jagow. '*Ah, ces sales Boches!*' she said to herself.

She felt a hand on her shoulder and turned to find a very tall elderly man looking at her.

'Madame Mata Hari?'

She was so surprised at this intrusion that she immediately stopped crying. His expression was soft and warm. He was roughly shaven, with a large moustache and sideburns. His snow-white hair and whiskers needed trimming.

'I thought it was you. I recognised your face.'

He spoke in French, but with a heavy accent.

'Are you Dutch?' she asked.

He was taken aback. 'Yes. How did you know?'

His dark suit was frayed at the edges and around the collar. His hands were weathered. She wondered what the chances were of meeting another Dutch person in Berlin at this very moment. She found it slightly absurd and began to laugh.

'Are you all right, madame?' the old man said. 'Would you like to sit down?'

She shook her head. 'I'm fine,' she said and dabbed her eyes with a handkerchief.

'My name is Jip Wijngaarden.' He made a little bow.

She tried to smile.

'You seem very distressed. Is there anything I can do?' he said.

This man was being very kind to her and she wasn't sure why. His manner was extraordinarily calm. The foyer was more or less empty now and she felt very alone. Standing there, in her expensive green dress, seemed slightly ridiculous. She had to get back to Paris quickly. She looked at Wijngaarden again. He struck her as a sincere man and she decided to trust him. Who else could she turn to? She told him everything that had happened that morning, but left out exactly how much money she had at the bank and who it was from.

He listened attentively and, when she had finished, told her that in his opinion it was unlikely she could reclaim her money or jewellery at present. She would have to wait until the situation was clearer. As a French national, she would not be allowed to return directly to Paris without the necessary transit papers. She stood more chance of travelling to a neutral country, like Holland, and then on to France.

Mata Hari nodded. 'What should I do?' she asked.

Wijngaarden thought for a moment. His brother, he said, knew the Dutch Consul in Berlin. His name was Van Panhuys. If she wished, they could visit him and obtain the transit papers for her to travel to Holland. In fact, he would be returning to Amsterdam himself that evening. They could at least try, no?

Mata Hari smiled and agreed. She thanked him.

Wijngaarden bowed again. 'It's a pleasure to help a beautiful lady such as yourself. And a compatriot too!'

As they left the hotel together, Wijngaarden explained that he was the director of a company that grew tulips. The company had many customers in Berlin and, every summer, he came to Berlin to renew his supply contracts. When war had been declared, his brother, who lived in Berlin, had advised him to leave at once.

They passed the French Embassy, where a group of demonstrators were holding up pro-war placards. The two German policemen standing guard by the gates looked uneasy. The crowd jostled them and shouted nationalist slogans. Wijngaarden and Mata Hari walked on.

After a long wait at the Dutch Embassy, they were seen by the Consul. He greeted Wijngaarden warmly and shook Mata Hari's hand when they were introduced. They all sat down. The Consul nodded as Wijngaarden explained Mata Hari's dilemma. He saw no problem with issuing the necessary documents for her journey and, opening a drawer, took out a form. What reason should he put for her wanting to return to Paris? Mata Hari explained that she wished to dispose of her property at Neuilly. He filled in the form with details of her age, height and religion, stamped it and added his signature at the bottom. Handing the form to her, he said that it would be easier still if she travelled on the same train as Wijngaarden. Mata Hari couldn't believe how simple it had been. There was relief in her voice as she thanked the Consul. He waved his hand in dismissal and said it was a pleasure to help such a famous artiste. He wished them a good trip.

In his room at the Metropole, Wijngaarden packed the last of his things. He was meeting Mata Hari at Bahnhof Zoo at seven o'clock. The overnight train departed at 19:20. He placed a call to his brother and told him about his meeting with Mata Hari. His brother asked if he was mad. 'Don't you know who she is!?' he asked. Wijngaarden listened in shock as his brother went on to explain that her name had been linked to all kinds of German military personnel and that she probably worked for the German Secret Police. 'Under no circumstances should you travel with her! Let her get on the train tonight and you leave on the sleeper tomorrow. Do you hear me?'

After promising to do as his brother had said, Wijngaarden replaced the receiver on its hook and stood still for a moment. Then he took off his jacket and laid it on the bed. He undid his collar and cuffs, rolled up his sleeves and settled into a chair. The evening sun fell on his neck. He rubbed his face and smelled the fragrance of tulips on his fingertips.

23
Zeppelin

> Whenever the airship flew over a village, or whenever it flew even over a lonely field where a few farmers were working, a really tremendous shout of glee rose into the air towards Count Zeppelin's miracle ship which, in the imagination of all those who saw it, suggested some supernatural creation.
>
> *Thüringer Zeitung*, July 1908

Count Ferdinand von Zeppelin was born in 1838 in Konstanz, a small town on the shores of Lake Constance in the Kingdom of Württemberg, Germany. He graduated from the military academy at Ludwigsburg and became a lieutenant in the Eighth Württemberg Infantry Regiment, but the routine of military life soon bored him. Instead, the capricious von Zeppelin wished to travel to America to observe the armies fighting in the American Civil War and, through a variety of connections and introductions, the twenty-four-year-old Count secured an audience with President Lincoln in Washington on 21 May 1863.

With the full military pass that President Lincoln granted him, von Zeppelin spent a year as a 'guest' cavalry officer with the Union Armies at their headquarters in Falmouth, Virginia. The general pace of the war, however, was slow and von Zeppelin soon became bored again. To divert his attention further, he joined a civilian expedition to explore the sources of the Mississippi river. During a scouting mission at St Paul, Minnesota, he took his first ride in a tethered balloon, which had been floated to survey the surrounding countryside. It was then that he first realised dirigibles would make excellent weapons of war.

He returned to Germany and remained a cavalry officer until his retirement at the age of fifty-two, in 1890. A few years later, he applied for a patent for an airship and began experiments near Lake Constance. For the next decade, he personally financed the construction of airship after airship, each better than the last and, in 1907, the King and Queen of Württemberg joined him on a short flight in the *Luftschiff-Zeppelin 3*.

By 1909, von Zeppelin had formed the world's first airship passenger service: Deutsche Luftschiffahrts Aktien Gesellschaft, or DELAG for short. Operating flights between Berlin, Frankfurt, Hamburg and Dresden, his airships carried 32,750 passengers on 1,600 flights in five years without a single accident. The short but athletic Count, with his ruddy face and a snow-white moustache, became a national hero. A Zeppelin craze swept across Germany – confectioners sold marzipan Zeppelins, a brand of cigarettes and prize flowers were named after him and he was awarded the Military Cross by the Kaiser.

When war was declared between Germany and France, the German navy acquired many of the Zeppelins, converted them so that they could carry three 100-pound bombs and began bombing raids over London. The bombs were held in place by ropes, which were cut as the airship drifted over its target. It was impossible to be accurate and direct hits tended to be accidental.

These raids over London caused little material damage, but they incensed Londoners. Every night there was a blackout in the city. The sight of the monstrous airships caught in the high-powered searchlights, cascading their bombs on to the capital, brought the people out on to the streets shouting in protest. During 1915, airships took part in more than thirty raids over London. The belief that the Germans could never reach London had been shaken.

It was feared that the Zeppelins would be able to target

Kensington Palace using reflections from the gilding of the Albert Memorial, so the gold leaf was stripped using a solvent and the glittering slurry dumped in a hole behind the Tate Gallery. The statue was then painted black. But from the beginning of the war, the Kaiser was careful to protect royalty among his enemies. He gave strict instructions that any raids over England should only bomb targets of real military importance and stipulated that places such as Buckingham Palace, Westminster Abbey and St Paul's Cathedral should not be bombed under any circumstances. The Allies, however, did not share his sentiments and later bombed Charleville and Stenay, where the Kaiser and Crown Prince often stayed.

Cold nights were preferable for airship raids over London. A drop in temperature of three degrees meant that an airship could gain three hundred feet in altitude. The airships were launched from their bases deep in Germany at noon and, by night, were approaching the English coast. Navigation was complicated because of the blackout of all landmarks on the coastline, but the beams of the lighthouses at Oostende and Steenbrugge formed a line that pointed directly at the mouth of the Thames.

There was no protection from the bitter cold. The gondola cars were open to the elements and the crew had only fur-lined greatcoats and heavy boots for warmth. They were issued with oxygen bottles for high-altitude flying, but kept below 25,000 feet because, above that altitude, blood ran freely from the nose, mouth and ears.

Storms were very hazardous for the Zeppelins. In one raid over England, an airship encountered such a colossal storm that it stopped moving forwards altogether. Winds pitched the airship up and down hundreds of metres. It was then struck by a bolt of lightning, illuminating the whole of its inside. Wires and cables glowed with bluish light. The look-out on the upper platform reported that his machine gun was spitting sparks and that, when he spread his hands, small flames spurted from his fingertips.

This phenomenon, known as St Elmo's Fire, was incredibly dangerous for the crew members, but as long as the electricity was distributed along the metal framework and provided that none of the hydrogen gas escaped, lightning in itself was no danger to the airship. Any puncturing of the shell by bullets or shrapnel, however, was fatal if combined with a lightning storm.

The lighter-than-air Zeppelins flew too high to be harmed by anti-aircraft batteries and could stay aloft for much longer than heavier-than-air biplanes. In response to the public panic over these airships, a reward of £4,250 and the prospect of a military decoration were offered to the first aviator to shoot down a Zeppelin over Britain, but none succeeded. The best they could do was pepper the gas-bags with holes. This made the airship heavier, but only resulted in complicating the return journey. As long as there was no fire or spark to ignite the hydrogen, the airship was damaged, but not destroyed.

In 1917, however, the British finally developed a new kind of ammunition against the Zeppelins – the ZPT 'tracer bullet', each of which was coated in burning phosphorous. It took only one hit from these green-sparking bullets to turn the airships into flying fireballs. The tiny BE 2 biplane fighters were now more than a match for the Zeppelins and the bombing raids were rendered useless.

During that same year, the seventy-nine-year-old Count died suddenly of pneumonia, contracted after a simple operation on his intestines. The burial took place at Pragfriedhof in Stuttgart in March, and was attended by the King and Queen of Württemberg along with thousands of other mourners. As his casket was lowered into the ground, two Zeppelins hovered overhead and dropped wreaths and hundreds of thousands of petals on to the grave.

24

Picardie, France, 1915

Captain Keith Hogg leant against the earthbags and looked through the periscope while he waited for his major to arrive. It was 06:10. The Major was late. No man's land was quiet; there had been no exchange of gunfire for two days now. Large craters pitted the one hundred and twenty yards between him and the first line of German trenches. All he could see were stakes rising up from the ground, *chevaux de frise* and shattered tree trunks. A flare was still smoking. The sky was blank.

A squad of Moroccans filed past, dressed in goatskin overcoats. Hogg watched as they staggered along the duck-boards without talking. He told them to watch out for the wire, but they hardly noticed him. He wondered how they'd cope when winter really set in. Behind them came Major Windley and Corporal Dick Chandler, followed by the early morning patrol. Hogg noticed that the Major's uniform was dry and his puttees clean. He saluted the Major perfunctorily and told Chandler to fetch the night patrol's report.

The Major looked through the periscope for a few minutes and grunted, as though he had found the answer to a question. Hogg waited. The Major turned to him and asked about the previous night's activities. Hogg gave his report that there had been none and then listened as the Major recounted the orders he had received. There was going to be a night raid on enemy lines. He made it sound as if the whole war effort depended on it.

Hogg asked about training, and the Major explained that an area behind the mess halls had been sectioned off. The ramparts of the old trenchline would be reversed and the trench used for training, which was to be done in daylight.

To simulate combat by night, the whole company was to be issued with dark glasses.

'Dark glasses?' Hogg said.

The Major nodded. 'Your orders are to go with one of your men to Paris and requisition one hundred pairs of dark glasses – I don't care where or who from. The raid is scheduled to take place on the twenty-ninth, six days from now. You're to return no later than 18:00 hours tomorrow. There's a munitions truck leaving for Amiens in an hour. Understood?'

Hogg nodded. 'I'll take Corporal Chandler,' he said.

'Fine,' the Major said and left.

Chandler returned holding the night patrol's report. 'What's up?' he said.

'You won't believe this.'

'What?'

Hogg lit a cigarette. 'Fancy a trip to Paris, Chandler?'

Amiens was twenty-five miles to the south-west. Hogg and Chandler were sitting in the rear of the truck as it passed the field hospital and left the village. Hogg filled Chandler in on what the Major had told him. Chandler kept smiling and said it was the most ludicrous thing he'd ever heard. 'But I'm not complaining, mind,' he said.

They watched as the bustle of the forward zones gave way to quieter clusters of stores, dumps and temporary barracks. This far from the front line the land was intact. The Somme, which they would follow all the way to Amiens, flowed quietly. Ditches and thickets sped by; one or two low farmhouses among pasture fields. Ten minutes later, Chandler said he could hear a bird singing and to Hogg the war seemed unreal.

Nearly two hours later, the driver dropped them off at Amiens railway station. He told them to have a drink in Paris for him and drove off. Hogg worked out from the timetable on the wall that there was a train to Paris in ten minutes. They sat on a bench on the platform and looked around the station. Chandler couldn't sit still; he said he felt strange being there. Hogg lit a cigarette. A thin white dog with yellow eyes approached and started howling at them. It wouldn't stop. Chandler said that a howling dog was bad luck and, when the train arrived, he almost ran to get on board.

The train travelled slowly through the northern suburb of St Denis and arrived at Gare du Nord at 3:40 p.m. As he wandered down the platform, Hogg tried to think of the best thing to do. Chandler was repeating 'Loonet noowah' to himself, like a mantra. The driver had told him it was French for 'dark glasses'. Chandler explained to Hogg that he had to keep saying it to himself, or else he'd forget it.

As they crossed the concourse, they passed a *tabac*. Chandler said he wanted to buy some cigarettes. While waiting, Hogg saw a rack of magazines outside. He picked up copies of *Le Miroir* and *L'Illustration* and flicked through them. There were portraits of dead French soldiers and of whole companies standing in rows in training grounds. There were also pictures of another raid over London by the 'New German Military Weapon' – the Zeppelin. Hogg studied the balloon. He'd heard about these machines from soldiers recently arrived from London. All of them said how terrifying they were. The middle spread was a 'photo record' of a battle, but not a real battle, just some men in clean uniforms running around. Hogg stuffed the magazines back in the rack and shouted at Chandler to hurry up.

They walked out on to rue La Fayette. Both men were quiet as they looked at the huge buildings on either side and the motor cars and street trolleys moving between them. Everything seemed so normal, as if the war was a thousand miles away. Hogg realised how hungry he was.

'Lunch?' he asked Chandler.

'Are you joking?' Chandler replied.

They went to the nearest café terrace they could see and sat down outside, facing the street. It was just about warm enough to sit there. A waiter in a long white apron came outside and smiled warmly to them.

'*Bonjour*,' he said.

After some confusion, they ordered some hot soup and sandwiches. Hogg lit another cigarette.

'How the bleedin' hell are we going to get those glasses?' Chandler asked.

'We'll ask the waiter.'

'What about a bit of vino to go with the soup?'

Hogg looked at Chandler, whose expression was saying 'why not?', and sighed. 'All right, but let's keep a lid on this, agreed?'

'Absolutely, Captain.' Chandler rubbed his hands.

The waiter came out with their food and served it to them.

'*Excusez-moi*,' Hogg said, trying to remember his French from school, but Chandler cut him off.

'Loonet noowah,' he said, making glasses around his eyes with his fingers.

'*Comment?*' the waiter frowned.

'Loonet noowah,' Chandler said.

The waiter blinked and listened as Chandler repeated the phrase several times. Then it dawned on him. '*Ah, lunettes noires*,' he said.

'Oui,' Chandler smiled.

'*Pour ça, vous devez aller à la place de Clichy, il y a un magasin là-bas.*'

'What?' Chandler said.

The waiter repeated himself. Chandler turned to Hogg. 'Did he just talk about magazines?' he asked.

'I think he said Clichy Place.'

The waiter took out his pen and pad and drew a little map for them. He talked quickly, nodding at them to check they understood. Hogg looked at the map. He thought they could find it. He nodded back.

'Merci beaucoup.'

'I didn't understand a word he was saying,' Chandler said.

'Neither did I, but we'll find it.'

'I'm starving.'

After checking the map and asking several passers-by for 'Clichy Place', they finally arrived there. It was getting dark. The square was little more than a huge roundabout (Chandler counted seven exits) with shops in between. They walked once around the square, but couldn't find a shop that they thought would sell dark glasses.

To warm themselves up, they went into a bar that they had already passed several times. The counter was made of metal. They ordered two coffees and, after persuasion from Chandler, two cognacs. While the bartender was getting their order, Hogg noticed that the bar was busy.

'We're going to have to ask again,' he said.

'All right.'

When the bartender placed their drinks on the counter, Hogg showed him the little map and, first in his limited French and then in English, asked him where the shop was. The bartender waved at him to wait and then walked away. Hogg watched him make a telephone call. When he had finished, he returned and gestured for them to wait five minutes. Hogg nodded.

'What's up?'

'Dunno,' Hogg said. 'But I suppose we'll find out.'

Chandler drank his coffee and reeled off what the others in their company were probably doing at that very moment. He shook his head. 'Unbelievable,' he said. Hogg watched Chandler for a moment and realised Chandler was actually getting used to being away from the front line.

'Whatever they're doing right now is exactly what we'll be doing tomorrow at the same time. Don't forget that,' Hogg said to him.

Chandler shrugged and drank his cognac.

The bartender addressed them and pointed to a woman, who had just entered the bar. She was wearing a long red dress and Hogg sensed that she didn't often enter bars such as this. She came over to them.

'Hello, I'm Lady MacLeod.'

Hogg introduced himself. Chandler almost bowed when he shook her hand.

She smiled at them. 'I'm sure I can help you find some glasses. I suggest we look around Clichy; there must be a shop not far away.'

Both men agreed. The woman talked to the bartender for a few moments and then gave him some change.

'According to Jean-Louis, there's an optician's on boulevard des Batignolles, just over there.' She pointed. 'Shall we go?' she said.

'We still have to pay,' Hogg said.

'Don't worry about that. It's the least I can do,' she smiled.

'Well, thank you, madame,' Hogg said.

'Thank you,' Chandler said.

They left the bar and walked down boulevard des Batignolles. On the way, Hogg felt the cognac warm his stomach. The woman asked them for details of the glasses – what type? how big? how many? Hogg answered as best he could and explained to her that they needed one hundred pairs.

'One hundred!' she said. 'My God, what are you going to do with one hundred pairs of dark glasses in October?'

'I don't know,' Hogg replied.

When they arrived at the optician's, the woman asked them to wait outside while she talked to the proprietor. She remained inside the shop for several minutes, talking to a small man in a dark suit. There were several bustling restaurants and cafés all along the boulevard. Chandler was watching the women in the street. He nudged Hogg and pointed to a young woman in a silky black dress. She couldn't have been more than seventeen, Hogg thought. She smiled at Chandler as she walked by.

The woman came out of the shop and told them that the proprietor had several pairs of dark glasses, but not one hundred. It was out of season, he explained. However, he would be able to contact his supplier the next day and order them.

'What would you like to do, *messieurs*?' she asked.

Chandler looked at Hogg. 'When would he be able to get the glasses?' Hogg asked.

'Not until the day after tomorrow,' she said.

'That's too bad; we have to leave tomorrow.'

'Oh, no problem,' she said. 'Just give me the address of your company and he can dispatch them to you.'

Hogg wasn't sure if he should. He thought about the Major's reaction if they returned without securing the glass-es. He looked at Chandler, who was waiting for him to say something, and realised this was the closest they would come before they would have to leave. He looked at the woman.

'All right,' he said.

She motioned him into the shop, where he wrote the address down for the proprietor. When he had finished, the proprietor read the address, smiled and shook Hogg's hand. He said something, which the woman translated as: 'I am happy to be of help to the Allied forces.' Hogg thanked him.

To celebrate, the woman took them to a nearby bar, where, she said, she knew some friends. Once there, she bought them both another cognac. Hogg drank it and felt relieved. A small band, made up of an accordion and fiddle, played 'It's a Long Way to Tipperary' when they saw the English soldiers. Chandler was singing along at the top of his voice.

Several women were introduced to them. They sat down, asking about the front and listening as Hogg told them about it. They said, *'Mon pauvre,'* and embraced him. One of them said that the woman in red was a famous dancer. She repeated her stage name to him, but he'd never heard of her. He looked for Chandler and saw him talking with her. Perhaps Chandler knew who she was. The walls of the bar were red and the woman's dress blended in with the colour. The interior was warm. Hogg drank the cognacs bought for him.

The first thing Hogg saw when he woke up was a window with bright sunlight pouring in. He looked at his pocket watch: 10:25 a.m. He cursed under his breath and sat up. The world slipped up and over him. He stayed still and had to swallow whatever had risen from his stomach.

He was in a small, well-furnished bedroom. Chandler was out cold next to him. He had no idea where he was. He felt vaguely under threat, but everything was quiet, except for the sound of cars outside the window. He got up carefully, his head pounding, and looked out of the window. He was two floors up on a busy street. He knew they should make their way back straight away and started to shake Chandler to rouse him.

On the night of the twenty-ninth, Hogg and Chandler, along with the rest of their company, stood leaning against the earthbags in the dugout, waiting for the signal to go over the top. Everyone was silent. Hogg stood ankle-deep in mud, breathing slowly to keep calm. It was so dark that he could hardly see the man next to him. He wished he could smoke a cigarette.

The glasses had indeed arrived when the proprietor had said they would and in enough time for the Major to order two days of full-equipment training. All artillery and rifle fire had ceased in order to pacify the German front lines. It had worked: there had been no night-time exchange of fire for the past few nights. Hogg waited.

When the tap on his shoulder came, he climbed up the

ladder and crawled over the rampart through the breach in the wire. He fanned out to the right, as in training. He could hear the faint sounds of others slithering as quietly as possible over the mud and into the bomb craters, where they halted for two minutes. Then, when all the men were spread out in a line, they crawled quietly out of the craters towards the first enemy trenches.

When Hogg reached the rise, a dozen flares went up and, suddenly, it was as bright as day. Hogg blinked and looked to either side of him. He saw five men fall; then he saw that every German gun emplacement was manned and firing. He ducked and rolled over on to his back, breathing hard. More flares went up. He felt a warmth in his chest and had the sensation of being drunk. He realised he'd been hit and closed his eyes.

When he opened them, it was still night. More flares went up and he realised no time at all had passed. Chandler's face came into view, looking down at him. He saw Chandler's lips moving, but he couldn't hear a word. Chandler was crying. All Hogg could hear was the sound of his own breath, which gurgled when he breathed in; then Chandler disappeared. All he could see now were the flares rising brightly. He imagined them rising for ever and falling into a different land, one that was clean, dry and quiet. His eyes closed.

25

Vittel, France, 1916

Her eyes were puffy and bloodshot; her nose was rather flattened, and her mouth, with its thick lips, stretched almost from ear to ear, revealing yellow and uneven teeth. Her hair was dyed, but this did not prevent streaks of grey from being visible. In short, she bore little resemblance to the seductive dancer who, some twelve years before, had dragged a host of admirers in her wake.

Robert Boucard, 1916

When I awoke, I couldn't see anything and, for a while, I didn't know if I was dead or alive. But gradually, I felt my chest and legs and wiggled my toes and realised that my body at least was unharmed. I was in a rock-hard bed that smelled of menthol. Sunlight was shining on my face and I could hear footfalls echoing around me. There were low murmurings nearby and faraway conversations, all in French. I reached up to my eyes and felt a bandage around them and, with that, I knew I was alive. I said my name aloud, in Russian. 'My name is Vadime de Massloff, of the First Regiment of the Special Imperial Russian air force!' Someone answered me in French. 'Hey, no need to shout, *mon ami*, we can all hear you. You're surrounded by a dozen *blessés*. Get a nurse, someone; the Russian bear is awake.' I asked the voice what day it was. Thursday the fifth, he said. What month? July.

The man next to me was called Favourier, a *poilu* who loved to talk. He had been injured at Verdun, a bomb-blow to the chest that had left him with one lung. He told me that I had been brought in two days previously, the day after him. There had been so many wounded at Verdun that all the hospitals there were full. Everyone had been brought a hundred kilometres to here, a makeshift field hospital just outside Vittel. It was still in the Zone of the Armies, he said, so it wasn't entirely safe. I asked about the menthol. 'It's not menthol,' he said; 'it's anise. They used it when they made absinthe.' He explained that the hospital used to be an absinthe factory before the government banned it and that all the beds in the hospital were stacked absinthe crates, which still reeked of anise. He laughed and told me not to worry – the smell was good for the fever.

He asked what had happened to me. I told him I had been at Verdun too, on reconnaissance. I had been flying over German lines to take aerial photographs of their trench systems. It was dangerous work avoiding their anti-aircraft battery and passing through the plumes of smoke from artillery fire. I had taken the last photograph during one sortie when I saw a large smoke cloud ahead. As I passed through it, I had to lift my goggles to turn the aircraft around. The smoke smelled like a *bon-bon*, or perfumed soap, and I realised that it was a cloud of gas, not smoke. I quickly put my goggles back on and straightened up, but it was too late. Seconds afterwards, there was the dreadful itching and stinging sensation in my eyes. I knew I was safely behind our lines so I tried to land. I remember the bumps as the wheels hit the ground. I also remember thanking God that I had cotton-wool in my mouth, which was soaked in my own urine to stop the gas entering my lungs. Favourier said it must have been mustard gas, because of its smell. 'You were lucky,' he said, 'too long in that gas cloud and you would've been a dead man.'

The next few days were filled with interminable boredom and pain in my eyes, particularly my left eye. I found out how difficult it is to remain lying down for days on end. The nurses were busy, too busy to stay by my bedside for more than a few moments, and I passed the time listening to Favourier. My ears became my eyes. Every so often, someone would touch my toes and tell me his name and I would reply. By the time I'd put names to all the different voices, there would be a new voice and a new name to learn. Many died, most were sent back to the front. Only a few were sent home and everyone was jealous when they said goodbye. They took letters to post and promised to return belongings. The nights were the worst. Surrounded by the sleeping, I heard private miseries being uttered, or subdued crying. In reality, no one slept very well or for very long, but everyone left alone the men who chose the night-time for grieving.

I didn't tell Favourier anything about Mata Hari; she was the one thing I wanted to keep for myself. I carried a photograph of her tucked inside my sheepskin on every sortie I flew. I had met her in Paris, in April – just three months previously. I had been spending a few days there before being sent out to Verdun. Two acquaintances of mine, officers in the French air force, had told me they had a lunch appointment with Mata Hari. They wanted to introduce her to me; they said she loved meeting officers of all nationalities. I waited in the Jardin des Tuileries one warm afternoon, and I soon saw them walking among the trees and symmetrical paths towards me. She was wearing a white flannelette dress and a wide-brimmed hat. She was as beautiful as a gypsy, with long dark hair and huge eyes. As my friends introduced us, she held out her hand, which I took. It was warm and soft. The Frenchmen treated her with grave respect, as though she were untouchable, but I could see by her expression that she was timid and craved love. I'd thought about her a lot since then – too much probably.

After four weeks in the hospital, the nurses removed my bandages. The room was too bright. The sunlight shone from the *coiffes* of the nurses, obscuring their faces, and the walls were blocks of burning white. I still couldn't see out of my left eye, so I was given a patch for it. Favourier immediately christened me 'the Russian pirate'. He asked me if he was as handsome as people said. I looked at his blond hair, sunburnt face and clear eyes and told him he was ugly as hell. He laughed. Later that day, a letter came for me. It was from her. She wrote that she had only just heard I was in hospital and was making arrangements to come to Vittel. She asked me to keep her visit a secret, as she didn't want any undue attention. Of course Favourier grilled me about the letter, but I said nothing. Her letters to me at the front line had kept me going through the worst days, but the prospect of seeing her was almost too much to bear. A few days later, I was deemed fit enough to be moved upstairs, where inpatients stayed before being sent back. The nurses said they needed the bed. I told Favourier not to worry, that I'd be back to see his ugly mug soon.

I spent August walking in the grounds of the factory, where the wormwood plants had grown wild and unkempt, and playing *vingt-et-un* with Favourier. Sometimes I tried to read the French newspapers, but my French is not so good and, anyway, the news was too depressing. The doctors kept checking my left eye and telling me it wasn't healed enough for me to resume flying. Late in the month, when the sunlight was at its strongest, I stayed indoors and watched the shadows move round the room. One hot afternoon, a nurse came with a telegram for me. It was from her again. She was expected in Vittel within twenty-four hours! I was to meet her in the morning. I couldn't believe it. The nurse was standing over me, smiling. She asked me if I wanted a haircut for the big occasion and produced a comb and a pair of scissors from her pocket. I took off my patch and leant my head back. My fine black hair fell in little clumps.

On 1 September, I left the hospital a little early and took my time walking along the quiet, tree-lined streets into the town centre. In a café in the main square, I ordered a glass of spa water. There were many civilians sitting outside in the square, enjoying the sunshine. I sat with my arms folded, feeling nervous but calm. Somewhere out of sight, a church bell struck eleven times. I paid and crossed the square. Down a side street, I came to a small park. In one corner, I saw a wooden shed and a bench nearby, where a woman was sitting. It was her. When I walked over to her, she stood up and touched my face. She asked me how my eye was. I said I didn't know. Her lovely dark eyes looked at me, openly. I smiled and said that we always seemed to be meeting in parks. And then she said a curious thing. She said that parks were the only place away from prying eyes.

She had taken a room at the Grand Hotel, on the periphery of the town. The hotel was isolated in its grounds and surrounded by small trees shaped into cones. We walked slowly up the curved steps to the main entrance. Her room was lined with walnut and painted in a soothing green. Through the window, the lawns sloped down to a line of poplar windbreaks and, beyond it, you could see the Vosges mountains. Somewhere among the mountains was the front line. It seemed a lifetime away. She was standing by me, the light shining off her pale yellow dress. She asked me what I was thinking and I kissed her. Her mouth opened to me and I put my arms around her. She took off her dress for me, watching me all the time. Sheets of silk and mousseline fell from her until she stood naked, except for her brassière. Her hips and legs were smooth and round. She pulled back the covers of the bed and slipped inside. I took off my uniform and placed it on a chair, then slipped into bed beside her. I could feel her warmth on my body, as she pushed me back and spread herself over me. She kissed my wounded eye. Her hand on my waist was like an electric shock. She smiled and said I was too thin. She rolled on to her back. Her dark hair fell open on the pillow and she smelled of strange, delicate flowers.

Later, much later, we lay side by side and looked at the ornate ceiling. She said she had known she would see me again after we had first met; she didn't know why exactly – it was just a feeling. 'You looked so impressive in your uniform,' she said. I asked her to describe it to me. She said I had had a black cap with a shiny peak and a gold emblem in its centre. My dark-blue jacket had a white ring of chenille around each cuff and down one side of the buttons. My trousers were also blue. I wore two medals, one shaped as a cross and pinned to my uniform, the other a round golden disc hanging from a green ribbon. Not bad, I said. She laughed and told me she had an eye for detail. Then, after a while, she said my expression that day had been both sad and proud. It had intrigued her. I asked her how she had managed to get to Vittel – it must have been difficult to arrange. She said a friend of hers had warned her that a permit was necessary to travel to Vittel and that she should see a certain Captain Ladoux, who was authorised to grant such a permit. So she did. At his office, she told him she had applied to the Red Cross to become a nurse and care for me. After listening to her case, this Captain Ladoux had agreed to grant her the permit. She leaned over me and opened the bedside-table drawer. 'See for yourself,' she said. I read the piece of paper she handed me.

> The restriction of personal liberty within the army zone is a measure which we enforce upon our own nationals, but we do not feel justified in recommending a similar course against neutrals whose friendship we desire to promote. Such a ruling, for example, would prevent Mata Hari, the prominent young Dutch artiste, from undertaking the highly meritorious mission she proposes to perform for the benefit of one of our wounded heroes.
> Captain Ladoux, Chief of the French Intelligence Service.

I was amazed and impressed. I said her reputation must really count for something. She shrugged and said that once she had an impulse, she acted on it quickly. I asked her if I was one of her impulses. She kissed me again and again, saying that I was, but a good one and a correct one, at last. We stayed in her bed for two days.

*

When we eventually ventured outside, it was to a restaurant. As we walked to the town centre, she sensed my nervousness and asked what the matter was. I said that I didn't have any money to pay for the meal. She squeezed my arm and told me not to worry – it wasn't my money she was after.

By the time we reached Les Nuages, the light was beginning to fade. We were shown to a table by the maître d'. The doors and windows in the restaurant had been opened up to let in the late summer air and the restaurant was only half-full. When we had settled, the maître d' handed us two menus and said how pleased he was to see Madame again. He bowed and left. I asked with some surprise if she had been here before and she said that, yes, she had been here in 1911, to take the waters – she had had a little arthritis in her knees after all her dancing. Did it work? I asked. Not really, she smiled. She went on to tell me that during her stay, she had seen a fortune-teller, who had warned her that the thing for which she was famous would one day come to an end. I remarked that the prediction was so vague, it could mean almost anything. She shook her head and said she had taken the old woman's words to heart; indeed, she told me that she had decided to stop dancing altogether. When I asked why, she sighed, saying that she didn't like dancing as much as she used to. In fact, she hated it. She went on to explain that she'd had some bad notices when she was performing *Lucia di Lammermoor* in The Hague two years previously – bad enough for the show to be taken off. She had been so distraught she hadn't danced since. I said she should dance in Paris, where they still loved her, but she took my hands and repeated that she didn't want to dance ever again. She was tired of it. She wanted to go somewhere far away from the war. She told me she would soon have enough money for the both of us and asked me to come away with her. She was looking at me so intently when she said this that I believed she meant it. I realised this was the moment when I had to say either yes or no, that after this moment, the course of my life would alter. I looked her in the eye and said that nothing in the world would make me happier than to be with her.

We left the restaurant in a hurry and went to her hotel room. There, we undressed each other and made love quickly, almost brutally. All my thoughts and feelings were centred on a spot somewhere in my lower back. She said nothing throughout; she seemed shy. She held on to me. Afterwards, we lay quietly. I asked her why she hadn't let me take off her brassière. She blushed and said that she was ashamed of her breasts. I asked why. She mentioned a painter, long ago, who had been less than kind about them and, ever since, she had been self-conscious. I could see by her expression that she felt exposed. I touched her breasts through the muslin for a long time before pushing the material up and kissing her. She held on to my head and sighed. After a while, her breathing became deep and regular. I thought she was asleep, but when I looked up, I saw that she was staring out of the window into the night. She looked like a child, not a woman who had just turned forty. I thought about her former husband, of whom she had told me many stories. I didn't know much else about her; she was mysterious to me, but I wanted to protect her. She turned her head to me and smiled. Unable to stop myself, I asked her if she would marry me. At first, she didn't respond, but lay absolutely still. Her eyes seemed to shine, taking in all the light there was in the room, and her mouth was agape. It was several moments before she uttered a quiet 'Yes'. 'When the war's over, let's do it,' I said. And then she broke into a smile and hugged me. 'Yes, yes,' she said.

I went back to the hospital the following morning: I had to show my face. A nurse scolded me for missing my appointments and sent me up to the doctors' offices. A doctor there examined my eye for half an hour, shining lights into it and asking me to follow his finger. He told me that my eye was nearly healed and that I would be reassigned soon. I went downstairs and found Favourier. He wanted to know where I'd been. I winked and said wouldn't he like to know. He laughed. I asked him how he was. So-so, he replied. He was being invalided out – a *grand blessé* with a full pension. So the war's over for me, he smiled. I patted him on the leg but couldn't say anything. Favourier understood. Then he asked me if I'd heard about the new aerodrome. I didn't know what he meant. Some captain or other had been looking for me, he said, to give me my new posting. There was an aerodrome being built at Contrexéville, not far from Vittel. Reconnaissance had already started as part of a new offensive.

In the evening, I arranged to see Mata Hari. We met in the park, by the small shed, and wandered around as I told her about my new posting. She seemed very interested in hearing the details and asked me many questions. I was touched by her concern for me; it was pleasing to have her suddenly so involved in my life. As the daylight faded once again, she asked me if I still wanted to marry her. I turned her to me and replied that I did. I took her in my arms and looked out over the green lawns, which seemed to glow greener in the half-light. We stayed still for several moments. I said softly that I had to go: it was Favourier's last night in the hospital and I had promised to be back. She nodded. As I was leaving, she stopped me and said she had been thinking: she thought I was right that she shouldn't give up dancing. She had spoken to her agent about the matter and he was busy trying to secure a performance for her soon. But afterwards, she said, 'We'll be together, won't we?' I said we would.

At the hospital, Favourier was in a great mood. For the first time, I saw him sitting on his bed, not lying in it. He was excitedly telling me all the places and people he would see back in Paris. One of the other *poilus* had had some whisky smuggled in. We waited until lights out, then cracked open the bottle out on the balcony. We had to whisper. The night air was moist. The outline of the trees below us hardly moved and the factory walls kept their yellowness in the dark. My night vision was getting better all the time. Favourier asked me if there was anyone he could see for me, or if I had any letters to post. 'All my family are in Russia,' I said. He went quiet and asked if I was afraid to go back into action. His question made me think about it, as if for the first time. He was right, I had to start thinking about it properly. I put my hand on his shoulder and told him I would be fine. We drank to that, then skulked back in, bumping into beds as we went.

Favourier was moved out the next morning. It was odd to see him in uniform. He had a twinkle in his eye when he left; I'm not sure if it was a twinkle or a tear. He never said a word, just raised his hand and disappeared with the others. His departure was sudden. A part of me left with him and I was left wondering what would happen to me. As I was sitting on his bed, a nurse came by and told me I had a telephone call. It was the Grand Hotel. They said Madame Mata Hari was leaving on the 11:01 train to Langres and asked me to meet her at the railway station. She was on the way there herself. I thanked them and replaced the receiver. I looked at the clock: 10:37. As the station wasn't far from the hospital, I could make it if I ran.

As I came on to platform 2, I could just see the train further down the line. The station was busy. I glanced up and down the platform, looking for her, and saw her standing by her piles of suitcases. She shouted my name and waved. I ran to her, out of breath. She smiled and put her arms on my shoulders, apologising for her sudden departure. She said she had to go to Madrid immediately because her agent had organised a performance at the Central Kursaal. I was trying to take this in when she asked me if I would be all right. I nodded. The train pulled into the station and we watched it come to a standstill. Blasts of steam issued from the engine car. I helped a porter with the luggage while she got on to the train. She leant out of a window and handed me an envelope. Open it later, she said. We stood looking at each other while the train built up steam. I told her to have a drink of absinthe in Madrid for me. She nodded. The guard waved a red flag from the other end of the platform and the train began to pull away. She remained leaning out of the window, waving, until I could see her no more.

I left the station feeling as though I'd just had another part of me suddenly cut away. People were leaving me. The sunshine was so bright outside that I had to squint. As I walked back to the hospital, I opened the envelope. Inside was a photograph of her, sitting sideways, but facing the camera. Her dark eyes were calm, her lips glistening with rouge. She had on a wide-brimmed white hat that was fluffy on top. A parure of pearls lay gleaming around her neck and hanging from her earlobes. She was wearing a simple white dress, sleeveless and low-cut, so that her milk-white chest and arms were bare.

I remembered the past few nights with her, the way she was always quiet when we made love. Was she that shy? Or was she frightened? I wondered if such a sudden departure meant anything. The photograph of her was delicious and I vowed to carry it on all the sorties I would have to fly from Contrexéville. I glanced at the back and saw that there was an inscription:

> Vittel, 1916 – In memory of some of the most beautiful days of my life, spent with my Vadime whom I love above everything.

26

Oleum Absinthii

Absinthe is a bitter spirit made from the leaves of the wormwood plant, a member of the huge *Artemisia* genus native to Europe and Asia, which also includes tarragon and mugwort. To make the drink, wormwood leaves are grown, harvested, dried and then mixed with angelica root, fennel, oregano, star-anise seeds, anise, hyssop, Melissa and balm mint. This mixture is left to macerate in alcohol for eight days, after which it is distilled and anise oil added. The large number of aromatic herbs is needed to hide the bitter taste of wormwood and the drink has a strong liquorice-like flavour, which comes from the anise. The drink is pale green, almost emerald-green in colour.

In bars and cafés, the drink was prepared by following a little ritual. From the bottle, an inch of absinthe was poured into a tall glass. A lump of sugar was placed on to a two-pronged fork, which was then balanced on the glass. Water was poured slowly on to the sugar lump, dissolving it into the absinthe and turning the whole drink cloudy. This was the mark of a pure absinthe – cheaper imitations would curdle when water was added.

The drink was used by the Egyptians, Greeks and Romans as a vivifying elixir. Pliny the Elder (23–79 AD) recommends *absinthium* as an aphrodisiac as well as a relief for headaches, flatulence and coeliac trouble. He also noted that it was customary for the champion of a chariot race to drink a cup of wormwood leaves soaked in wine 'to remind him that even glory has its bitter side'.

The word 'absinthe' derives from the Greek word *apsinthion*, which means 'undrinkable', because of its bitter taste. The common English term is 'wormwood'. The German word is *Wermut*, or vermouth, a drink originally distilled using wormwood leaves or drops of wormwood oil. This progenitor of absinthe had been distilled in Germany for centuries before absinthe was established as a drink in its own right.

The first person to do this was Pierre Ordinaire, a French doctor who fled the French Revolution in 1792 and settled in Couvet, a village in the west of Switzerland. While exploring the region on horseback, he discovered wormwood plants growing wild in the hills and began using them in his homemade remedies. His 136° proof elixir became popular with the local community as a stomach tonic and was known as 'La Fée Verte' – the Green Fairy.

The first medical study of absinthe was completed in 1864 by Dr Valentin Magnan, who was then a physician at the asylum of Sainte-Anne in Paris. He found that the effect of absinthe differed from alcoholic delirium tremens in that it provoked an *état vertigineux* resembling the *petit mal* form of epilepsy. In large quantities, he concluded that the drink could lead to 'absinthe epilepsy', caused by brain tissue lesions.

But what caused Magnan the most medical concern was the bitter oil, *oleum absinthii,* extracted from wormwood, which contains a powerful narcotic poison called thujone. Magnan concentrated his studies on thujone and found that it profoundly affected the motor centre of the cerebrum, producing convulsions and hallucinations of sight and hearing. Chronic absinthistes, he declared, were prone to automatism and amnesia, as well as violence and epileptic seizures, all caused by damage to the central nervous system.

As a result of studies such as Magnan's, absinthe was banned in every European country except England, Spain and France during the years leading up to the First World War. In England, the drink was never that popular, while in Spain production levels had always been low. But in France, absinthe was drunk in prodigious quantities and any attempt to ban production was met with hostile lobbying from the absinthe industry. In 1912 alone, the French consumed 221,897,000 litres of absinthe.

With the Franco-German war looming, however, the French government and military were worried, since much of the population was unfit for military service owing to the effects of absinthe. Ironically, it was as a fever preventative that the French military had introduced absinthe during the Algerian War in the 1840s. Two weeks after the Germans declared war on France, the Minister of the Interior, Louis Malvy, was compelled to ban the sale of absinthe. The Chamber of Duties followed suit and, in March 1915, banned the production, circulation and sale of absinthe in the whole of France.

At the height of its popularity, absinthe consumption was particularly heavy in Paris and Provence, and particularly popular among the artists and writers of the time. Picasso's Blue Period paintings are said to have been inspired by the effects of absinthe; Toulouse-Lautrec was committed to a sanatorium because of it, and Verlaine shot Rimbaud while under its influence.

But perhaps the most famous absinthiste of all was Van Gogh. According to Gauguin, it was while drinking absinthe that Van Gogh threw his glass at Gauguin's head. The auditory and visual hallucinations, epileptic-type convulsions and attacks of delirium that Van Gogh experienced during the last ten years of his life in Arles fit exactly the symptoms of toxic poisoning by thujone.

While in Arles, Van Gogh once had to be restrained from drinking a quart of turps. Shortly after cutting off his own ear, he wrote to his brother that his cure for insomnia was 'a very, very strong dose of camphor in my pillow and mattress'. Like thujone, both camphor and turpentine are terpenes, and Van Gogh may well have developed a strong addiction to all chemicals in this group.

A thuja tree, which is another source of thujone, grew

over Van Gogh's grave for fifteen years after his death. When his casket was disinterred for reburial in a larger plot of land, it was discovered that the roots of the tree had completely entwined themselves around the casket, as though embracing it. The thuja tree was replanted in the garden of Dr Gachet, Van Gogh's friend, and is reportedly still flourishing in the Provençal sun.

27

London, 1916

In November 1916, Mata Hari travelled by steamer from Vigo, in Spain, to neutral Holland. Owing to increased enemy submarine and mine-laying activity in the English Channel and North Sea, the British Admiralty had ordered all neutral shipping to make a port of call in England to be searched. The French authorities had informed the British of Mata Hari's presence on the Hollandia *and, when the steamer docked at Falmouth, she was arrested by officers from Scotland Yard. She was taken to London and interrogated for two days. What follows is the verbatim transcripts of the two interviews. When Scotland Yard had finished with her, they prevented her onward journey to Holland and chose instead to send her back to Madrid. At the time of her arrest, Mata Hari was carrying no fewer than ten pieces of luggage. The contents were listed as follows:*

One small wooden box containing a gilt clock.

Hat box containing: six hats, two hat pins, white feather boa, one veil, two fur necklets, two fur hears, two hat decorations, one imitation peach, one dressing gown.

Trunk containing: one pair gent's boots, one brush, one bundle wadding, one pair puttees, one pair spurs, three pairs shoes, three chemises, one napkin, one pair leggings, three veils, one box of ribbons, two brass shells, two belts, two underskirts, three skirts, one dress, four pair gloves, one umbrella, three sunshades, one douche, three scarfs, one night dress case, one coat, one costume, one bag of dirty linen, one bundle sanitary towels, one box contg. four hair ornaments, one hat pin and false hair, three fur necklets, one bottle Vernis Mordore Dore, one box of powder, one bottle of white fluid.

Boot trunk containing: six pairs slippers, one box face cream, three pairs boots, two pairs shoes, one pair stockings.

Trunk containing: two pairs corsets, 30 pairs stockings, one lavender packet, one veil, eight under bodices, one shawl, 10 pairs knickers, three princess petticoats, three combs, two dressing jackets, 11 chemises, one dressing gown, one towel, one garter, two coats, one petticoat, two pairs gloves, two powder puffs.

Trunk containing: one handbag with mirror inside, one hair comb, three coats, one fancy box, one box contg. copper plate and visiting card in the name of Vadime de Massloff, Capitaine, 1er. Regiment Spl Imperial, Russe.

Wooden box containing: china tea service.

Gladstone bag containing: one pair shoes, nail polisher, two boxes contg. cigarettes, eight hair nets, box visiting cards, box soap, sachet contg. 21 handkerchiefs, one empty cash box, pearl necklet in case, monocle in case, two earrings in box, two pearls in case, green stone ring in case, green stone necklet and two earrings in case, three fans. Holdall of cotton, needles, etc., handbag contg. cigarette case (two photos inside), powder puff and rouge stick on chain, boat tickets, sterling, francs, gulden, pesetas and Russian notes, two pieces of music, Spanish and French dictionary, bundle of photographs, crayon drawing.

One travelling rug.

One fitted lady's dressing bag.

New Scotland Yard, S.W.
15th November, 1916.

5′5″, medium stout, black hair, oval face, olive complexion, low forehead, grey brown eyes, dark eyebrows, straight nose, small mouth, good teeth, pointed chin, well-kept hands, small feet. Handsome, bold type of woman. Well and fashionably dressed in brown costume with racoon fur trimming and hat to match.

MARGARETHA ZELLE MACLEOD was seen here today by A.C.C., D.I.D., and Lord Herschell, and interrogated as follows:-

M.Z.M. My real name is Margaretha Zelle Macleod. I married Macleod and was afterwards divorced from him.

A.C.C. *Where were you born?*
In Frisia.

That is your photograph?
No, it is not my photograph.

I put it to you that your real name is Clara Benedix.
I swear to you that it is a mistake.

I put it to you that that passport is a false passport on which somebody has written the upper part.
No.

Just to show you are not speaking the truth – there is writing under the photograph.
Send it over to Holland and you will see that it is right.

Are you ready to account for the fact that that seal does not meet?
I did nothing with my passport, Sir.

Can you account in any way for that seal not meeting? Do you wish to say anything about the writing coming under the photograph?
That is my passport.

You wish to say nothing?
Nothing.

You say you were born in Frisia?
Yes.

What was the name of your father?
Ardum Zella.

Living where?
He is dead. He was born in Laeuwanden.

When did he die?
In 1913. I think in March.

Where?
In Amsterdam.

What address?
He died in a hospital: I do not know which. I have not seen my father since my divorce from Macleod.

What was the date of your birth?
The 7th August 1876.

Are you 40?
Yes.

You were born at that same place?
Yes.

At what age did you leave home?
When I married Macleod in 1895 in Amsterdam.

Where were you married?
In the Consulate. I have two children by Macleod, one born in Amsterdam in 1897 and the other child died in India. My daughter is 16 years old and is living with Macleod in Holland. I have not seen her for ten years, and she does not want to see me.

Had you begun your stage career when you married Macleod?
No, I left him in 1903 to go to Paris, and my divorce was taken out in 1907.

You never went under the name Clara Benedix?
Never, but I have been in the same compartment in a train with that woman.

When was that?
As I went from Madrid to Lisbon.

Was that the 24th of January of this year?
Yes, it must have been.

Have you been at Seville at all?
Never. I know Barcelona, San Sebastian and Madrid.

But you were working in Malaga, were you not?
I never saw Malaga.

Where were you when the war began?
I was in Italy. I danced in the Scala at Milan; then I had an engagement at the Metropole in Berlin. Then the war broke out and I went back to Holland.

Where did you stay in Holland?
In my home.

Do you speak Dutch?
Yes.

When did you leave Holland?
I left Holland to go to Paris: you have my French passport. I came to London, to Folkestone and then to Paris.

Were you in Holland in 1914?
Yes. I have a friend in Holland who is with the 2nd Regiment of the Fusiliers and I lived with him.

In November 1915 you got a visa for London. It was on the 27th November 1915 that this passport was issued No.312. And you were in Paris on the 4th January 1915?
Yes.

Did you ever have inflammation of the left eye?
No, I have never had anything the matter with my eyes.

You know that one of your eyes is more closed than the other?
Yes, it has always been so.

This photograph also has that peculiarity.
It is possible, but that is not me.

There are also other similarities. Is this your photograph?
(photo in small red book)
Yes. That was taken in Madrid this year.

You then left Paris, on what date?
I do not remember, it was 1916.

I notice that your visa is for Holland via Spain and Portugal: why was that?
Because I had a great deal of baggage and my Consul advised me to go that way as there were good boats going from Lisbon.

Was it less expensive to go that way?
I think a little more so. The agent looked after the forwarding of my luggage.

What did you actually do – did you go straight through Spain and Portugal, or wait?
I left Paris on Sunday night, 5th February, arrived in Madrid on Wednesday and Vigo on Thursday. Then I went to a French gentleman in Barcelona Juan Caris Januona (?)

Why did you stop a fortnight in Barcelona if you were on your way to Holland?
To see the place.

What was happening to your baggage all the time?
It was with the agent.

Have you got the bill for this baggage?
Yes, in my home in The Hague.

Are you wearing a bracelet?
Yes (this was shown).

(An inspector was instructed to speak to her in Dutch, and he stated that she spoke the language well, but with a northern accent.)

You went to Barcelona in February for a fortnight, then to Madrid and on to Lisbon?
That was not with this passport. The passport is in Holland.

Have you any proof at all of your alleged movements in Spain other than this passport?
No. The other passport is in The Hague at the Passport Bureau.

What we propose to do is to bring somebody from Barcelona who knew you were there under the other name.
You cannot do that.

If you are going to be put on trial as a spy you can then send for any witness you like from Holland, but in the meantime we shall keep you in custody on suspicion of espionage and on the charge of having a forged passport.
I hope I shall be given opportunities of proving my identity.

Oh certainly. If there is anybody now that you wish to call as to your identity, we shall be very pleased to see them.
I have Mr. Albert Keyzer and his wife: they have known me for twelve years.

What is his nationality?
English. Then there is Monsieur Rudeaux, who knows me well.

Did you say you have never been in Hamburg?
I swear it.

Not in a stage capacity?
No.

Where did these pearls come from?
From Paris.

It is a very rare thing that two people should have a droop in the left eye and the peculiarity in the left eyebrow exactly identical, as they are in this photograph and yourself.
That is not my photograph, Sir.

Then you are a victim of circumstance. There is another circumstance in which you are the victim. There is handwriting under the photograph on this passport, and if it is forged it is a very clumsy forgery.
It is not a forgery. Can I be visited by the Dutch Ambassador?

You can communicate with the Consul. I am going to write to the Dutch Embassy as we have grave doubts as to your passport. I shall also tell him that I believe you to be Clara Benedix, a German. Could you tell me what Clara Benedix is like?
She is younger than me – much the same height or a little shorter, of stout build. I could not see the colour of her hair.

Did she talk to you?
Yes, we talked together all the time.

What did she say she was doing?
I did not ask her.

What hotel did you stay at in Madrid?
Always the Ritz.

What hotel in Barcelona?
Hotel des Quatres Saisons, under the same name as is on my passport.

Did you ever stay at the Hotel Roma in Madrid?
No.

Is this the passport you signed?
Yes.

Did you sign it when it had the photograph on it?
Yes.

Very well, you explain the fact that the writing goes up underneath it.
That is my passport: that is all I can tell you.

(She was told to write her signature, and it was found to be the same as that on the passport).

She was sent over to Cannon Row and instructions given that writing materials be furnished her.

16th November, 1916.

Madame Zelle McLeod was seen here to-day by A.C.C, D.I.D., Lord Herschell, and Major Drake, and stated as follows:-

Who wrote you that letter? (Showing letter)
That is a Mr. Higby, of Madrid.

Did you ever go to Liverpool since the beginning of the war?
No, never.

It is a most interesting case of identity, because a lady of your name did go to Liverpool, and was seen by this Officer, and you are not the lady. That is interesting.
I have no family, so that is funny. I am quite alone.

First of all you came with Zelle's passport, now we have a Clara Benedix, who met you in the train, and then we have another Madam Zelle who was seen at Liverpool by this Officer.

I do not understand. I have had the same trouble in Paris. Not so gravely. In Paris they asked me if I ever went to Antwerp. I was never there. The same Captain, I gave you his name, said it was a Dutch woman. She was always called McCleod. And one day in the Grand Hotel in Paris I received a love letter from somebody for Mrs. McCleod, in English. It was not for me. I went to the Manager of the Hotel, and he said, 'That is the Grand Hotel in London.'

Then there is another lady going under your name.
Yes, it must be. I would be happy to see her. Clara Benedix is the woman I have seen in the train. We had the same compartment from Madrid to Lisbon.

The same eyes?
I do not know.

Do you know a Mr. Hans Sagali, or some such name?
No, I have never heard of his name.

He never paid you any money?
No, I do not know the man.

He did pay Mata Hari some money.
I do not know the name of the gentleman. When did this lady travel to Liverpool?

I cannot give you the exact date?
I know where I have been all that time.

Just before you went to France, did you receive the sum of 15,000 francs from anybody?
No.

That was in Holland.
No, but I took my 15,000 francs from a Bank and gave it to another Bank. I have two Banks in the Hague.

What was the bank you took it from?
Londres, and I have another Bank, Sch.

Londres Bank is the Bank of the German Embassy.
I do not know.

We have information that Mata Hari received 15,000 francs from the German Embassy.
That was the amount I took to go to Paris.

Is your father alive?
No, my father is dead. I told you yesterday. He died on 13th March, 1910.

Do you remember your life-story being published in a certain paper?
In many papers.

This was a paper owned by Mr. Veldt, in Amsterdam.
Yes, I remember.

Who wrote your life for that paper?
Sir, that is a dirty story.

Was it your father who put it in?
My father left my mother twelve years ago. He went to Amsterdam and lived with a woman, one of the common class. My family then sent me to school. I married to become happier. He was twenty-two years older than I. Then my father married this woman. I always sent my father money, and then, as I left McCleod, I went to Paris and became a great dancer. Two writers went to my father, and asked him if he would give his name, and she wrote the book, and my father gave my photographs. I have been very unhappy through this horrible book. She wrote this book, and my father gave the name, and one day 60,000 books went to India, where I am known very well. I took the train to Holland, and a great lawyer from Amsterdam said it was no good for me. All Paris thinking I was twenty-eight years, and this said I was seventy-six or something like that. He said 'Do nothing. You will only make trouble for yourself.

Say nothing.' I saw this book always. It was at The Hague, and there was always a new edition. I went to a lawyer. He said 'Do nothing. You can give money to buy this book out.' All the people bought it. It was the great unhappiness of my life.

Have you had an illness this year?
Yes.

Were you ill in Holland?
No.

Last March, the 17th?
Yes, I remember. I stayed in bed for many days. It was not serious, but I stayed in bed.

Is that your picture? (Showing it)
Yes. That is the picture M. Rudeaux made for me. You know to-day that I am not Clara Benedix, I hope.

Well, rather a curious thing has happened. We were in doubt. We have got to get evidence from Spain as to whether you are a separate person from Clara Benedix. We have been in communication with Holland, and there we find that Madame Zelle is a German agent, and Mata Hari is truly a German agent, and so is Clara Benedix, so now comes this new complication, that a third lady appears to have been seen by this Officer, who is also travelling on a passport of Zelle, and she is not identical with you.
Now I have something to tell you that will surprise you. I thought it was too big a secret. This Captain, Captain Ladoux, asked me to go in his service, and I promised to do something for him. I was to meet him in my home at The Hague. That is why I sent a telegram.

You ought to have mentioned this to me yesterday. Where did you meet Captain Ladoux?
That is old history. In the lawyer's Office. He said 'There is a lady of your name in Antwerp.'

When was that?
Now. No, I will tell you. I was not well in Holland, and I went to Paris to go to Vitol. Vitol is in the zone of the Army, and to go there you must have a special permission. I went to the Police, and they made my paper out, and asked me my reasons, etc., and then one day I received a note from the Lawyer, to go to his Office, and saw Captain Ladoux on the second floor. He was very polite. He said 'I know you very well. I have seen you dancing. There is a lady under your name in Antwerp.' I told the Captain I never was in Antwerp. The last time I was in Brussels was in 1912. One day the Captain said to me 'You can do so many things for us if you like,' and he looked me in the eyes. I understood. I thought a long time. I said 'I can.' He said 'Would you?' I said 'I would.' 'What would you ask?' I said 'If I give you plenty of satisfaction I ask you 1,000,000.' He said 'Go to Holland, and you will receive my instructions.' 'If it is for Germany I do not like to go.' 'No,' he said, 'it is for Belgium.' So I waited his instructions in my home.

Then you went to Spain after that?
Yes.

Will you describe Captain Ladoux?
A fat man with very black beard and very black hair, and spectacles.

How tall?
He was tall and fat. Fatter than a man of fifty years.

Has he any peculiarity of speech; any particular habits? Did he speak loudly, or softly?
I did not make any impression of that. He smokes all the time. He always has a little cigarette in his lips.

When you went to Spain was that part of Captain Ladoux's instructions?
No. Captain Ladoux let me through to go which way I liked.

I went to the Prefect of Police, who signed my passport, and I told Captain Ladoux I was going to Spain.

When you got your passport vised at the Consulate in Rotterdam on the 27th March, 1915, you said you were going to an address in London.
Yes, I have a letter. I do not remember. I stayed at the Savoy Hotel. I telephoned to the place. It was in Tottenham Court Road. I do not remember the name.

Did you go there?
No.

You were staying at the Savoy?
Yes.

How long?
Four or five days.

You were a very short time in Spain this time.
Yes, half a day.

I do not understand why, in October, you came through Spain on the way to Holland.
I have ten trunks, and I like to do this.

That was on the former voyage.
The Dutch Legation, they said you must go quickly back. You must have a permit. I said 'It is not necessary. I go the other way.' I have not finished my story. When I was in Vigo, I met the French Consul from the Dutch Legation. He came to me. 'You love a Russian Officer. You would give him the pleasure of sending a telegram to see if he is wounded, and work a little with me. Will you do something for the Russians?' I did not tell them about the French. He said 'Can you go to Austria?' He said he wanted to know what Reserves they had, to fight. He said 'Do you know Austria?' I said 'Yes, I have danced in Vienna.' I was to go home and await his instructions.

That would have been rather awkward, and when the Germans asked . . .
I do not understand.

I was only asking you.
The Germans did not ask me.

It would be awkward to have a levée of all the belligerent countries in your room. Who was the Russian who saw you?
He was not Russian. He is the French Agent from the Oi. He gave me two cards.

How disappointed these people will be in Holland if you are late for the appointment at your home.
I do not know.

In any case they will knock at the door and find nobody at home. Did Captain Ladoux or the other man give you any money?
No.

Just a promise that if you were useful . . .
I would not make anything out of the Russian business. If I gave Captain Ladoux plenty of satisfaction, then I would have 1,000,000.

Well, we are sending a telegram to Spain. We are going to get over here somebody who knows Clara Benedix, and I have got a list of people to whom you think we should refer, people that know you. I will have some enquiries made, of them, and that is all we can do, except that you can look up Mr. Keyzer.
He is a Belgian Correspondent for the Daily Mail.

28

Madrid, 1917

At the Ritz Hotel, Mata Hari was reading a letter that had just been delivered to her room. It was from Vadime. It was the first letter she'd had from him for several days. They had kept up an exchange of *billets doux* as she had travelled around Spain looking for work. In this latest letter, he began by saying that his eye had completely healed and that he was well. He was still flying reconnaissance sorties, but the new Fokker fighter planes had made these sorties pure hell.

He was also writing, however, to tell her something far more serious. His superior officer had called him in two days ago and said that he had received a warning from the Russian Embassy in Paris that one of his officers was having an affair with Mata Hari. The Embassy had named Massloff and claimed that Mata Hari was a spy working for the Germans. His superior officer said that this situation was intolerable and he expected him to break it off immediately. Vadime couldn't describe how this news had shocked him. Of course, it was out of the question that they could meet again. He was sorry, for her as well as for himself. He would always remember Vittel but he couldn't forget her deception and dishonesty.

Mata Hari got up from the wicker chair and opened a window. She was weary. Below her were terracotta rooftops, all differently angled. Above them hung the winter sun, more white than yellow, more bright than hot. It would be cool tonight, she thought. A pigeon cooed on a nearby ledge. She sat back in her chair and took out from the writing desk a sheet of paper and an envelope. She wrote to Massloff saying that she denied the accusation of spying and could not imagine who was behind such slander. You must believe me, she said. Her chances of obtaining a performance in Madrid, it seemed, were slim – no one wanted to see Mata Hari dance any longer. She was afraid because she wasn't sure what was in store for her. She loved him and missed him terribly. She signed off by writing, '*Après la guerre . . .*'

She addressed the envelope, sealed it and rang room service. A few minutes later, a maid appeared with a tray, which she placed beside the wicker chair. Mata Hari gave her the letter to post and dismissed her. From the thin bottle on the tray, she poured an inch of absinthe into the tall glass. The green reminded her of Massloff's eyes. She placed the sugar lump on to the two-pronged fork and the fork on to the glass. As she poured the water on to the sugar lump, the whole drink turned cloudy. She said Vadime's name out loud and took a sip.

Georges du Parcq climbed the steps of the Ritz and stopped for a moment at the entrance to catch his breath. He made way for a man in a grey suit before pulling open the heavy glass door. In the foyer, footsteps rang out on the tiles and he was puzzled for a moment before realising that the footsteps were his own.

Du Parcq was still working for *Le Monde*, but had long since been promoted to Crime Editor. His job involved more time in the office; the hours were fewer and the pay better. He liked it and it was nothing less than he deserved, he thought. To cap it all, he had married Jeanne, his secretary, two years ago after a six-month affair that they had managed to keep secret from their colleagues.

When the war broke out, the French Secret Service had recruited him as a courier. They had told him he should continue working on the paper, but that every now and then, he would make a little trip to the French Embassy in Madrid to deliver some dispatches. Well, he was a patriot so that was fine by him and, despite being a little concerned for his safety, Jeanne agreed.

He had just delivered some such documents without mishap and, as ever, was greatly relieved it was all over. He wanted to lie down in his hotel room, but first he wanted to take the edge off his heartbeat by drinking a sherry and smoking a Havana cigar.

The bar was an open area near the foyer, cornered by four enormous pillars of marble and clusters of potted palms. On the walls were mosaics of tiny coloured tiles in the forms of large parakeets and birds of paradise. Sunlight fell downwards from a glass roof so that the bar was a kind of atrium. As du Parcq filed through the tables, he noticed a striking-looking woman seated at one of them. She was deep in conversation with Lieutenant Hans von Krohn. As he passed their table he recognised her: it was Gerda.

When she happened to glance up, he saw the flash of recognition in her eyes too. She held his gaze for a split second before returning to her conversation and paying him no further attention. Du Parcq felt slighted. He carried on past her table and ordered a large sherry at the bar. Von Krohn was the naval attaché to the German Embassy and an extremely senior figure in Madrid's military circles. He couldn't imagine what Gerda was doing in Madrid, or why she was talking so intimately with von Krohn. His sherry came; he sipped it and rolled the liquid around his mouth. How long had it been since he last saw her? Twelve years? Thirteen? No, fourteen years! He knocked back his sherry in one and ordered another. When he turned round, Gerda and von Krohn had gone.

After his nap, du Parcq met his contact at the Embassy, a young attaché whose name he could never pronounce. All he could remember was that it sounded Spanish and began with a B. The attaché gave du Parcq some documents to take to Paris. As he was leaving, du Parcq mentioned seeing his old acquaintance.

'Oh really?' The attaché arched his eyebrows. 'These days she is considered a dangerous woman, you know.'

'Nonsense, she's just a dancer.'

'Not just a dancer. She does other things too.'

Du Parcq smiled. 'Well yes, everyone knows she is also a courtesan.'

'No, you misunderstand me. She is working for Abteilung III.'

'What?' du Parcq said.

'Believe me, she is.'

Wearing a long lily-white dress and carrying a matching lace-edged parasol, Mata Hari left the Café de Platerías and walked quickly along Calle Mayor. Men tipped their boaters as she passed, but she took little notice. When she arrived at the French Embassy, she announced herself and demanded to see Colonel Denvignes.

A few minutes later, she was shown into an office, where a short elderly man with a dark moustache stood behind a wide desk. Mata Hari waited until the receptionist had closed the door before she spoke.

'Is there a Captain Berruguete working here, Colonel?'

'Please sit down, madame.' Denvignes offered a seat.

'Does Berruguete work here?'

The Colonel sighed. 'Yes, he does. What is it?'

'I've just been talking with my friend Senator Junoy, who tells me he was advised by Berruguete to break off his friendship with me. Is this true?'

'Madame, you worry too much. I'm sure it's nothing. Please, sit down,' he smiled.

'I will not allow some insignificant attaché to tell my friends to stop seeking my company!' She was breathing heavily. Her dress rustled as she sat down. Denvignes settled in his own chair. She took out a handkerchief from her cuff and patted her mouth.

'I don't know if you are aware of what happened to me in London,' she said; 'it's only because of Ladoux that I was in England at all and still I wait to hear from him. It seems I'm not allowed to leave Spain!'

'Madame, if you had allowed me, I could have told you that I have indeed received your orders from Captain Ladoux.'

She glanced at him. 'Oh, I see. What are they?'

'Germany is about to prevent any possibility of an early peace by declaring unrestricted U-boat warfare. Captain Ladoux wants you to find out German submarine positions along the Moroccan coast from von Krohn.'

She nodded.

'As soon as possible,' he added.

She nodded again and rose. 'I'm sorry, Colonel.'

'Think nothing of it. Before you go, may I ask you something?'

'Of course.'

'May I have your handkerchief as a souvenir?'

In one of the reception rooms at the German Embassy, Hans von Krohn was mixing two vermouth cocktails and thinking back over the message he'd received that afternoon. It was from Berlin, ordering him to instruct H21 to return to Paris, where a cheque for 15,000 pesetas would be given to her. Straightforward enough, but what intrigued him was that the cipher used for the message was old. Von Krohn was sure it was one that the French had cracked many months previously.

Her recruitment by the Deuxième Bureau as a double agent was an open secret. Up to now, she had remained at liberty, a result either of incredible luck or incredible aptitude. Von Krohn had known from the very beginning who she was and what she was doing, so it wasn't the latter. What did it matter? Either way, the game was up for her. Von Krohn felt a pang of regret. They had spent many nights together since he had first let her seduce him. She was a delicious creature in bed – passionate and uninhibited. He resolved to concentrate on the evening ahead and put the whole affair out of his mind until morning. He would pass on her final instructions then, after their last night together.

Von Krohn had almost finished his cocktail when she finally arrived. She was a quarter of an hour late. He sucked in his breath at her long rose-red dress. It whispered to him as she walked into the room. She looked exquisite, as ever. He kissed her hand and complimented her, then handed her a vermouth. She drank it quickly and they left for the Café Gijon.

The open-brick restaurant was only half full and they took a table near the back. 'Have you ever noticed', von Krohn said, 'that there isn't a straight line in here?' She looked around the interior: all the doors, window frames and walls were curved. 'Only the floor is flat,' he said.

For dinner, they both ordered *cocido a la madrileña* – chickpeas and boiled potatoes with bacon and chicken. She complained about the food in Madrid compared to Paris. He said Paris was overrated, he liked the simplicity and spice of the food here. They drank strong red wine from a bottle wrapped in sackcloth.

During the meal, von Krohn pointed out three hatless young men in long black jackets who had just entered the café and were talking together at a table by the window.

'Anarchists,' von Krohn said. 'They're organising against Rivera. The Moroccans are beginning to rise as well; we heard today that there was some trouble in Annoual. This country is headed for disaster.'

Von Krohn couldn't help but notice her efforts at restraint. She let an appropriate few moments pass before inquiring further. Inwardly, he smiled.

'There's going to be a landing of German and Turkish troops on the coast of Morocco. They'll land in the French zone and use the political unrest as cover for a counter-offensive.'

She took this in. Von Krohn knew that she would think this information important. As it was, it was useless. No such troops were going anywhere near Morocco. Now, she would relax, imagining she had her intelligence, and he could get what he wanted from her. He sipped his wine and glanced at the outline of her breasts.

After dinner, they took an open carriage up to Palacio Real and around Plaza Mayor. The sky was purple to the west and there were few sounds apart from the horse's tired walk. Their guide didn't say a word throughout the trip. When they returned to the cobbled plaza, the guide edged his carriage into a line of a dozen other carriages, all waiting for customers. Von Krohn handed him some notes and said goodnight.

They walked to von Krohn's apartment near the Museum of Natural History. The city was almost dark at night because of the poor street lighting. Once in the apartment, he shut the door, put his keys down and told her to undress. When she had done so, she lay on the bed, waiting for him. During their sex, she seemed to be searching for something in him, but he knew she was just pretending. All the same, he made sure he wearied her, and himself. He insisted on fucking her three times through the night, making her flush and him sweat. She complied each time, finally leaning over the side of the bed and talking to him while he manoeuvred himself behind her.

He slept badly and was awake when it grew light. He lay still, watching the east-facing window as it gradually grew less red. When she woke, she smiled and laid her arm across his chest. He told her that she had to go back to Paris immediately. She replied that she missed Paris. She seemed not to have heard him.

'Are you awake properly?' he asked.

She opened her eyes.

'You have orders to go back to Paris,' he said. 'Some money is waiting for you there. You have to go straight away.'

She rubbed her eyes and sat up.

'Paris?' she said.

*

A few days later, on 13 February 1917, Mata Hari checked into her usual room at the Élysée Palace Hôtel on the Champs-Élysées, Paris. While she was unpacking, six men entered her room without knocking. Alarmed, she demanded to know who they were and what they thought they were doing. A man who identified himself as Police Chief Priolet informed her that she was being arrested. He indicated to one of his inspectors to read the accusation. The inspector took out a piece of paper from inside his jacket. He coughed and said:

> The woman Zelle, Marguerite, known as Mata Hari, living at the Palace Hôtel, of Protestant religion, foreigner, born in Holland on 7 August 1876, one metre, seventy-five centimetres tall, being able to read and write, is accused of espionage, tentative complicity and intelligence with the enemy, in an effort to assist them in their operations.

PART III

29

St Lazare, Paris, 1917

> If you ask whether I thought her guilty, I should be compelled to answer 'Yes, against my will.' It does not seem logical to me that a creature of her nature, with her pride, her imagination, her love of art, her beauty, her culture, and her contempt for money could debase herself to the point of seducing drunken aviators to betray secrets of military importance. However, there is no doubt that the evidence before the court-martial was too strong for her defence. I recall paying her a visit on the day the death sentence was read to her. I can assure you that her calm, her indifference, amazed me. Had I been her confessor I should have been tempted to sound the depths of her soul and offer her the consolation of faith, but my role was merely that of medical adviser and for that reason I was compelled to maintain a reserved attitude.
>
> Dr Bralez (Mata Hari's assistant prison doctor)

When she received her death sentence in July, Mata Hari became calmer. She seemed to accept her fate, but in the first few weeks of her imprisonment, this wasn't so. She was feverish and intractable and often displayed a violent temper. As one of the nuns who care for women prisoners at St Lazare, my duty was to stay with her, no matter how difficult it proved to be. And I stayed with Mata Hari until her last breath.

On the day in May when I began my ministrations, she told me her world had fallen apart. She said everybody had turned their back on her. I told her that God had not forsaken her. She looked at me with cruelty in her eyes. I have seen the same look many times before. She said that my presence was an offence to her more fastidious taste in companions. She told me that she was not Catholic and therefore had no need of me. 'As I go down it will be with a little smile of contempt,' she said. I told her my duty had remained the same for fifty years – I would not leave her side. How she fought with herself, poor child.

She was very ill in the beginning. It happens to all new prisoners. Every morning, when I got to her cell and relieved Sister Maria of her night ministrations, she was often not well enough to stand up. Sister Maria told me she spent many nights quietly crying. On one occasion, she vomited blood and Dr Bralez had to be sent for. Sometimes she shouted suddenly and involuntarily and looked at me with anguish in her eyes and said that no one had heard her. At these moments of despair, I took her hands in mine and prayed for her. Often, the Abbé Doumergue and the Protestant pastor, Arboux, visited her. In June, she asked to see Captain Bouchardon. When he came, she told him she was going mad and she hoped she wouldn't have to stay in the cell for very long. Captain Bouchardon said that he would not improve the conditions of her imprisonment unless she revealed the names of other foreign spies. She begged him not to be so hard on her and said that no matter how much he made her suffer, he couldn't make her tell him what she did not know. With a terrible lack of compassion, he said that he was going to make an example of her.

In the days leading up to her trial, she was regularly visited by her agent and lawyer, Maître Clunet, who gave her great hope for an acquittal. On each of the two days of the trial, I sat alone in her cell, number 12, and looked up through the window and prayed for the souls of Mme Steinheil and Mme Caillaux, whom I had attended to previously. I regarded the strong shaft of sunlight coming through the window that lit a square on the cell floor. It was a hot July, but the cell itself was cool. It had the same chilliness as the chapel in the convent I was sent to as a young girl. When she returned from hearing the verdict, I made sure to exert greater vigilance. We sat together on her bed. Dr Bralez paid her a visit. She said only that she would like to sleep well that night and asked Dr Bralez to prescribe some veronal. He said regretfully that he was not permitted to do that. I do believe her sentencing was the moment in her great spiritual struggle when she let peace suffuse her soul. Prison is a model of the soul. To find peace in such confinement is the search for love in dark places. To find liberty in such a small space is the largest understanding I have seen of God.

Maître Clunet stopped visiting her afterwards and this upset her deeply, for she was greatly brightened by his news of her friends and acquaintances and his perennial hope. He sent word to her that he was arranging for an appeal against the decision, which would surely secure her acquittal or a mitigation of the sentence at least. She took heart from this, but the weeks went by. In September, she requested to see a journalist friend of hers called Georges du Parcq. Together, they smoked small cigars and she passed many hours dictating her memoirs. Mostly, the things they discussed were not for my ears, but I remember one memory which struck her oddly. She said that when she was a young girl, her father had been in the habit of calling her 'an orchid among buttercups'. I remember this because of the beauty of the sentiment and because she seemed distressed by the memory. The journalist asked her if she had any regrets and she looked at him with great reflection and said she would like to have known her daughter better. She hadn't seen her Non since 1903 and it was only now that she realised just how much she'd missed her. She asked him to visit her daughter and he said he would. This man seemed to me to be considerate. After he left, she was quiet. The only thing she said to me that whole evening was: 'Dreams are silver, Sister, but memories are pure gold.' During her sleep, she twice uttered a name: Norman.

She remained quietened for many days after this meeting. Noticing this, Dr Bralez suggested that she take to reading. He advised her of the wonderful writings of Prévost, Bourget and Rosny. I have never read any of these writers but the doctor assured me they were marvellous. She admonished the doctor and told him she could not tolerate European things, not even the religion. She said, 'I am a Hindu, although born in Holland. Hindu? Yes, certainly. You who are an intelligent man will say that there must be something European in me. No, there is not. I am absolutely Oriental.' However, she told the doctor that there was indeed one book she wished to read, *Lotus of Faith,* which I am told is a book of Buddhist instruction. Dr Bralez returned with it and, in the days that followed, she took great delight in reading aloud long passages to me. She revelled in the book's contempt for everything in life and I saw that she was once again fighting against the workings of God. I prayed for her while she read.

The day before the execution was a Sunday. There are never any executions on God's day of rest. Despite the imminence of her terrible ordeal, she awoke brightly that morning owing to Maître Clunet's promise of news. The evening before, he had sent word that he had an audience with President Poincaré and was confident that his personal friendship with the President would result in the mobilization of his powers of clemency. She prattled all morning that her friends in high places would secure her release and I silently prayed that she was correct. By the mid-evening, Maître Clunet had still failed to appear. Major Julian arrived and told her that the President had refused to exercise clemency. Oh! How her happy disposition was thwarted with those words and she fell into a deep gloom. I did not know how to combat such despondency. She desperately needed something to hold on to, to overcome the gravity of her soul. The true fight against oneself is against one's gravity. Only by effacing it could she then be spiritually light and clear and so be nearer to God. I thus requested that she dance for me. At first, she did not believe that I was in earnest, but I convinced her and she eventually acquiesced. She stood opposite me and for several moments held a pose rather like a ballerina's. Then she twirled her arms up and down and gyrated her body round and round, opening her arms to heaven and then sinking on to the hard floor of the cell. I told her it was a splendid example of her art. She thanked me and, after a few moments, she asked if it was true I had received the Légion d'honneur. I replied that it was. She looked at me with great reflection and said that we were not so unalike after all. I was happy that she had made some use of me.

The warden came then, accompanied by the prison photographer. The warden explained it was regulations that she have her photograph taken for the records. She nodded. The photographer set up his tripod in the cell and directed her to sit on the bed in front of the bare wall. She did as she was instructed. The photographer disappeared under a black hood and soon there was a loud pop and a flash. He took a second photograph, of her profile, and left with the tripod over his shoulder. She asked the warden if she was permitted to write her final letters and was soon furnished with paper and a pen. She spent the rest of the evening composing and writing two letters, one to her young daughter, to whom she offered much motherly advice, and one to her lover, who now resided in Russia. She told me that she would have walked through fire for this young man, but that even he had betrayed her. Dr Bralez came to ask if she wished for a sleeping draught. She said she did and drank all that was offered. Her spirits seemed greatly restored as she lay down on her bed. As is my custom, I told her I would not leave her side and prayed for the deliverance of her soul as she slept. The prison was quiet that night. I have often observed this phenomenon and know that the guards and other prisoners are keeping silent.

At a quarter to five, Major Julian arrived with Dr Bralez. She was still asleep, poor child. Dr Bralez admitted that he had given her twice the usual dosage and woke her gently. Major Julian told her that Maître Clunet had just arrived hurriedly and announced that he opposed the execution and invoked Article 27, Book 1, Chapter 1 of the Penal Code. I became greatly agitated over this development. He asked her if she understood what this meant. She admitted that she didn't and he explained that it meant she was pregnant. Maître Clunet claimed to be the father. The warden cried that it was impossible and, indeed, I knew it to be impossible as well. Major Julian said if she could prove that she was an expectant mother by submitting herself for medical examination, her life would be spared. She burst into laughter and dismissed the claim, saying that Maître Clunet was just a dear old man who was trying very hard to help her. My heart fluttered at such bravery; she was truly finding the lightness and clearness within her soul. Major Julian said, '*Ayez du courage, l'heure de l'expiation est venue.*'

Two *matonnes* helped her with her corset and pearl-grey dress. She asked what the reason was for executing prisoners at dawn? In India it was not so. 'There, death is a penalty that is made into a ceremony – in full daylight, before crowds of guests, and to the sweet scent of jasmine. I would have preferred to lunch with friends, and then go to Vincennes in the afternoon. But you choose to shoot me on an empty stomach! It is unreasonable!' I recommended a cordial, but Dr Bralez suggested a tot of rum. She smiled at me and said she would take the rum, which the warden duly produced. After drinking the rum, she donned a long black coat and a black tricorn hat, without pins in case she tried to do damage to herself. She turned to me and asked, 'My hat becomes me, does it not?' The ease with which she accepted her fate that morning was courageous in the extreme and moved me so greatly that, against my will, I began to cry. I reminded her that the Protestant pastor was in attendance and urged her to make her peace with God. She smiled a most gracious smile and said she would if it pleased me. The Protestant pastor, Arboux, was sent for and, kneeling before him, she was baptised according to the rites of Anabaptism. I was happy for her delivery into the hands of God and could not control my weeping. When the ceremony was finished, the *greffier* came forward and asked if she had any declaration to make. She declared that she was innocent and a victim of murder. The *greffier* said he would record it. Major Julian asked if she was ready. She looked at me and I saw a great calmness in her eyes that made my tears flow freely. She comforted me and said, 'Don't fear, Sister, I shall know how to die without weakness.' Together, we left that dreaded cell and she walked with her head high, into His arms.

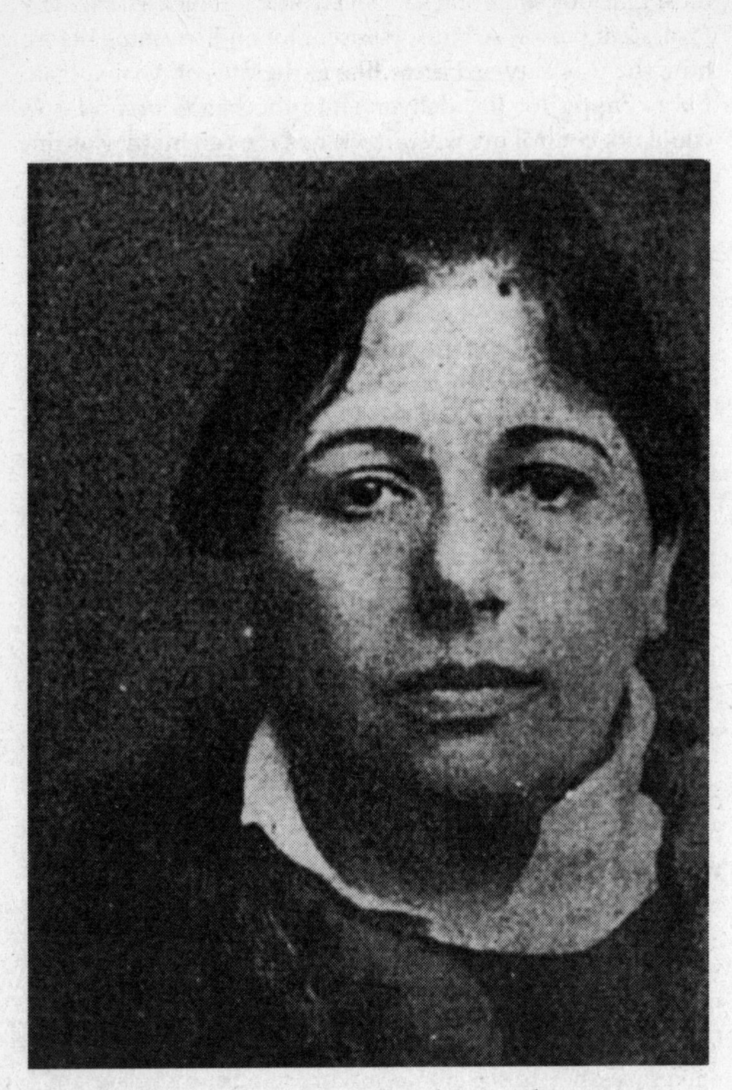

Prison photograph of Mata Hari on the eve of her execution.

30

Vincennes, Paris, 1917

> PARIS, OCT. 15. Mata-Hari, the dancer, was shot this morning. She was arrested in Paris in February, and sentenced to death by Court-martial last July for espionage and giving information to the enemy. Her real name was Marguerite Gertrude Zelle. When war was declared she was moving in political, military and police circles in Berlin, and had her number on the rolls of the German espionage services. She was in the habit of meeting notorious German spy-masters outside French territory, and she was proved to have communicated important information to them, in return for which she had received several large sums of money since May, 1916.
>
> *The Times*, 16 October 1917

Sergeant Célestin told me that I was one of the firing party the night before the execution. He said if I was going to see any action, I needed to be hardened up. I asked who the other eleven were. He said they were all *chasseurs à pied* from other divisions here in the barracks. The Captain had told him to choose either wounded men or young men because it might be the only action we ever saw. I felt sick. The Sergeant told me to look at him. His face is big and round. He's built like an ox but has the tongue of a lark – always talking. He said it was natural to feel all churned up over something like this. Every man who had ever been in a firing squad was sick to the stomach with it and if they said anything different, they were lying. I asked if I could choose not to do it. No, he said. You're a soldier, it's your job, just think of it like that. He told me to get my rifle and go over to the canteen at 20:00. He punched me on the shoulder and left. I smoked a cigarette.

The others call me *le gosse* because I'm the youngest in the whole of the regiment. I don't like it, but when I tell them to stop, they just laugh. They all know I'm not twenty yet. My real name's Jean, identification number 5793. I signed up in June with Gaston and Angel at the recruiting office in Nation. This was after the disaster at Chemin des Dames. The recruiting officer asked me how old I was and I said twenty, but the truth is I'm not sure. Because I didn't have a birth certificate, the officer said he couldn't send me for training just yet because it was against the law. He told me to wait a bit. Gaston and Angel are both older than me and were sent straight to Picardie and I ended up here, at Vincennes, in the 4th Regiment of Zouaves. The Colonel turned a blind eye to my age because the war was going badly. Shit, the only reason we joined up was to stick together. The last time I heard from Angel was three months ago, Gaston five.

We all grew up in Nation. It's near Vincennes, so I've always known about the barracks. You heard stories of desertions and reprisals. The soldiers came into the local bars on Saturday nights, which was their night off once a month. Mainly, they used to go to Little Louis's bar on rue Amelot – he imported English cigarettes for them. He didn't charge too much; if he did, he knew the soldiers would go to another bar. You never saw the same soldier's face twice. Little Louis looked after me, gave me work unloading the beer barrels. Sometimes I slept in the *cave*, but mostly I slept at Angel's place. His mother didn't mind. Louis used to be a boxer and he's always punching people. In a playful way, I mean. Behind all the bottles above the bar are photos of him in shorts and gloves, ready to punch someone just out of the photo. Louis has always said that I must be the son of a welder because my eyes are pale blue with flecks of red in them. He said that all welders have eyes like mine, but the truth is I'm not sure what my father did. My mother died bringing me into the world. Her name was Jeanne – I was named after her. I never knew my father and, by the sounds of it, neither did she. The old women who hang around Louis's say he was from Italy originally, but I don't believe a word – half of everything they say is made up and the other half makes no sense. People pity me when they hear I'm a foundling, but it's normal for me. How can you miss something you never had in the first place?

Anyway, I went over to the canteen with my rifle just like Sergeant Célestin said. It was dark. All the tables had been cleared except for one and I found out later that no one else was allowed in that night. The others were there already; I'd seen one or two of them around. I nodded to Corporal Estrangin. Sergeant Célestin was sitting on the table with his feet on a chair. There was a bottle of brandy open on the table and about twenty glasses. Packs of cigarettes too, English ones. Where d'you get these? I asked him. Captain's orders he said and threw me one. A pack for each man. Shit, English cigarettes! I opened the pack and lit one. It tasted good.

Sergeant Célestin told everyone to shut up and listen. Everyone did. He said he hated the *sales Boches* just like everyone else, but he hated the whole lying lot of our officers even more for not knowing how long this fucking war was going to last and for lying about the numbers of casualties. But most of all, he hated Clemenceau. The dirty bastard was doing a terrible job and, if he had his way, it would be Clemenceau that they were going to shoot tomorrow, not some second-rate dancer. But that's neither here nor there, he said. You have a job to do, no matter how much you dislike it and if anyone failed to carry out their orders, he would personally see to it that his life wouldn't be worth living. Only that morning the Captain had told him that this dancer was personally responsible for the deaths of 50,000 French soldiers. So forget any feelings you have about shooting a woman and think about those dead. And besides, everyone knows she's just a jumped-up *putain*. But, because it's a woman you're going to shoot, the Captain has ordered one blank to be issued among the twelve bullets. So, you'll never know if your bullet was the one. Got that. Everyone murmured something. *Bon,* let's have a drink. Brandy was poured into everyone's glass and we all drank.

Sergeant Célestin put a box on to the table and handed round rags, oil and barrel sweeps. We all started taking our rifles to bits and cleaning each part. The others asked Sergeant Célestin about the trial. They all called him Célestin. I could never do that – Sergeant Célestin, or just plain Sergeant, but never just his first name. Anyway, someone asked if it was true she danced naked and had sex with twenty men a night. Everyone laughed. Wouldn't you like to know, the Sergeant said and everyone laughed again. Someone said something about a new invisible ink and someone else said yes, that was one of the things she was convicted for. Where is she from? someone asked. Somewhere tropical, the Sergeant said. Someone shouted as though he was introducing her at the Folies Bergère – 'She's a Lotus-Eater! A High Priestess! Madame Mata Hari!' What the fuck's a lotus-eater? I thought and drank another brandy. It made my head explode. 'Easy on it, *gosse*.' Sergeant Célestin tapped me on the shoulder. 'We don't want you shooting the Captain tomorrow morning now, do we?'

At 04:30 hours, a bell rang and the Sergeant came into the dormitory shouting at us to get up, but I was already awake. The dormitory was not the one I usually slept in – all twelve of us had been placed in it for one night only. My head had a little black cloud in it from the brandy. I got up with the others and put on my uniform. It's known as 'horizon-blue'. No one spoke as we filed out and congregated by the armoury room. The Sergeant opened the door from the inside and let us in. He handed our rifles back to us and told us to line up outside. We marched across the inner court and the polygon to the rifle-range and stood at ease. It was just light, not too cold. The clouds in the sky were low, with a little bit of mist. They didn't help how my head was feeling but, by then, my stomach was worse. The klaxon in the factory on the other side of the embankment sounded for the morning shift. It used to make pistons and axles, but it made munitions now. The Sergeant walked up and down in front of us and told us he was expecting every man to carry out his duty without a hitch. 'Remember what I said last night, lads,' he said; 'think of all those dead.' I wanted him to shut up, he was only making it worse. Then our Captain and the Colonel arrived in their longcoats and kepis and talked with him for a couple of minutes. The Sergeant kept on nodding his head and looking in our direction. I couldn't hear what they were saying, but I thought it must be about me. All of a sudden my stomach felt awful and I had to swallow three or four times before it passed.

By 05:15 I could hear murmuring in the crowd of spectators behind me. Then I heard cars approaching. Sergeant Célestin ordered us to attention. The guy standing next to me was breathing heavily. I wished he'd stop, but I couldn't say anything. Everybody stood still for a few moments while we waited and, when a bugle sounded, I saw her. She was treading over the puddles in the mud – the cars must have got stuck further back. She had on a long black coat and a triangular black hat. There was a nun with her. We all knew these nuns; we called them the Sisters of Mercy. She told the nun to hold her hand tightly. In front of her was Major Julian from the barracks who must've gone to get her. Behind her was a pastor, a doctor with his bag and old Maître Clunet wearing his medal. I knew him from the papers. He was a lawyer for actresses and the like and always wore his medal. He was crying. So was the nun. Shit. Behind them, I could just make out the newspaper men and their cameras. How they got wind of this is beyond me. To the nun she said, 'Embrace me quickly and let me be. Stand to the left. I shall be looking at you. Goodbye.' Clunet, the nun and everyone else were all pulled to one side while she walked right past us with her head held high. God, she was beautiful. I'd never seen a woman like her before. She carried herself like a princess. When she looked at us, my stomach started up like a mixer. Anyway, she was tied to the post and Major Julian offered her a blindfold, but she turned it down. Then the *greffier* read out the court's verdict and the nun went down on one knee in the mud. Old Clunet was still crying and I kept swallowing. Sergeant Célestin ordered us to get ready and aim and I raised my rifle and looked down the barrel at her. She was standing so still it made me tremble. I swallowed and aimed straight at her heart. She looked so small against the bank of earth behind her and I prayed I had the blank. The Sergeant raised his sword and looked at the Colonel, then swiped the air and shouted 'Fire!' I squeezed the trigger. The recoil jolted my shoulder and she slumped to the ground. The sound of our rifles volleyed around the barracks, then everything was quiet. Not even a bird sang. Sergeant Célestin walked up to her and raised his pistol to her ear and fired a single shot. Her head wobbled under the impact and blood sprinkled in the air. I felt sick and fought hard to stay upright. The doctor came forward. He undid her clothes and, after examining her, announced that she was dead. He said ten bullets had passed through her body and another right through her heart. Shit! Shit! My vision went all blurry and that's the last I can remember.

Oh, poor little *gosse*, can't stand up for a pretty woman! Hey *gosse*, did the recoil knock you over? They kept it up all that night, drinking and laughing at me because I had passed out. I thought about telling them where to go but it's no use, it would just make it worse. I just drank and kept quiet. Corporal Boffi was the only one who didn't laugh – he has kids of his own, not like the others. They're all small-time crooks and thugs, especially Kléber – he's a pure sadist. We stayed in the canteen. Some played cards, others picked their teeth and everyone drank the wine Sergeant Célestin had got in specially. I asked Estrangin what happened after I'd passed out. He told me that no one came forward when an official asked if anyone wanted to claim her body. Imagine that, he said. I didn't tell him I could imagine it very well – I've always been on my own in this world. He saw two gendarmes load the coffin on to the wagon and sit smoking on it as it was wheeled away. If your body's not claimed, he said, it gets given over for medical research. I imagined her body being carved up on some slab and took a drink of wine. Shit. She was too beautiful to deserve that. Donnay said he'd heard rumours that she wasn't dead at all. He'd heard that all the bullets were blanks and the coffin she was taken away in was perforated with airholes. Everyone was in on it – the Colonel, Clunet, the doctor, everyone. She was going to be buried in a shallow grave and, after a few hours, they were going to dig her up again and then she would run away with that guy she wouldn't name at her trial – Monsieur M—y. He was slurring his words. Isn't that supposed to be Malvy? someone said. No, no, it's not him, Boffi said, it was another Minister – Messimy at the War Department. Kléber nudged me. Maybe she's going to run away with you, eh, *gosse*? he laughed. I could see the gap between his front teeth and felt like smashing his face in. Boffi told him to lay off and poured some more wine into my glass. Drink up, he said. Chardolot said that maybe she would be pardoned when the war was over and everyone was dead and gone. Look at Dreyfus, he said, only the other month that Schwartzkoppen lay dying in a Berlin hospital shouting that Dreyfus was innocent all along. Maybe the same will happen to her. It's a bit late for that, someone said, and everyone laughed. My head was spinning. I drank some more wine and turned to Estrangin and asked him why wasn't a beautiful lady like that sent to Devil's Island instead of being shot? Estrangin shrugged. It's the war, he said, they wanted to make an example of her. But what if she's innocent like he says? He just shrugged again. Kléber nudged me and breathed wine fumes into my face. You're in love with the exotic dancer, aren't you, *gosse*? he laughed, and emptied his glass. Donnay looked like a cushion that's had the stuffing knocked out of it. Chardolot was still arguing with some others about whether or not she was guilty. Estrangin said he had to go. I was seeing double of everything so I put my head on my arms. I wondered if my mother had been as pretty as Mata Hari. The next thing I remember is Sergeant Célestin picking me up and lifting me on to his back. He carried me to the dormitory. I asked him if my rifle had the blank in it. He said he wasn't going to tell me and, besides, it was better if I didn't know. He told me to forget about the whole thing. '*C'est un grand nom, mais c'est rien,*' he said and flung me on to my bed. If he noticed that I'd called him by his first name, he didn't mention it, just left without another word.

Author's Note

Although this book is a work of fiction, it was necessary to draw on many sources for detail about Mata Hari's life. In particular, I am indebted to the following biographies: *Mata Hari* by Major Thomas Coulson, *Mata Hari* by Ronald Millar, *Inquest on Mata Hari* by Bernard Newman, and *The Murder of Mata Hari* by Sam Waagenaar.

I also wish to thank Axel Libeert and Marie Mandi for their support and especially for *De Naakte Waarheid*, Jon Cook and Russell Celyn Jones for their kind words of encouragement, and James Mckenzie for his warm friendship and his unerring critical eye.

Special thanks are due to all at Faber, particularly Jon Riley for the faith he showed in this book, and Lee Brackstone for his infallible editorial suggestions.

And, lastly, to Christine, for the walks and talks.